LURiNG THE PRiNCE iNTO THE OPEN...

Operation Retribution Part 3

PALADiN SHADOWS SERiES, BOOK 9

A Novel

by **Aidan Red**

⋏

Edited by Tina Perdue

To my wife for her patience, tolerance and encouragement. Many thanks to my family and friends for their past and continued encouragement and assistance.

Luring the Prince into the Open...

There is only one sure way to deal with a bully. No matter how big he is or how small you are, you have to face him and take a stand. Suddenly Shara knew it was to be her hand on the thrust levers and her finger on the trigger.

Chapters

Ninety-Nine
Wednesday, January 11

Stran had landed STSX just south of Obscure's launch bay in the same manner he had when Cheral and the previous supply ship arrived two weeks prior, with the launch portal abeam to STSX's left. He and Casi stood just outside STSX's aft portal and watched as the Peace Force's Class X supply freighter settled into a hover just above the partially open launch portal, it's length almost a match for the width of the portal. Kiile's loadmaster lifted to the man-sized hatch just forward of the main freight portal and conversed with the ship's loadmaster, arranging all of the details necessary before unloading could begin.

KKLC14 landed behind STSX as Kiile came out of the hatchway to the left of the portal and walked over to them. Together, they greeted Major Kooich and Leeana when they joined the group.

Kiile turned to face the ship and the troopers preparing for the coming tasks. "We're supposed to be getting a number of spare parts to help in repairs, but you've been bringing the ships home with almost no damage, well, minor at the worst."

"They're not supposed to come back all beat up, Kiile," Stran said tersely. "The crews are usually happier and more eager to engage in the next mission that way."

"Yes, sir," Kiile said and smiled. He winked at Casi.

Cheral, Ani Tigs and Wilm Moss came out of the portal hatchway and hurried across the clearing to join up with them. Cheral slowed and stopped beside Kiile. Ani and Wilm saluted the Colonel and Lieutenant Casi, the Major and Lieutenant Leeana, then Ani said, "I hear we're getting two more cadets."

"Yes, Cadet Tigs," Stran said with a smile and glanced at her. "They are advanced cadets, which means they are about the same training level as you, but without actual combat experience." He turned and looked at her and then at Wilm. "Remember how you felt before your first engagements, eager and nervous at the same time? So don't go putting on airs or do any boasting. Help them learn, just like you were helped. Even if they act like they don't want it."

"Yes, sir," Ani said, followed quickly by Wilm. "We'll remember, sir."

"Good." Stran smiled. "Especially since you three have more combat kills than any other cadets in the Force. They already know who you are. Just don't let it go to your heads."

"Yes, sir," Wilm said and caught Casi's smile.

"They're opening up," Casi said and pointed as the large hatch swung away from the freighter's side, exposing the huge cargo hold to the morning light. "They should move the fighters out first."

Enthralled, the cadets watched as the first of three Class 1 fighters drifted out, passed overhead and slowly landed in nearly the same spot that Captain Iims had two weeks prior. The second and third Class 1s drifted out and settled beside the first, and they all turned as a Class 2 fighter followed the group out and landed just past the group of Class 1s.

Stran turned the group of eight to face the new arrivals as they slipped down their ladders and Cadet Instructor Pilot Captain Iims led them towards the colonel and the waiting reception line.

"Colonel Geaardt," Captain Iims said, "I'd like to introduce Cadet Gill Kast and Cadet Loni Grenn." They saluted and then Captain Iims continued, "Cadets, this is Colonel Geaardt, the campaign commander for this operation and your commanding officer. Lieutenant Casi Geaardt, the co-commander and Q-Ship pilot and the colonel's nav-com and mate." Both of the cadet's expressions changed to surprise and then to awe as they put faces to Stran and Casi's names. Captain Iims continued without hesitating. "Marine Squad Leader Kiile, who is in charge of the facilities and the Marines protecting our emplacements. Major Kooich, the colonel's wing commander and wing leader responsible for all flight operations except practice and drills under myself or the second instructor pilot. Lieutenant Leeana Kooich, the major's nav-com, mate and Q-Ship pilot in training. Cadet Captain Cheral Haak, Apache Patrol Two, Cadet Ani Tigs, Apache Patrol Three and Cadet Wilm Moss, Apache Patrol Four."

"It's my pleasure to greet you," Stran said to the new cadets. "Captain, please take the cadets inside, get them settled and briefed on what they've gotten themselves into. We will join you in the Mess in thirty."

"Yes, sir," Captain Iims said with a quick salute, turned and led the way into the portal hatchway.

"They sure seem young," Stran admitted softly to Casi as they marched to the hatchway.

"They're seventeen," Casi said, nudging his ribs. "You were fifteen or barely sixteen when you graduated from the cadets."

"I guess my perspective has changed a little since then," he smiled and put his arm around her shoulder. "Kiile, let's see if any of our special orders came in with this shipment."

▲ ▲ ▲ ▲ ▲

"I almost didn't recognize you, Thom," Eddie said as they followed the young woman leading them to their table, "dressed in regular clothes. No deputy's jacket or fur lined cap."

"I guess I do usually look like I've been left out in the cold too long," Thom admitted and smiled at her.

He adjusted her chair as she sat down at the table near the large stone fireplace where they both could enjoy its warmth and the view of the rock canyon behind the steakhouse. Colorful artificial lighting beyond the window highlighted the snowy cliffs on the far side of the Lynx Creek. The evening was a couple of hours old when they sat down and he smiled and inhaled the look of her.

"If I remember correctly," Thom started softly, "you were drinking wine with Wally and Carole when I interrupted your New Years' evening. Is it safe for me to say you might like wine over other cocktails?"

"Yes," Eddie said and cocked her head slightly as she looked at him.

"I suppose a chilled white was in the chiller, probably Chablis for Carole," he continued, "and there were two bottles of a red from a new Idaho winery, Snake's Grapes."

She smiled at him. "My, my, but weren't you the observant one?"

"A little, I guess. You know, they produce three very nice dry reds," he smiled. "A Mouvèdre Grenache blend, a Mouvèdre Syrah blend and a Grenache Syrah blend. I believe you had the Grenache Syrah blend that night."

Eddie just stared at him. "What're you doing?"

"What? Sorry, Eddie," he said, startled by her sudden concern. "I don't mean to upset you. I simply noticed what wine you were drinking and did a little research on the winery. I thought you might want wine with dinner tonight." He looked down at the table and then back at her. "I'm a little nervous, Eddie, and just making conversation. I really don't want to upset you."

With concern deeply coloring her expression, she asked, "How can you remember specifically what I was drinking nearly two weeks ago?"

"It's a bi-product of the job, I guess," Thom said and glanced at the view beyond the window. "I've always had a knack of remembering things I see, the ability to recall them in great detail sometime later. Since I was ten or twelve. It comes in handy sometimes, on the job I mean."

"It's a bit scary," Eddie admitted and hesitated a moment longer. "Do you remember everything you see?"

"Usually," Thom said, "but it's better when I concentrate when I see it. You know, actually stop and look at something for a second, rather than just glancing at it in passing. Then I just have to remember the when and recall the images. Please don't take this the wrong way, but I will remember how nice you look tonight for many years." He wanted to tell her he would remember how very beautiful she was, how much he liked the flattering cut and pattern of her blouse, the graceful look of the long, flowing, layered skirts, the way she had pulled her long auburn hair back into the wide clasp that let it fall down to her back, her manner and poise and the way she moved. But he knew telling her that would violate his promise, definitely push her too far.

"I see," she said softly and watched him carefully for another moment. Then she picked up the wine list. "Okay then, let's see if they have anything in a nice red. Since you seem to know something about wines, do you have a preference?"

They reviewed the choices and finally decided on an Australian Syrah and then quietly discussed Thom's hobbies of camping, hunting and refinishing and restoring old furniture and how she got started in flower arranging over appetizers. Over their main course, Eddie asked how Thom saw his future as Wally's deputy and what he planned to do besides law enforcement, to which he said he wanted to settle in a place like this, especially once they have cleaned up the Family influence and people felt safe again, and run his own furniture and refurbishment business.

Thom asked about Eddie's thoughts for her future, whether she would stay in the valley and try to continue her education, or move to a warmer clime with better paying job opportunities and she remarked that she had not thought much about it, essentially being trapped in a day to day existence. But she had to admit that if the time came for her to decide, she would base her decision on a number of things that she did not care to enumerate.

For desert, Eddie had a light Amoretto and Chocolate Mousse with shaved almonds and a cream topping and Thom sipped a Grand Marnier served neat. Their conversation drifted to the things she liked about the town and the valley and things she thought he ought to see or do to get a better feel for the area.

The waiter scanned Thom's card for the bill and Thom keyed his remote fob to start his sport utility vehicle, hoping it would be warm by the time they got out into the cold. He entered his code into the waiter's hand-held processor, selected an electronic receipt and when the waiter had gone, he helped Eddie out of her chair.

"I really don't dislike the winters and I do like the flower business," Eddie said as they drove out of the parking lot and Thom turned toward Main. "At first, it was something to get my mind off everything that was going on at the time." She looked at Thom as he concentrated on the snowy road. "But it didn't really do that. I mean, I couldn't put Dad's leaving out of my mind. And as Mom's health worsened, it became a daily reminder of how bad things really were."

"I'm sorry, Eddie," Thom said and looked at her as he turned south toward the north bridge.

"Me too," she admitted. "I feel like I've missed so much in those lost years."

"I must admit," Thom continued, hoping he was taking a good track, "that you learned the flower trade very well. I've never seen anyone do anything as beautiful as the arrangements you make."

She looked down for a second and then glanced at him. "Thanks."

"You're very welcome," Thom said and grinned at her. "It's the truth."

"That's right," she chuckled, "you did say you wouldn't lie to me."

As they passed the marshal's office, before they turned on Birch, Thom noted the absence of patrol cars. The lights were on, but the office looked deserted. "Strange to see everyone gone," he said

5

absently and Eddie caught his look at the office.

"Are they on rounds?" Eddie asked as he turned onto her street.

"Wally's usually in the office at this time," Thom said, thinking out loud. "He doesn't close up until he goes to meet Carole when she gets off at midnight."

He pulled into her driveway and hurried around to open her door. Then he escorted her to her front door and was about to turn and leave when she asked if he'd like some coffee.

"It'll warm you up a little for the drive home," she said with a coy smile.

"Okay," he said, "only if you're comfortable with that."

"Thom, stop that!" she said firmly. "If I wasn't comfortable with it, I wouldn't have asked." She unlocked the door and led him in.

"Sorry," he said and closed the door behind them.

She dropped her coat across the arm of her living room couch and turned to the kitchen. "I'll get a couple of cups started. Toss your coat anywhere."

He hung his coat on the back of a dining room chair and stared at the Victorian Style Claw-Foot sofa with her coat draped over one arm. Then he looked at the ornate chair under his coat and more closely at the intricate carvings around the edge of the round pedestal table. "My word, these are gorgeous," he said softly as he touched the edging. "Maybe from a grandparent?"

"What?" Eddie asked as she turned and saw him studying the table. "Oh. I figured you'd notice that set. Yes, it was Mom's mother's set as well as a few other pieces I have stashed here and there around the house. Mom sold me all of the furnishings with the house."

"They're really, really nice," Thom said as he straightened up and smiled at her. "The finish has held up nicely too."

"Yes, it has," she said as she walked into the dining room. She noticed the message indication was blinking on the phone console and froze.

Thom saw her sudden change. "What is it?"

"I only get messages from..." She keyed the replay.

"Miss Collier," the female voice said from the speaker, "this is Nurse Kelly at the Hospital. Please come as soon as you get this message. It's about your mother."

6

She stared at Thom for a stunned moment.

Thom grabbed her coat and put it around her, forcing her to put her arms into the sleeves. "Let's go," he said as he hurried through the kitchen and turned the coffee machine off. "I'll take you." He gently pushed her out and locked the front door behind them.

⋏

Thom held Eddie's hand firmly as they half ran through the hospital's front doors and to the elevators. When the doors opened on the third floor, they quickly crossed to the nurse's station and asked for Nurse Kelly. The nurse behind the counter paged Nurse Kelly.

"Miss Collier," Nurse Kelly said as she stopped beside them. "I'm sorry, but your mother passed about a half an hour ago. I tried to get you on the phone, but..."

Eddie's knees went weak and Thom scooped her up in his arms to keep her from falling, Eddie absently wrapped her arms around him and buried her face against his shoulder. He stepped aside to a row of chairs along the wall and sat down on the edge of the first one. The nurse hovered over them, and someone brought a cup of water and a vial of ammonia salts.

"Eddie, Eddie," Thom whispered as he held her tight, not letting her move or pull away. "I'm so sorry, so very sorry."

After a very long moment, she slowly lifted her head and he gently held her tear filled eyes. He was surprised when she did not pull away. She laid her head on his shoulder and he felt her tighten her arms around him.

Finally, after many long moments she relaxed and tried to sit up. Thom helped her straighten and when she realized she was on his lap, she forced herself to stand. Thom got up with her and kept an arm around her shoulders until he was sure she could stand on her own.

"Can I see her?" Eddie asked when Nurse Kelly was beside them again.

"Certainly," Nurse Kelly said softly. "This way. We moved her to a preparation and waiting room. Take as much time as you need." At the door, she gestured for them to go in.

Thom turned to the nurse and said, "I'm Thom Baine. Would you please call the marshal and tell him that we're here?" Then he turned to Eddie.

"I'll wait out here if you want," Thom said as he gently pushed her

7

through the door, but Eddie caught his hand and pulled him with her.

She sat down in a chair that Thom pulled up beside the gurney and he stood beside her. She did not let go of his hand as she sat and looked at her mom.

After nearly a half an hour, Eddie turned and looked up at Thom. "Maybe now, she can stop worrying and stop blaming herself for doing something wrong. Maybe she can find happiness again."

Still holding his hand tightly, Eddie stood up, leaned over the gurney, kissed her mom's cheek and whispered her goodbyes.

When she stood up and they turned to the door, Wally was leaning against the jamb, quiet and patiently waiting for them.

"If there's anything we can do, Eddie," Wally said. "Please don't wait to tell us."

"Thank you, Wally," Eddie said.

"I've been down with the Coroner and the Hospital's admin office," Wally continued. "The Coroner's report is complete and whenever you feel up to it, all of the paperwork is ready for you to sign, releasing your mom's remains so you can arrange services and to close out the financial items. All of the financial items have been covered, but it still requires a signature. Come back and see them when you feel up to coming in. It doesn't have to be done tonight."

Eddie nodded and glanced at Thom and he knew that she was ready to go.

"I'll take Eddie home now," Thom said and gently turned her down the hallway.

Wally nodded, touched the side of his head and whispered, "When you're available."

⟁

Thom stopped just inside Eddie's closed front door and watched as she tossed her coat on the arm of the living room sofa. She turned, surprised when he stood there without taking his coat off.

"Please let me know if I can do anything, Eddie," he said as she watched him. "If you need anything..."

"I want to thank you for a very nice dinner and evening, Thom," she said and stepped back to stand in front of him. "Would you like that coffee now?"

"Eddie, I shouldn't," he said heavily. "You've had a difficult past hour and some, and I should let you have some time to yourself."

"Thom," she said softly and looked into his eyes. "I've thought about the coming of this night for a very long time. It's hard to accept, but it wasn't unexpected. I've known it was coming."

"I know," he said with a tight smile. "I've known as well, but that doesn't make it any easier. I'll just talk to you tomorrow."

Her expression did not change, but she stepped closer, slipped her arms through the open front of his coat and around him. She pulled him to her and let her body press firmly against his. She laid her head beside his and he felt her warmth on his cheek. He knew if he stayed, he would most certainly break his promise and take serious advantage of her situation.

"Thanks for being here tonight," she whispered. "I don't know what I would've done if you hadn't been."

When she relaxed her hold, he took a card from his wallet. "This has my home number as well as my desk at the office. Call me, anytime, night or day, if you need something, anything, anytime."

"Thank you, Thom."

"Good night, Eddie," he said and turned to the door. "I..." He stopped and did not finish voicing his thought. It would be too hard to keep his promise if he continued. "Just good night."

⋏

As Thom started back toward the office, he slipped his earpiece on and tapped it.

"Wally," he said, "What's up?"

"Can you stop by the office for a minute?"

"Yeah," Thom said, "I'm almost to the lot now."

Thom parked his SUV and entered through the back door and found Wally leaning back in the chair behind his desk.

"What's up, boss?" Thom said and pulled another chair up beside his desk.

"Before you had the hospital call, I had a meeting with that Marine, Kiile." Wally explained his conversation with Kiile and described the network of tunnels that were uncovered after the night the sheriff and his deputies disappeared and the attack that happened at the place in the woods.

"It seems this network connects somewhere here in town to that facility and Clay, Hawthorne, Grants and a ranch complex some thirty miles east of Grants." Wally spread a small map out on the desk. "Kiile said they are opening up a collapsed area southwest of the facility and are going to investigate the extent of the system."

"Wow," Thom said as he studied the map and the lines indicating the known tunnels.

"Kiile and Greg's group think we should use them to keep a check on what's happening in Clay, Hawthorne and Grants." Wally looked at Thom with a gleam in his eye. "Kiile expects to take their first sojourn down to Clay and Hawthorne tomorrow. He wants to station a couple of Marines at each place where the tunnels access the surface."

"When will you be checking them out?" Thom asked.

"Next few days, I suspect," Wally said. "Kiile will tell us when he thinks it will be okay."

"Very interesting," Thom said. "Keep me in mind."

"I am," Wally said, then changed the subject. "How's Eddie doing? It looked like she had a good hold on you tonight."

"She did," Thom agreed. "Dinner was nice, very comfortable conversation except for a few sticky points. Then she got the message the hospital left on her phone console and we hurried to the hospital."

"She had to know it was coming," Wally said, almost as a question.

"She did, but it was still a shock. She nearly collapsed when the nurse told her and I caught her before she fell. I held her on my lap until she regained her self-control, but then she wouldn't let go of my hand."

"I'm not surprised," Wally said with a slight smile. "I think she's beginning to like you."

"Probably not. She just needed someone to lean on tonight and I happened to be there." Thom stared at Wally. "I told her there are no strings—"

"Well, it looked to me like she might be willing to have a few strings between the two of you."

Thom started to argue but remembered her parting hug, which was no more of a friendly hug than a kiss would have been. She had definitely made sure he felt every inch of her, but he quickly reminded himself of her strained situation, her lowered defenses caused by her mother's passing. No, he could not let himself believe the feelings she showed were real.

"Okay, maybe," he said instead, "I'll see you in the morning. Tell Carole 'hello' for me." Thom got up, returned the chair and stepped out through the back door.

▲ ▲ ▲ ▲ ▲

"Well," Abe said to the phone console as he studied his notes, "the marshal and his deputies seem to run pretty random routes around town. With four of them working, they have at least two patrol cars moving almost all of the time."

"What are the other two doing while those are out on patrol?" Don's voice asked.

"Meal breaks," Ben said over Abe's shoulder, "or they are in the office doing paperwork, making phone calls, just about anything."

"Yesterday and today," Abe continued, "their routines were shuffled around some. One deputy took yesterday morning off and one took tonight off. Then tonight, when the marshal is usually in his office, he was nowhere to be found."

"What does that mean?" Don asked in a suspicious tone.

"Just that," Ben said. "From six to eleven, when he is usually in his office working, we could not find him anywhere."

"One of the deputies had taken the night off, and went to dinner with the girl from the flower shop," Abe added, "and the other two deputies drove the evening rounds, but not the same routes they used previous times."

"Do they take breaks at the same times each day?" Don asked, puzzled.

"Yes and no," Abe said. "It depends on who you are watching and what he is doing. If they are driving their trips around town, breaks tend to come when they are finished, but even that varies in time and place. If they are walking around the main part of town, they are very casual and do not have a fixed schedule."

"And what is the marshal doing when the deputies are driving or walking?"

"Either driving a patrol or walking a beat," Ben said, "eating or visiting someone or working in the office, or..."

"Don?" Abe finally asked, "it seems the marshal is doing a very good job of making their presence felt around town, all of the time, and a lot of the people I have talked to seem to like it. They feel they can contact the marshal's office and they get immediate support, any time of the night or day."

"Is Kenny still running the jail and the dispatch communications?" Don inquired.

"Most of the time," Ben answered, "but usually only during the day. The marshal lets him have most evenings off, unless they have someone locked up."

"And yet you say people can call any time and get support?" Don was skeptical.

"Somehow," Abe said, "the marshal has the phones set up to transfer directly to whoever is on duty."

Don chuckled. "Well, we know that only works over a short distance."

"Yeah," Ben laughed softly.

"I guess I need to think about setting up distractions to spread them out some," Don said, half to himself.

"What are you planning, Don?" Abe questioned.

"Just thinking of options, Abe," Don said softly. "I need a way to keep the marshal in line when he starts going against our needs and wishes."

"It looks to me like he has pretty well stopped looking at the missing people issues," Abe commented, "if that is what you are thinking about. He's stopped asking questions and has not gone searching the papers or the library."

"But his deputy was down in Clay and Hawthorne asking about some of the names he found in old newspapers," Don corrected him.

"Okay," Abe said, "I did not know that. When?"

"On the Friday and Saturday of New Year's weekend. Chief Parks got very agitated."

"Chief Parks gets agitated if his coffee gets cold," Abe said tersely.

The console remained silent for a long moment before Don said anything more.

"There is no easy way to stop the marshal from investigating cold cases," Don finally admitted. "But the chief is certain that if he continues, he will find a way to pin the disappearances on the Council."

"But Don," Ben said surprised, "the Council does not exist anymore. You are all that is left of the Council, and the two chiefs and two others are all that's left of the governing committee, and they only manage nominations and resources."

"Ben! That does not make me feel any better," Don said, hitting something they could not see. "If the marshal decides to point to someone responsible, the list of names is getting pretty short."

"Sorry," Abe said.

Silence poured from the console again.

"I have a meeting in a few minutes. I'll get back with you," Don finally said.

Concerned, Abe and Ben looked at each other as the connection broke.

One Hundred
Thursday, January 12

Greg looked out of STSX's aft portal and glanced around for KKLC14. He knew before he looked that Major Kooich and Leeana had already gone to Obscure for his mission briefing.

'Bren, we need to talk to Hench and Leeana,' Greg said as he turned back to look at the main house.

'Coming, love,' Shara said as she stepped out onto the back porch and hurried toward him. *'Five just told me that Wally, Thom and Eddie were at the hospital last night. Eddie's mother passed.'*

'Is Eddie doing okay?'

'I think so. Five said Thom took her back to the hospital this morning to take care of paperwork.'

He stepped to one side and she slipped past him and through the aft portal. "STSX, please take us to Obscure," he said as the portal closed and Shara scurried up the ladder to the cockpit.

⋏

"What's the forecast?' Shara asked as STSX settled in the clearing just below the closed launch portal. "I didn't look this morning, sorry."

"Snow will be getting thicker as the day goes," Greg said as he dropped through the floor portal and turned aft.

Shara was right behind him as the aft portal opened and they stepped out into the shielded atmosphere covering Obscure. They entered the portal hatchway and followed the curved corridor of steps to the launch bay inside.

"They're still in their mission briefing," Shara said as they entered the office complex across the north side of the launch bay.

"Yeah, but I think they're almost done," Greg said as they stopped just outside of the meeting room and the sounds of chairs scrapping on the concrete floor reached them.

They smiled and returned the numerous salutes as the cadets and pilots passed them in leaving, then Shara slipped in to catch the major and Leeana before they left by any other door.

"Major," she said as Major Kooich closed his notepad and looked up at their arrival. "We need to talk with you and Leeana if you have a minute."

"Sure," Leeana said and sat back down at the head table.

Greg and Shara took seats across from them as the major sat down beside Leeana.

"We just got a message from the director," Greg began. "It seems that one of our agents in the palace on Knobaal heard of the prince's plan to provide us with a surprise the next time we go after a freighter."

"Any idea what sort of a surprise?" Major Kooich asked as he leaned forward to hear more.

"Yes, well, sort of," Greg said with a smile. "We don't know the exact details, but it sounds like he's thinking he can set up an ambush."

The major smiled as Greg explained the few details he actually had.

"I told the director," Greg continued, "I wanted a second group of Q-Ships, eight if possible, suitably marked and available to rendezvous ahead of the intercept. We will have the second Wing watch our flanks."

"Well," Major Kooich said and glanced at Leeana, "until we have more details, that plan will have to do. With Shara and your long range scanner, we should be able to see what they're up to before the main Wing is committed."

"We hope," Shara said softly.

Greg smiled, "One more good intercept may rile the prince's ego enough."

Major Kooich raised an eyebrow.

"We have to get the prince someplace where we can get to him," Greg said soberly, "if we're ever going to slow the slavers down. I thought you'd figured out that I also have an ulterior motive behind our attacks. I'm hoping to upset the prince enough that he'll rise to the bait and decide to take matters into his own hands, personally join the fight."

⋀ ⋀ ⋀ ⋀ ⋀

"That looks like one of those two train cars you found in the storage area northeast of Obscure," Seventeen whispered to Kiile. Investigating the tunnel from Obscure to Clay, Kiile's small squad stopped before they entered the illuminated connection chamber at Clay and cautiously approached the mouth of the tunnel.

"Yeah," Kiile said, "It has five seats and a small cargo bin."

Seventeen motioned for two of the squad behind them to move forward and two Marines hurried up to the car and positioned themselves at both ends. They slowly rounded the ends and the Marine near the far end of the car checked the open hatch and found the car empty.

With a quick hand signal, Seventeen sent the last two Marines to join the first and directed one of the first to check the stairs leading up from the platform. One of the second pair of Marines attached a locator transmitter to the near end of the car and activated it.

"Do you want to apprehend whoever came here?" Seventeen asked. "You weren't clear on that point."

"No," Kiile said. "I want to know who it is and I want to know where he's going. I also want to know where he came from if we can determine that."

Seventeen touched his earpiece and muttered softly, "ID only."

⋀

The Marine slowly crept to the top of the stairs and peeked around the corner using a small mirror; the hallway was clear. He stepped into the hall and listened for activity; a clink and the closing of a door somewhere above him caught his attention.

He hurried down the hall and crouched behind a large potted plant and a cabinet in the alcove beneath a curving staircase; the footsteps approached the stairs from above. He turned his head and aimed his head mounted video recorder at the foot of the stairs.

Don Nikle hurried down the stairs carrying a small box, turned down the hallway and then down the stairs to the waiting car. The door in the hallway began to slowly close and the Marine jumped to catch it.

Kiile and Seventeen had withdrawn two of the three Marines,

leaving one in place, hidden from the staircase by the tunnel car, when Don hurried down the stairs.

"Thirty-One," Kiile said as he tapped his earpiece as the car began to move. "Send the second squad to Clay and the third south, and tell Major Kooich the tail has been planted." Then he turned to Seventeen. "Let's go and see where he was and check out the house."

⁁ ⁁ ⁁ ⁁ ⁁

Four turns had passed since Kela received the mental list of names from Agent Kilp in Angrilat and she had started the systematic search in Dangcee's staffing data base. With her duties in the mine's 'Production Assessment Office,' her daily routines and requirements did not allow her time or the opportunity to search often.

Kela watched the wavering traces as the screen scrolled to her left, dragging the lines with it, exposing the new data as if the lines were pulled from behind the edge of an invisible sheet laid across the display's right half. The traces flowed, simultaneously revealing the current outputs for the eighteen different ores extracted from the mines. Each ore, precious to one market or another was either painfully hand-chiseled from the tough mine faces or it was manually collected behind a powered drill where the faces were too hard for manual penetration.

She knew well the tedious, redundant manual processes required to move the raw materials from the mine face to the lower levels of the crusher mills and the separators, where the first steps of the refining process began. The whole system was heavily reliant on manpower, physical, inexpensive, involuntary manpower. In her galactic year of deepening awareness here, more than a thousand standard turns of agonizing waiting, quietly doing both of her jobs, her hatred for the process grew daily. But then she got Kilp's message and hope began to glimmer faintly. Maybe they were trying to do something to help the slaves after all.

She glanced around at the others on staff in the assessment office, hoping her thoughtless musings had not betrayed her semblance of attention to the screens. But seeing the others were deep in concentration over their own screens, she refocused on her displays of statistics, the finished outputs from the multiple refineries.

Calculated from the running averages of the individual traces and biased for the previous ten turn averages, each trace displayed a narrow light green line beneath the current output, the lowest acceptable output limit, the company's instantaneous minimum. But the mine floors, the working areas away from the face, were hot with stale atmospheres, and though low gravity made lifting and carrying easier, it also made hammering and shoving more difficult. The conditions wore heavily on the basic capabilities of the manual work forces. But the bosses did not seem to care. The bosses did not care if the process was efficient, only that it was productive. If the traces fell to or crossed the green line, alerts went to the shaft masters and corrections demanded within a ten centipar window of time.

As least, Kela reminded herself, that as much as the bosses wanted continually increasing output, they had further adjusted their expectations for shift sizes and times of the turn. There were periods when there were physically less bodies doing the work or the mix of individual origins made it less productive. To the bosses' displeasure, some of the species pressed into service in the mines were just not as capable as others. Some required a different atmosphere, more controlled temperatures, or simply shorter work cycles.

During the first turn after Kela received Agent Kilp's list, she was excited that the Force might be doing something about the continuing number of slaves imported into the mines. She knew it had been a long time since the Force had looked deeply at the issue and wondered what had happened to cause the sudden inquiry. She took Kilp's request as a positive sign that something was afoot.

Dangcee's surface complex for the Pico Mining Consortium was a series of joined, semi-cylindrical containers arranged in connected rectangles to ease movement within, linked to the main city by wide, underground company access tunnels. The rest of the city was a combination of above ground structures, shipping and receiving ports, and below ground tunnels, chambers, dwellings and city squares, all pressurized against the planet's very low atmospheric pressure. Dangcee was a veritable metropolis with all of the services and entertainments deemed necessary, especially when one considered it was company-owned and located on a company-owned mining planet, one of four in the somewhat inhabited Greel System.

Kela had taken an early half-turn break and was on her way back to her office from the surface canteen. She stopped to check on her private files on a public system terminal, then she switched logins and using one of the few user codes she had 'borrowed,' she checked on the name Kilp had identified as his first priority, but the search was blank, the name was missing. She *replied* to Kilp and sent the requested list to another agent she knew was working in Tissl. Then later, during her late half-turn break, she checked on another.

On the second turn, she used a different user-code and checked two other names and was able to repeat the routine on the third turn, each time passing the results to Kilp. That was yesterday, the previous turn and she realized her ability to search was going to take eight turns to complete. She did not want to admit it, but the suddenly repeated access was going to come to someone's notice and raise some suspicion. Discouraged, she forced herself to be cautious, getting caught would not be beneficial to her or to the slaves the Force was seeking. She *told* Kilp her search would take more time, maybe a lot more time.

Friday, January 13

Eddie was about half finished with her lunch when she looked around Connie's dining area and realized that Thom had not stopped like he usually did. Her thought surprised her, though she knew his timing could be off for any number of reasons. She privately admitted that she was beginning to like seeing Thom when he stopped to eat or to pick up a to-go order. She admitted he was cute, well built and muscular, maybe even more than his uniform or her embrace had revealed.

She smiled at the audacity of her thinking, expecting him to stop just because she was having lunch. She certainly had no reason to think he ate at Connie's every day, or even ate there more often than at Jerry's or his occasional stop at the Rusty Saw.

She turned her attention back to her meal and the booklet she was reading when the conversation at a nearby table caught her attention.

"...it certainly seems funny," a woman with a blue scarf said to the woman with her.

"Well," the other woman said, "who knows what Mr. McWilliams is doing."

"I know," the blue scarf said, "but Marry Ann at the Bank said that new deputy, Deputy Baine she said, was in and asking a lot of questions about Charley's Craft Shop, you know, the one down between Main and Webb."

"He talked to her about it?"

"No. No," the blue scarf said. "The deputy was in the office talking with George Hattle about the place and Mary Ann overheard part of the conversation."

"When was this?"

"Last Thursday or Friday," the blue scarf said. "And no one's seen Charley since Saturday."

"How do you know no one has seen him?"

"I asked his neighbor, that Mr. Green. He said Charley hasn't been around and when I drove by, the place was closed up and dark."

"It's off season. It will be closed up."

"Even the house is closed up," the blue scarf said. "It makes me feel sort of nervous, like when Sheriff Black was here, bullying people, asking lots of questions and then people would suddenly just disappear and he could never find a trace of them."

"Disappear? Like I said, he could be anywhere. I wouldn't jump to that conclusion."

"So where would he be?" Blue scarf insisted. "He's always here, never goes on vacation or anywhere. Not in the six or seven years he's had the craft shop."

"So you think that just because the deputy was asking about his place, there's something sinister going on?"

"I said it makes me nervous when someone just leaves, disappears, or whatever." Blue scarf took a sip from her cup and finished the last of her sandwich. "Especially after that deputy was asking a lot of questions, and you know a lot has been happening since the marshal and his deputies came to town."

"Sure, but what's been happening has all been good."

"Good?" Blue scarf questioned. "How can you say that? The marshal's only been here a couple of months and suddenly he and that Carole Davis announced they are getting married in what, another two weeks or so? Sounds like the marshal found out about Carole's inheritance, if you ask me. Just like something the old sheriff would try to do."

"Yeah, why else would he want to marry a cute blonde that likes him and only thinks about him and horses, right?"

Blue scarf wadded up her paper wrapper and stuffed it into her empty cup. "We'll see. You ready? We've got that meeting at city hall in about ten minutes."

Eddie stared, disbelieving her ears as the women got up, tossed their trash and slipped out into the blustery, snowy day. She quickly finished her cup of soup and coffee and got up. She knew what Carole had said about Wally not knowing about her grandfather's conditions and knew she was completely satisfied with Wally's response when she told him. So, what business was it of those two anyway? But Eddie wanted to talk to Thom about his interest in the craft shop and to see what he knew about Charley McWilliams.

She tossed her trash as she pushed the door open and then crossed Main.

▲ ▲ ▲ ▲ ▲

Matti had just cleared the breakfast dishes and Leeana and Shara had joined Jill and Nick in the living room when Shara suddenly felt the new prescience.

"Greg, Hench," she called as she turned to look at him and Major Kooich. "We've got two new intruders coming from the west."

Greg turned and faced west and *felt* for them. "Still a ways off."

"Are you sure they're intruders?" Jill asked and glanced at Nick.

"Yes," Shara said as Major Kooich told KKLC14 to alert TTYF8.

"Major Mooren will have someone aloft in a couple of minutes," Leeana said as she hurried to the back door. Already in their Blues, she stopped at the door and waited for Hench.

"We'll go to Obscure," Hench said as he joined Leeana. "Cadet Tigs is topside, MKCC5 is monitoring the Indian Ocean and everyone else is waiting for the morning's briefing. You're welcome to join us, but it isn't necessary."

"Thanks," Greg said as he glanced at Shara. "You go on. We'll join you shortly."

Hench nodded and gently pushed Leeana through the door.

▲

Ani listened to the normal communications traffic between QuickSilver and the planet-side QCC, still impressed by the volume of information sent automatically back and forth. She had settled into a trailing position early in her mission, high and to the right of the station's path giving her a breathtaking view of the station and the planet below. She checked the scanner's display and noticed the two blips far to the west of the valley and Obscure when the broadcast codes tripped their cloaking transmitters.

"Apache Base, Apache Patrol Three," she said into her helmet mic. "Two bogies inbound from your southwest. Just above the atmosphere."

"Thanks, Apache Three," Apache Base answered. "Apache Two will launch and join you. TTYF8 has been alerted."

Ani absently looked back over the fighter's right pylon, but knew they were too far away and too far east in the station's orbit to see anything visually. She turned back to the scanner as the two red dots slowly separated.

"Apache Base," she called again. "Looks like they're splitting up. One is going your way and the other is coming my way."

"Confirmed, Apache Three. Better alert QuickSilver."

"Will do," Ani replied and then switched transmitter channels. "QuickSilver Apache Watch. This is Apache Patrol Three in high, right echelon. Inbound intruder illuminated."

"Apache Three, Captain Nesbit here," the voice responded in her headphones. "We have you and see the intruder. We also have another Apache IFF approaching."

"That is confirmed. Apache Two is joining us," Ani explained. "I show the intruder will reach us in about twelve minutes. Suggest activating your shields."

She heard Captain Nesbit call Lieutenant Riviera to activate the shields. Then he had a subordinate verify the cannon turret's status and readiness.

"Apache Three, QuickSilver defenses are ready," Captain Nesbit said after a moment.

"Thank you, Captain," Ani said as she slowly turned Three to face in the direction of the oncoming intruder.

"Apache Three, Apache Two here," Cheral's voice filled Ani's headphones. "Joining up on your right."

"Thanks Captain," Ani said as Apache Two drifted into position. "Do you have a confirmation of the intruder's type?"

"Negative. Casi says it's of Angrilat origin," Cheral added, "and I figure she knows."

"Agreed," Ani said with a smile to herself. "Six minutes. QuickSilver is on Alert, Shields Up and Weapons Ready."

"Apache Watch," Ani called again and relayed the strategy position Major Kooich had taken in yesterday's post mission briefing. "This one feels different from other intruders. It's your move. Apache Two and Three will back you up if you need it."

"Understood, Apache Three," the captain said.

Ani watched as the intruder swung around, following the station and aligned itself with the station's path.

"Apache Two," Ani commented, "This one looks like he's lining up for a strike."

"Yes it does," Cheral agreed, "A high speed pass. I don't like it. Confirm your shields are up and full, Ani,"

"Confirmed." Then Ani called QuickSilver. "Apache Watch, this one looks like he's setting himself for an attack run."

"Roger that," the captain's voice replied.

"Apache Two?" Ani asked, "Can you drop his cloaking?"

She had no more than asked when its veil fell. The ship coalesced and it instantly fired a double cannon volley at the station. In the same instant that the shields deflected the bolts, QuickSilver's upper and lower turrets unleashed a volley and the intruder vanished in a burst of fiery smoke.

A long silence prevailed until Cheral called QuickSilver. "Apache Watch. Good shooting."

"Thank you," the captain's voice came back, then paused briefly. "I think I like those shields."

"We do too," Ani remarked.

⅄

"This one's yours," Major Mooren said as he followed Franni through TTYF8's aft portal and up the ladder. "I had yesterday's."

"I know," Franni said, then turned to smile at him. "Thanks."

Major Mooren turned aft and quickly switched on the necessary systems and monitors. "He's up and ready when you are."

"Ignition," Franni said as the pilot's chair adjusted and she swung it to forward facing and buckled herself in.

"IGNITION," TTYF8 said.

"Put the target on the forward scanner display," Franni said as she pulled TTYF8 up and through Obscure's shield dome, into the snow filled, blustery air buffeting the ship and jostling them. She focused on the incoming scanner dots.

"Looks like Ani was right," Franni said. "They have definitely spilt up. Captain Haak went up to relieve her on escort duty, so we'll have two up topside for a little bit."

Franni maneuvered TTYF8 into a waiting position high above Obscure and watched as one of the targets drifted lower and lower, until it had slowed almost to a stop below the mouth of the valley. She closed the distance between them as it approached and drifted around Grey's Peak and up into the valley just east of the highway. Franni followed about a mile in trail as the fighter turned east just south of Grants.

"It looks like it's going out to the farm that we've been watching for Major Kooich."

"Sure does," Major Mooren agreed and brought up the magnification on the monitors.

Franni had TTYF8 record the scanner images as they followed, but decided against dropping its veil. She knew they wanted to find out what it was doing and unveiling it would only let it know it was being watched.

"I sure wish I could bring up the details like Casi does," she whispered to herself.

'Didn't Casi do something with Captain Haak to help her?' Major Mooren asked, *'I thought I heard someone mentioning that she was able to see targets more clearly after Casi did whatever she did.'*

'I don't know, Crem,' Franni answered absently. She had finally accepted the fact they heard each other and that he seemed to always be listening for her. *'I haven't heard anything.'*

'Looks like it's landing beside that large building south of the main cluster,' she continued as she swung TTYF8 around the ranch. *'They don't have cloaking over the ranch.'*

'No shields either," Major Mooren said. 'They're pulling it inside.'

"TTYF," she said out loud. "Do you have any specs on the ship?"

"LIMITED. FIVE PERSON FIGHTER. SMALLER THAN A Q-SHIP AND OF ANGRILAT ORIGIN. MKCC5 INDICATES

25

IT LEFT THE INDIAN OCEAN LAUNCH FACILITY FORTY MINUTES PRIOR TO ARRIVING HERE."

"Thanks, TTYF," she said and thought about his words. "Crem, do you suppose they are moving small groups of people on these ships to that facility?"

"Could be," he agreed, "but why? They can't get a transport in to pick them up."

"Workers?" she asked absently. "Major Kooich said they haven't finished the facility. And to get them off planet, why wouldn't they just take them up in these fighters and rendezvous with a freighter in a high orbit?"

Major Mooren turned and looked forward at the back of her chair. "Of course! We're not looking for fighters going out, and we might not pay attention to it coming back since it belonged here in the first place."

"I think we need to discuss this with Major Kooich," she said and then changed her thought. "TTYF, drop our Remote Six to monitor this area. Report any activity concerning that ship or any increases in people in the area. Keep Six fully cloaked and in Alert mode. Confirm actions before any aggressive responses."

Suddenly Franni looked up. "Did you feel that?"

"What?" Major Mooren asked, puzzled as he turned around and saw her looking up through the canopy.

"THE SECOND FIGHTER FIRED ON THE SPACE STATION. THE SPACE STATION SHIELDS DEFLECTED THE SHOTS AND THE SPACE STATION RETURNED FIRE. THE FIGHTER HAS BEEN NEUTRALIZED. APACHE TWO AND THREE WERE READY AS BACK UP. APACHE THREE IS PREPARING TO DESCEND."

'Franni,' Major Mooren said, surprised. '*You felt that before TTYF told you.*'

She turned her chair aft facing and stared at him. '*I... did, didn't I?*'

⚔ ⚔ ⚔ ⚔ ⚔

Eddie pushed the front door to the marshal's office open and stepped inside, closing it quickly behind her. She looked around the room and only saw Wally.

"Wally? Where's Thom?" she asked as she stopped in front of his desk and he looked up.

"He's on an assignment," Wally said as he straightened up in his chair.

"When did he go?"

"About Ten," Wally said. "Anything wrong?"

"Not really," she said and glanced at Thom's desk, neat and cleared of any loose papers. "Maybe."

Wally waited.

"I just wanted to talk to him," she admitted, "about some gossip I overheard. I guess it's really not important."

"Gossip? What kind of gossip?"

"Just normal stuff," she said. "Nothing important."

Wally watched her and caught her eyes.

"Some of the town's folks think you're marrying Carole for the land her grandfather set aside for her." She sighed. "I know that's not true because Carole told me so on New Year's Eve."

"I'm glad she did," Wally said. "How she handles her land is up to her. I have no say in it."

"Do you know if..." she hesitated, "if Thom is buying any property here in town?"

"No. Recently, he's talked about wanting to buy a place some time," Wally said, "but he hasn't told me if he has picked anything out. Why?"

"Just something someone said," she sidestepped the question. "Thanks Wally. Do you know when he'll get back?"

Wally hesitated again. "Probably late Sunday night or very early Monday morning." He saw her shoulders drop. "I'm sorry, Eddie, but he's doing something important."

"I know." She sighed again. "I know all of you are very busy right now, and I do hope things will go well for you and settle down soon."

"Thanks."

She nodded, turned to the door and left.

▲ ▲ ▲ ▲ ▲

Greg and Shara with Hench and Leeana finished their debriefing of Major Mooren and Franni's encounter with the interloper. Cadet Tigs joined them and gave her account of the attack on QuickSilver.

"Thank you, Cadet Tigs," Major Kooich said and turned to look at Greg. "I certainly don't like this change of tactics, colonel."

"Nor do I," Greg agreed. "But it wasn't unexpected. Attacking the space station was surprising, but expected. What is more of a concern is the ship that you followed," he nodded to Major Mooren and Franni, "to the ranch east of Grants. I agree with Lieutenant Kaal that it is most likely here to transport personnel rather than for a defense."

"It could be an attempt to begin rebuilding their strength here in the valley," Leeana said.

"Maybe," Greg admitted. "But they don't have many fighters left. We know that from the data we captured with Ahaar's facility, so I'm thinking their intent is more likely what Lieutenant Kaal suggests, that they are moving people either to provide workers for the facility or so they can regain a position in the slave markets. They haven't been able to ship anything off-planet for quite a while."

"Has your remote sent any further information?" Shara asked Franni.

"Nothing of significance," Franni replied. "There are thirty-four individuals identified, scattered around the complex of buildings, including those we can see inside the buildings."

"Major," Major Kooich said, "TTYF8 has sub-terrain mapping capabilities. Would you go back and map that ranch in ten foot slices down as far as you think makes sense? Two or three stories at least."

"Certainly, Major," he said. "How soon do you want us to go?"

"I have sent three squads of Marines into the tunnels from here," Greg said. "They have searched all of the tunnels down to and east of Hawthorne and are now moving south. One team with one of Wally's deputies is headed straight to the ranch from the north. A second team, with a second deputy, is approaching the town of Grants." He looked at Major Mooren firmly. "They encountered a tunnel car in use and put a tracking transmitter on it. My last information said the car was stopped in Grants. If there's anything we can give the squads, especially the one moving in on the ranch, anything that will help them when they get there, I want them to have it."

"Yes, sir," Major Mooren said quickly.

"TTYF is still on full Alert, Colonel," Franni said. "We can be away in minutes."

Greg was about to tell Major Kooich to send them when STSX called him. He and Shara both turned their attention to his message and the group waited.

"STSX has just informed us," Greg said when the connection was broken, "the director expects another intercept mission as early as Monday morning our time, galactic day 400." He turned to Major Kooich. "Please focus on the south valley as much as you can between now and when we have to leave for the next mission."

"Will do, Colonel," Major Kooich said and then smiled at Major Mooren and Franni. "Go find out as much as you can. KKLC14 has given TTYF8 the communications links to the two squads. Work with them directly and use a second ship if you need it.

"Thank you, sir," Major Mooren said, stood up and saluted. Franni was close at his side as they turned and left the room.

"You know, Colonel," Major Kooich said after they left. "I'm going to have to leave a second ship here when we go this time. With new activity in the Indian Ocean, here in the valley and concern for the space station, one ship won't be enough support."

"Only if you have to, Major," Greg said and looked at Shara as he pondered the situation. "QuickSilver has demonstrated it can, if need be, defend itself. That relieves the need for full time escorting, especially if intruders can be detected and monitored like they were today. Please keep that in mind in making your decision, Major."

"Yes, sir," Major Kooich said, feeling the concern Greg was feeling.

⋏

As Shara and Greg stepped out of the portal hatchway and started across the clearing to STSX, Shara smiled and nudged Greg with her elbow. "I think you're going to be asked to perform a joining."

"What?" Greg stopped and looked at her. "A joining? Who?"

"Crem and Franni," she said and leaned close to him. "I don't think they know it yet, but I think it's coming, soon."

Greg thought back on how they acted in today's meeting and how they acted the first time they met them. He smiled at Shara. "I guess I've been too busy to notice, but you might be right."

"STSX tells me they've been *linked* for over a month now," Shara added, "and that their communications are becoming more frequent and natural."

"My, my," Greg said. "Are you having STSX eavesdrop on our crews?"

"Only enough to be sure we are not having any trouble in the ranks," she admitted. "While you and the major have been dealing with the more technical, logistical aspects of the campaign, Leeana and I have been keeping the spats and quarrels under control. "A happy squadron fights better."

"You are a surprise," he said and leaned down to kiss her.

She wrapped her arms around him, kissed him fully and held his embrace as long as she dared. "Thank you, love."

▲ ▲ ▲ ▲ ▲

Kiile adjusted the night vision goggles and sent two of his Marines up the narrow staircase leading out of the tunnel's connection chamber.

"M-Four," the Marine beside Kiile said softly to the remote following them outside, "can you see the door at the top of the stairs?" The Marine waited and then turned to Kiile. "It cannot see the door. It says the door is inside a small building set apart from the others, away from the ranch's main house yet near a large animal shelter. The snow is high around the small building. It has not been accessed since the snow started."

"Well that's good in one way," Kiile said with a tight smile as he looked at the three Marines and Deputy Baine, their expressions hidden by the goggles. "Six," Kiile called the Marine at the top of the stairs and gave him M-Four's assessment. "M-Four says there's no one around the building, so put a lock on the inside of the door."

The second Marine quietly descended the stairs, collected a small utility carrysack and then returned up the stairs.

After a few minutes, Six reported in Kiile's earpiece, "Two hasp halves securely in place. Lock installed." Kiile repeated the news.

"What kind of lock did he use?" Thom asked out of curiosity.

"Once they find out the door's locked, won't they come in through a maintenance hatch nearby and break it loose?"

"It's not that kind of a lock, deputy," Kiile said with a smile. "It's digitally controlled," he tapped his forehead, "and completely covers the hasp halves. It looks like a large box set across the edge of the door and the jamb. It will also alert the remotes if someone tries to open the door from either side."

"Wow," Thom said softly and quietly stepped back to watch.

"Okay," Kiile said as the two Marines descended the stairs and regrouped. "This is the Niles Reeds Ranch, twenty-five point one miles east of Hawthorne as the crow flies." He tapped the screen on his notepad. "Secured and M-Four has an aerial map. We'll get one of the ships to do a sub-surface investigation of the ranch and the surrounding area."

He put the pad in its pouch and turned to the waiting sled. Once everyone was on board, he had one of his Marines start them off.

"Squad Leader Kiile," the Marine at the back of the sled called, "Major Mooren has a message for you. Remote M-Four can link you."

"Thanks," Kiile said and then tapped his earpiece. "Major Mooren, Kiile here."

"Yes, sir," Major Mooren's voice said into his ear. "We have a series of sub-surface maps completed of the John Reeds Farmstead east of Grants and south of Community. I believe that's your next stop."

"Yes," Kiile said. "We are enroute now, just leaving the Niles Reeds Ranch. Anything we should know about?"

"Yes," the major said. "We show Thirty-nine persons above ground and another fifty-six below in an underground complex. Looks like five large rooms surrounding a single central chamber with one tunnel connecting to a room with most of the persons, possibly billeting."

"Ninety-five in camp," Kiile said, half to himself. "Can you tell if any of them are armed? Or if they have any security at the entrances?"

"Negative," the major admitted. "But it is wise to assume so. The billeting area may be for security forces. There is also a chamber in your tunnel about a mile north of the main complex, which could be a security check-point. A similar one exists in the tunnel leading to Grants."

"Thanks," Kiile said. Then he asked, "Where's the other squad?"

"They are just north of Grants, watching the tunnel car that is stopped there." The major paused and Kiile could hear muffled discussions in the background. "That car has started to move toward the Farmstead. There is one individual in the car. Your squad has moved in and is checking the connection to see where it comes out at surface level. We have a remote following them as well as one of your own remotes. We are presently above the farmstead and are available if you need assistance."

"We'll try to stay unseen," Kiile said. "But we'll call you if you are needed."

"We'll be here," the major said and the connection went silent.

Kiile turned to the men and recounted his conversation with Major Mooren, and stressed the fact that they were on a reconnaissance mission and did not want to engage anyone at this time and lose the element of surprise when they needed it. He watched the dark tunnel ahead of them and as they approached the bend in the tunnel north of the ranch, he turned to his men.

"Check your weapons, cloaking on," Kiile said and then looked at Thom. "Six, give Deputy Baine that extra cloaking transmitter and show him how to use it."

Saturday, January 14

Wally absently asked WL-One for a neighborhood status as he stopped his jeep in Carole's driveway. He glanced up and down the dark, snow covered street, noting the bright streetlight's illumination at the corner of Donovan and farther west at Fox as he got out. He was pleased when WL-One reported the night was quiet with no apparent activity and that no one had tried to place any new audio or visual sensors around the house as he opened the door for Carole.

"Thanks," she said as he closed the jeep door and she keyed the garage door open. "Did I hear you right, that you're off the rest of the night?"

Wally followed her in through the garage and opened the door to the house as the garage door closed.

"Yes," he smiled as he entered the kitchen and closed the door. "Dan will come on at four and walk Thom's beat on Main at seven and I will join him in the office at eight."

"Sorry to hear Dan has to come on duty so early, but I'm glad you're off until morning," she said, smiling at him as she hung her coat up and started down the hallway to her bedroom. "That means you can have a late snack and a glass of wine with me."

Wally hung his coat and utility belt on the pegs behind the front door beside Carole's coat and turned to the kitchen. He collected two stem-less wine glasses and a chilled bottle of Chablis from the refrigerator. By the time Carole returned wearing her sweats and a light robe, he had sniffed out a beef and a ham roll, sliced two different cheeses, and had plated the array along with a sleeve of thin rye crackers for a snack.

He unfolded a small round serving table, arranged the plate, wine and glasses and snugged it up in front of the couch. Then he sat down and Carole curled up beside him.

"I asked Hap about taking Wednesdays as my second day off," she began as he poured her a glass of wine. "Is that okay with you?"

He smiled at her asking for his opinion and handed her the glass. "Sure. I can probably work my schedule around to match that. Sundays and Wednesdays, I should be able to do that."

"You said two days off together would be difficult," she continued. "Maybe by summer, when school's out, we can change and take actual weekends off."

"Right now, even one full day off is difficult," he said as he stacked a slice of cheese, meat and cracker together.

"Are things getting worse?" she asked as she sipped her wine.

"Maybe. It's more of a feeling I'm getting." He ate his stack and took a sip of wine. "We've been hearing things around town."

"What sort of things?"

"Just some comments people are making, comparing the changes we are trying to make to the things the old sheriff and his deputies were doing." He smiled at her. "Old suspicions are resurfacing and we're seeing some folks withdraw."

"I'm sure they'll come around, Wally," Carole said and kissed him.

"Yeah," he said softly. "You'll hear some comments about me and my apparent designs on your land." He looked at her.

"I was sure I would," she said and sipped her wine with a wide smile. "Every fella I knew growing up here has tried to sweet talk me into a relationship so they could get their hands on it. And now, I'm certain there will be snide comments driven by jealousy and anger."

"Are you sure you want to hear all of that?" He knew she didn't really care, but had to ask anyway.

"You know I don't 'want' to, but even if I had of agreed to marry one of them," she said, "the others would have reacted the same way. That part of my future was set about the time my brother left. Dad let the conditions slip out one day after church. Then it was just Shelly and me and half the town knew she was engaged to Jim."

"That must have been hard to live with," Wally surmised as he fixed another stack of meat and cheese.

"Yes, at first, but then I ignored it," she admitted, "and realized I could never have a meaningful relationship with any of the local boys. I quit worrying about it and didn't let it concern me for a long time, and then one day you came into Hap's, remembered my name and asked me about a friend of mine."

"I still don't like people saying negative things about you," he said as he leaned over and kissed her.

"Well, you and I, and my family know the truth," Carole said and laid her head on his shoulder, "and that's all that matters to me."

One Hundred-One

"I can only take six at a time," the pilot said to Don Nikle as they reviewed Don's list of names. "If you look," he continued and pointed in through the side portal of the small fighter, "we have rearranged the interior with restraint seats. The passengers will be muffled and shackled to the seats for transfer."

"I am surprised you were able to get six seats squeezed into that space," Don admitted as he peered through the opening. "I thought these were designed for four seats."

"True," the pilot admitted. "There is not much room, but they will not be moving around once on board."

Don led the way back to the warmer accommodations at the front of the building and opened the door into a snug living area. At a round table near the kitchen, he sat down and gestured to another chair. The pilot looked around the room and then sat down.

"Well," Don said as he looked at the list again. He checked off the first six names on the list. "This list has eleven that are suitable for your workers, When can you come back for the last five?"

"I will check with operations," the pilot said, "but I should be able to return late this turn and leave early tomorrow."

"Very good," Don said and smiled for the first time since he met with the pilot. "Has your operations made arrangements for a rendezvous with a freighter?"

"I do not know about any arrangements concerning a freighter," the pilot replied. "That would not be for me to know. I am assigned to deliver persons to the facility and the facility distributes them. The facility contact information you need is in the sealed packet that I delivered when I arrived."

"Yes, yes," Don said, "I will make a call and make my own arrangements."

The pilot looked around the rustic living room of the old ranch house. "Is this a typical dwelling for this planet?"

"Yes, for this part of the country," Don admitted, pulling his thoughts away from the list and looked up at the room. "This is a worker's dwelling. It is made to look older than it is while masking the modern living features and necessary surveillance and protection devices. There are examples that are much more modern looking elsewhere. The main house is much nicer."

"Hmm," the pilot muttered, then he changed the subject, "When will the passengers be ready to load?"

"They are being prepared now," Don said and checked his watch. "They should be bringing them up in the next ten or fifteen minutes. You should be on your way about daybreak."

▲ ▲ ▲ ▲ ▲

Shara woke with a start. She slowly took in the dim room and feeling the comfort of Greg's warmth against her back, she focused on the sensation that woke her.

"Yes, love," Greg whispered, "the fighter is leaving the ranch down by Grants."

"You feel it too?" she asked and pulled his arm curled around her, tighter.

"Yes," he answered softly. "They loaded six men about half an hour ago and have just lifted off."

"TTYF8 is following it," Shara said as she recognized the other sensations.

"Yes. STSX says MKCC5 is watching the Indian Ocean Facility to confirm when the fighter returns there."

"What if they don't?"

"They'll let us know," Greg smiled and pulled her to him. "Otherwise, how are you this morning?"

"Good, I think," she said and rolled over to face him and wrapped her arms around him. She tightened her embrace and thought about the fighter. "Greg? Should we be letting the fighter take people out of the valley? I thought you wanted—"

"I do, Bren," he interrupted, "but this time I wanted to see if Franni might have the right idea. This trip the fighter is only taking men, and I'm thinking there is a chance they are needing workers for the facility."

"And if we stopped the fighter," Shara said, picking up on his line of thinking, "we won't know if they've set up a new way to move people off planet."

"I do think Franni and Major Mooren have a finger on it," Greg said softly and thought about the next steps, "and I'm very glad they mentioned what they thought. We may have become too focused on ships coming in that we could have missed one leaving."

"Could be. I almost missed those cloaked fighters on the last interception, too focused on one thing to see the other."

"You did just fine, Bren," Greg encouraged. "We can't see everything."

"I know, but that doesn't mean I have to like it." Shara pulled his head to her and kissed him.

C.3482.400

"Good morning, Apache Leader," the greeting said crisply from STSX's communications speakers. "B-Group, at your service. We're Major Amel Cleff and Lieutenant Pela Cleff, B Group Wing Leaders."

"Good morning, Major and Lieutenant. It's good of B-Group to join us," Stran answered as STSX slowed and led the Apache Squadron to join up with the waiting group of Q-Ships.

"Thank you Colonel," Major Cleff replied.

"Apache Wing, drop Visual Cloaking only," Stran continued.

STSX and Casi had verified the IFF signatures long before their arrival and had alerted the Wing to the eminent rendezvous. When Apache Wing dropped their visual cloaking, B Group followed suit. Stran smiled at the red bands they wore.

"QRTT7, what's your Wing status?" Casi asked when the Wing had settled into a loose formation beside B-Group.

"All ships are status Green," Lieutenant Cleff said. "The Wing is battle ready, Lieutenant."

"Thank you," Stran said. "Q-KKLC14, Major Kooich is Apache Squadron Wing Leader. KKLC14 is responsible for all ship pairings and special target assignments, as well as all of the engagement coordination. Major Kooich."

"Major," Major Kooich began as he confirmed he was

broadcasting to all ships. "This interception feels different than our previous missions. The intelligence we've received indicates the prince has set up some sort of a surprise for us. On our way in, we identified three battlecruisers and their associated fighters on our long range scanner. They seem to be waiting down course, cruising at a slower velocity as if they are expecting the target freighter and its escort to come to them and pass. Our estimate is an engagement with the freighter and its escorts that would reach their position approximately two decipars after we intercept. Our plan is for B-Group to follow Q-TTYF8's lead and engage the battlecruisers and fighters waiting in ambush. TTYF8 will act as the coordinator between our two groups. Any questions?"

"Yes, sir," Major Cleff replied. "We could not light up any of them on our scanners. We saw them when your group illuminated them. Do you have new codes?"

"My apologies, they are using a Kyddellan cloaking transmitter," Major Kooich explained. "KKLC14 will send the two codes we have to each of your Group's ships. We only recently uncovered them, one from a captured fighter and the other from an encounter with another fighter two turns ago."

"Thank you, sir," Lieutenant Cleff said. "We are receiving the codes now."

"Major Kooich," Stran said as the crews uploaded the codes, "Let's unload our patrol fighters."

"Affirmative, Colonel," Major Kooich agreed.

Stran turned his chair to aft facing and Casi drifted forward to take his place. She caught him as he drifted into the central chamber, kissed him and settled into the chair as it readjusted for her.

"Good hunting, Cheral," she said as she buckled in.

"Thanks, Cousin," Cheral replied and then twisted her helmet into place.

Casi watched the majors as they transferred the patrol fighter pilots to their ships and listened to Stran and Cheral as they transferred beneath STSX.

"STSX," Casi called, "what's the position of the freighter and its escorts?"

"FIVE POINT FOUR DECIPARS BEFORE THEY ARE WITHIN THE ENGAGEMENT SPHERE. THIRTY-ONE POINT ONE TERRAN MINUTES."

'Timing is getting tight,' Casi said softly to Stran and Cheral.

⋏

"Headbands on," Leeana said as Casi glanced around at the Wing clustered neatly behind KKLC14 on one side and B-Group on the other.

"Too bad the director didn't give out headbands when he painted the stripes on our support ships," Casi remarked casually.

"But, Bren," Stran smiled from the right side jump seat, "the navcom's are not flying B Group's ships."

She smiled at him for the reminder. "You're right. The director hasn't adopted your teaching methods. Yet."

Slowly Casi returned her thoughts to the mission ahead and reached out to feel the approaching freighter and fighters. "I see one battlecruiser and fourteen fighters in escort." She hesitated and studied the feeling she was getting as Stran ordered the Wing forward.

Absently, still concentrating on the battlecruiser, then the fighters, she pushed the thrust levers forward. "Apache Leader here, let's get close. Visual Cloaking On."

Something was bothering her and she stayed focused, as she looked around where she knew the Wing was accelerating behind her.

"What is it?" Stran asked, catching her concern.

"Don't know," she replied softly, "but something's wrong."

She studied the fighters one by one, but there were only the sensations she had felt on all of the other engagements. *Strange. Nothing odd there,* and she turned her focus to the freighter.

She embraced the whole of the ship and suddenly realized it was the source of her concerns. *'Something about the freighter, love.'* She probed the defenses and the controls, wondering if the ship had extra fire power, hidden fighters, something to enhance its defenses. But there was nothing and she turned to the crew and again everything seemed normal, a typical number of twelve manned the ship. Then she turned to the cargo and slowly felt each shipping container and pallet. Nothing.

'I don't get it,' she said as she took up their attack position with LTVC21 off to her left.

"Stay focused, Bren," Stran softly as they closed on their target. "LLRT12 will be sure the captives are all right."

"Damn!" Casi shouted. "That's it! There are no captives!"

"What?"

"We've been set up," she said and pulled the thrust levers back. "There are no captives." She turned her head and stared at Stran. "We have no reason to board or attack this freighter."

"KKLC14, Abort!" Stran shouted. "Abort! Disengage! Do NOT engage!"

Without question, Major Kooich repeated the command and the Q-Ships broke off. After a moment of discussion, Major Kooich regrouped the Wing and B-Group into an escort formation, paralleling the unsuspecting freighter and battlecruiser. Stran gave a terse explanation as they slowly reached and quietly passed the still cloaked second group of battlecruisers and fighters.

"Patrol Cruiser Brigstoan," Stran said into the com-link, "Apache Leader Colonel Geaardt here."

"Apache Leader. Good to hear from you," the Brigstoan commander replied. "Are you ready for us to hail the freighter?"

"Negative," Stran said and explained the situation. "There are no captives on board the freighter. We have no reason to attack the escorts at this time."

"Understood," the commander agreed. "No intercept. We do not have a report of any other illicit cargo. I'm glad you received intelligence on the captives in time. It would have been a large black-eye for the Force if we boarded and attacked a *peaceful* freight hauler, even if it was escorted by three battlecruisers and a hundred and fifty fighters."

"It certainly would," Stran said and smiled at Casi. "Our intelligence was timely indeed. If you have no further need of Apache Squadron, we will retire and prepare for the flight home."

"No further need," the commander admitted. "Thank you for your support. Brigstoan out."

"Thank you. Apache Leader out."

Watching Casi, his expression grew into a wide smile. *'You were incredible, Bren. Absolutely incredible.'* Then out loud, he said, "Major Kooich, let's collect our fighters and prepare to go home."

Monday, January 16

Thom stopped the patrol car in the wide parking area along

River Street between Fox and Julia and turned to face Eddie in the passenger seat. He left the car running for heat.

"I hope this is okay," he said as she handed him his sack with Connie's Chicken Panini, homemade chips and a cup of coffee. "I think it's a nice view of the river, and there are enough trees to block out most of the mill."

"It's nice, Thom," she agreed as she opened her sack and took the insulated cup of soup out. "I don't think I've ever had lunch in a police car with a view of the river before."

He smiled at her tease. "Well, you said you wanted to talk to me and I thought this might be a little more private than Connie's. But, it might get the town's ladies talking."

He sipped his coffee and was pleased to find it was still hot.

"That's one of the things I wanted to talk to you about," she said as she slowly removed the lid from her soup and stirred it.

"Oh? Ladies talking?" He took a bite of his Panini.

"Yes, but first," she said seriously, "can you come tomorrow at ten for Mom's memorial service? It's an open casket, come and go sort of thing at the mortuary. Don't know how many people will come, but I'd like it if you could be there."

"I'll be there, Eddie. I'll pick you up for breakfast."

"Thanks," she said and smiled at him. "I told Wally what I overheard some of the women saying about him," she said between spoonfuls. "How he was being deviously cunning, trying to get Carole's land away from her." She chuckled and he smiled at the soft, rich tones of her voice. "Anyway, I know he and Carole have all of that worked out and he's not after her land."

"I know too," he said.

"But I was curious about something else I heard," she said and sipped her iced drink, "a couple of things actually."

"Shoot," he said and smiled at her.

"I heard you were asking questions about Charley's Craft Shop." She watched him as she took another spoonful of soup.

"I figured someone would wonder what I was up to," he said absently and took another bite of his sandwich. "I was talking with Charley one afternoon when I stopped on my rounds." He sipped his coffee again. "And he told me he's buying a forty-acre place just north of the Jordan's ranch on the river. It has a nice, large two-story cabin

41

and enough trees to make him feel comfortable and secluded."

"He is?" Eddie stopped and stared at him. "Is he moving his craft shop?"

"No, he isn't," Thom said. "I wouldn't have believed it, but Charley said he's turning seventy in the spring and he wants to enjoy the money he's put away while he can. He said the craft shop wasn't holding its own, and he didn't like pouring more money into it if it wasn't going to be profitable."

"Wise thing to do," she agreed. "I knew he wasn't making a lot, but I didn't realize it was losing money."

Thom finished his sandwich and dropped the wadded wrapper into his sack. "He just had one little hitch in the whole deal."

"Uh oh, what's that?" she asked as she scooped the last of the soup from the cup.

"Seemed he needs to sell the craft shop, land and buildings," Thom said with a little frown, "before he can finalize the paperwork on the new acreage."

"So, are you trying to help find someone to buy it?"

"Nope," he looked at her over the rim of his coffee cup. "I'm not trying to find someone." His eyes started to dance. "I wasn't going to tell you yet, but I guess it is a small town. I close on the thirtieth of this month. I bought it. Well, the bank and I. George Hattle helped me get it all set up."

Eddie smiled as she dropped her empty soup cup back into her sack and took another sip of her drink. "I wondered," she admitted. "Your furniture business?"

He smiled. "Maybe someday, but not right away. Like I said, some things need to be finished up around here before I will have the time for that hobby. But this gives me a place of my own and room to work if I get time too."

"That's great, Thom," she said. Her smile filled her face.

"And," he continued, "it also turns out Charley has a lady-friend in the small town of Platte, South Dakota, a serious type of lady-friend. He left early a week ago last Saturday morning to go back and bring her out."

"That will certainly surprise a few of the ladies," Eddie chuckled. "Especially the ones that thought they had a special relationship with Charley."

"I bet it will," Thom laughed. "He said he'd be back sometime this week and she's going to help him move his stuff down to his new place."

"I suppose she's going to be staying there with him," she said with a raised eyebrow.

"He didn't say," Thom said and finished his coffee. "But we'll know what they're going to do soon enough."

"Thanks, Thom," Eddie said. "I knew there was a reason behind the gossip I've heard."

"There usually is, Eddie," Thom said as he put his empty cup in his sack. "Thanks for not jumping to conclusions before I could explain."

"When can you show me around?"

"The outside, anytime," he said, still smiling at her. "Unless George can move my Closing date up, it won't be mine for another two weeks, but Charley said that after he's moved out, he doesn't mind giving me the keys. Obviously, I just can't move anything in until after closing."

"I'd like to see it when you can and have the time."

"I can take you around the outside over lunch tomorrow," he said, and she saw the caution slip back into his expression, "if that's not too presumptuous of me."

"It's not too presumptuous," she said, her tone cooler than she meant.

Eddie leaned back against the door and faced him. With a confused smile, she studied him as he stuffed one of the lunch sacks into the other and set them in the door pocket so he would remember to throw them away. She had been very confident, knowing that he would be able to answer the questions the women in Connie's raised on Friday. And suddenly she realized she was very pleased he was buying a place here in town, a place that spoke of a future rather than an apartment that one takes for granted and can walk away from with little or no notice.

She thought about his manners from the first time she talked with him in the flower shop, how cool and impersonal she had been, and how angry she had been over the flowers. But she had to admit he knew what he was doing and his purpose was more for her benefit than anyone else's. She had worked through her issues, her feelings of loss and the realities of her mother's condition. Then, to find out he had actually started searching for answers to her father's disappearance and had found information that no one had uncovered before. When she thought about it, she was surprised at how much he had done for her without her realizing it.

She thought about his courteous, disciplined reserve, and she wondered if he was always so guarded, so polite and constrained in his actions, like he was just now, concerned that she would see an offer as an imposition or an intrusion. She wondered what it would take for him to let himself be less formal, more relaxed, warmer and tender. The word 'intimate' slipped through her mind and she wondered if he wanted intimacy. It was obvious he liked being with her, and she was feeling the same toward him, but he kept his distance, he kept... Then she remembered Wednesday night when he held her in the hospital, cradled her like a baby and patiently, tenderly waited for her to calm her emotions, softly sharing her heartache. He was there and comforted her when she needed it the most and she did not want to let those moments go. He knew she needed compassion and he gave it to her without obligation.

"You're suddenly very quiet," he said bringing her out of her thoughts, a concerned look on his face. "Have I done something wrong?"

"Stop, Thom," she said, again more sharply than she meant. "Sorry, but stop worrying about the little, unimportant things. When I think you've done something wrong, I'll tell you." She hesitated and decided. "Are you afraid of me?"

He stared at her, surprised by the question. "No, I'm not afraid of you. Why would you ask that?"

"Then what are you afraid of?" she asked. "Why do I feel like you're walking on eggs when you're around me?"

He looked out of the windshield and leaned back against his door as he licked his lips. "Okay," he started with a sigh. "Here's the skinny. I am a little afraid. Afraid of how I feel when I'm near you. Afraid of doing something you will see as breaking the promise I made.

"When I first saw you, I knew you were the most beautiful woman I'd ever seen and I wanted to meet you, to be with you, but you seemed very sad, distant, shutting people out. So, being what I am, I made a few inquiries and did a little research and found out what had happened to your family and to you after you moved to the valley. I researched your father and his job, trying to understand what might have led up to his leaving. I wanted to help, but every time I thought of something to do, it wasn't right."

She watched him and saw him glance at her and then look back to the windshield.

"From my searching, I knew about your problems with boys in school and after you graduated and I knew you had withdrawn into a world of work and worry over your mother. I uncovered the details of your financial problems and how you found the missing insurance policy, a blessing at a critical time. But when I saw you, I knew you needed a friend, a real friend, not just someone mouthing the words.

"I wanted to be near you and to let you know someone cares, someone understands, and I knew you did not want a relationship." He sighed again and looked down at the steering yoke. "I lost my dad before I was born, so I didn't feel the depression and despair of losing him, but my mother was in her early fifties when I was born and by the time I was out of high school, she was in her seventies. She only had one love in her life and without him and me grown, life finally became too much for her to continue alone. I was eighteen when she let herself die.

"So when I saw your sadness, I knew what you were going through, but I didn't, and still don't want to invade your privacy any more than you want to let me. I know men have tried to impose their feelings and to persuade you one way or another without respect and with complete disregard for what you want and care about. I don't want to be like that. I don't want you seeing me as being that way.

"Whose company you keep and hang out with, how you live your life and what you want and don't want to commit to are your choices, yours alone. I know you didn't ask me to be your friend, but I wish to be your friend, a friend first, before all else."

Eddie sat and stared at him for a long moment, thinking.

"I just want you to know you're loved and cared about, Eddie," he said softly and looked back out of the windshield. "There's no obligation and I don't want to take advantage of you."

She continued looking at him and finally, after another long moment, she said, "Okay, Thom Baine, let's cut to the obvious. You like me."

Startled, he turned and looked at her. "Yes, I thought I just explained—"

"And I like you too," she said. "And from the first time we talked and you gave me the bouquet, you made it clear your intent was 'no strings attached,' 'no obligations.' But," she leaned toward him, put her open palms on both sides of his face and pulled herself to him until their foreheads touched, "if this relationship is going to continue, Thomas, you ARE going to have to take advantage of me, more than a little and often."

She kissed him tenderly and he wrapped his arms around her shoulders and gently drew her to him.

Tuesday, January 17

Thom stood with Eddie at the door to the chapel room in Corby's Mortuary as she greeted the folks that came to pay their respects. He had picked her up early and they leisurely breakfasted at Jerry's Café before she needed to be at the mortuary to check on the last minute details for the service. When they arrived, Eddie decided she wanted to personally greet the arrivals as they came in and signed the guest book.

The mortuary opened the front doors early and the first family entered and stopped at the guest book. Eddie inhaled deeply and gently leaned back against Thom, reassured by the contact and his closeness. Then she composed herself, straightened and began thanking the guests as they entered. The line grew and she was surprised at how many people knew her mother and took the time to come. She knew she had become withdrawn, but their turnout reminded her how much of her life she had pushed out of her thoughts, focusing only on her here and now. She also noticed those that were surprised to see Thom, or anyone for that matter, standing with her to receive them.

She smiled when she saw Wally and Carole and the deputies behind them, all in their dress uniforms and polished leather jackets. Wally and Carole stopped and Carole hugged her. Wally took her hand briefly and nodded solemnly at Thom.

Dan Lupis took her hand and turned to the woman with him. "Eddie, this is my wife Mandy. Sorry I haven't introduced her before now."

Ted Marks shook her hand gently. "My sincere sympathies, Eddie," he said and nodded to Thom.

The greetings continued and as the last couple in the queue signed the book, a small crowd suddenly filled the doorway and entered in a hurry. They signed the book and lined up in front of them.

"I'm so sorry for your loss, Miss Eddie," the first woman said as she took Eddie's hand. "I'm Matti, Mrs. Shara's head woman."

"Miss Eddie," the second greeted, "I'm Cara, Mrs. Shara's house girl. Sorry about your mama."

Annie and Hank introduced themselves and made their sympathies known and then Shara reached out and took her hand.

"Sorry it has been so long since we've seen each other, Eddie," Shara said. "I wish now was under better circumstances."

"Thanks. Me too, Shar. Can you come to the reception?"

"I wasn't sure we'd make it back in time," Shara continued cryptically, then added as she turned to Greg, "This is my husband, Greg. What do you think?"

Greg leaned forward and took her hand. "Good to finally meet you, Eddie. Glad we could make it. I think we can make time to come by for a short while." Then he looked at Thom. "Good to see you again Thom. I understand you had an enlightening weekend."

Eddie looked up at Thom, questions dancing in her eyes as he turned her to the chapel room. Without answering, he guided her down the aisle to their seats in the front row of chairs.

C.3482.401

"Was the freighter intercepted?" Prince Kiese asked when his Naval Intelligence Officer answered.

"No, sir," the intelligence officer answered brightly. "It arrived at Gillac Freighters on schedule. It is the first one out of the last ten to arrive safely."

"Details!" the prince shouted. "Give me details! How did they get away? How many fighters did we lose?"

The intelligence officer hesitated before answering. "Sir, we did not lose any fighters. There was no conflict."

"What?" the prince shouted. "No conflict? How can that be? I sent three battlecruisers and one hundred and fifty fighters to escort the freighter, like I have with the last three freighters, and they were not intercepted?"

"That is correct, sir," the Officer said, timidly. "The fleet obviously was enough of a presence to deter anyone from intercepting them."

The prince stared at the console monitor.

"I thought that would please you, sir," the Officer said, "having a shipment make it without trouble."

The prince found his voice. "Not this time! It was supposed to be a trap you idiot!" He slammed his fist down on the console and disconnected.

He quickly keyed for his Naval Operations and shouted at the first voice to answer.

"Yes, sir," the voice stammered, "Commander Symns is available and he can explain the operation." The connection blinked and the mature face of the commander filled the screen.

"Yes, Sire. Commander Symns here," he said as the connection stabilized.

"I understand the latest freighter arrived without any attempted interception."

"That is correct," the commander said. "We dispatched one battlecruiser to fly continuous escort for the entire trip and had two more battlecruisers shadowing the first. They expected trouble at both navigational fixes, course change points, but nothing happened. They had no targets on any of their sensors and are positive they were not being shadowed."

Puzzled, the prince began pacing in front of the console.

"Sire," the commander continued, "we followed all of the same procedures as in the past shipments, used the same channels to process the shipping orders and even made sure the loading in Copus Two could be observed, since we suspect the Peace Force has undercover agents there. There is no reason they would think this shipment was any different than the others. We even required part of the shipment be loaded in Envirocubes. The trap was properly baited."

"Then how did they know there were no captives?" the prince asked in a loud voice. "How?"

"We do not know, Sire."

"Find Out!" he shouted and severed the connection.

▲ ▲ ▲ ▲ ▲

"I can't believe you handled that many people so calmly," Thom said as he opened the SUV's door and helped Eddie in. "It was a very nice reception, but there were a lot of people."

"Yes, there were," Eddie sighed as she sat down and flopped her head back against the headrest. "Mary from the shop was a great help with the organizing and keeping everyone moving, and Connie from the delicatessen was a marvel with the finger foods. I would've been lost without their help."

Thom closed the door and hurried around to the driver's side and got in. He slipped his earpiece on and adjusted it until it felt right.

"I know it went longer than you expected," he said, then turned and looked at her. "Are you doing okay?"

She waved his concerns aside. "Yeah, I'm okay. Just a little tired." Then she smiled and rolled her head to look at him, "There's going to be a lot more gossip, though."

"More? How so?" he asked as he started the SUV.

"Shar showing up in public and introducing her husband of over two months." Eddie chuckled. "And he's someone they don't know. The fact that she's alive and well would have been enough to set the gossip mill spinning, but to be married for two months and no one knew. That certainly ices the cake. Wait until they find out he's Jill's half-brother."

"I'm sure you're right," Thom agreed as he drove around the block and headed back toward Main.

"It's obvious that you already knew," Eddie said, her eyes asking for more details.

Thom smiled and glanced at her. "I knew. I met them the Tuesday after Christmas, when they openly came into town the first time since she 'disappeared.' I thought Carole mentioned that night to you, when they went into Hap's."

"She did," Eddie said, "but for some strange reason, I think there's more to the story. I think you and Wally know more about them than you let on."

Thom looked at Eddie, realizing she was very good at reading the subtleties in a mannerism or a conversation. Then he admitted,

49

"There is and I do. You're very good at sensing that, but right now, I can't tell you everything."

She studied his expression and held his eyes for a long moment. "Fair enough," she finally said and smiled as he turned south on Main. "Tell me, then, did you take the day off or what? How can you be with me all morning and now be on such a long lunch? It's nearly two-thirty."

Thom smiled at her. "This morning and through the reception, I took off to support you. Now, the long lunch is me taking time for me to show you where I'm going to live and to see what you think about it."

"As if I had a say in it," she chuckled.

His eyes danced, but he did not say any more. He drove down Main and after they passed Hap's, he slowed and turned into the snow covered parking lot in front of the craft shop. He pulled up and stopped beside the large, two story house.

"Glad you wore boots," he said as he helped her out of the car. "Charley hasn't plowed the lot or the drive in weeks. He lets the wind blow it away."

He guided her up to the house and onto the wide veranda that wrapped around its front three sides.

"You can look in the windows," he said and gestured for her to look. "I think it's modern enough and yet, will feel comfortable with a few older pieces of furniture and not be too contradictory. There are four rooms and two half baths on the ground floor and four bedrooms, three baths and a laundry room upstairs. The family room in the back has a large fireplace and the master bedroom is just above it with its own fireplace."

She smiled at his enthusiasm and candidness.

"What about the kitchen?" she asked as if he were intentionally ignoring it.

"Oh, it's great," he said quickly. "Fairly new appliances and room for a large refrigerator and a large upright freezer. Open plan into the dining room." He stopped and looked at her. "I know I'm acting like a kid in a candy shop, but I didn't think I could have a place of my own, at least not for many years yet. And never anything this nice. This place has things my mother only dreamed of having."

"Thom, I think it's wonderful," she said and hugged him. "But I'm going to be very upset if I don't get to visit now and then."

He wrapped his arms around her and held her close. "If you meant what you said yesterday, I'll be very disappointed if you don't visit very often. Besides, I think I'm going to need an understanding and complimentary feminine input for decorating."

She tightened her embrace and kissed him. "As long as you want me to be the feminine input, I will."

"That could be a long time, Eddie," he said, then slowly relaxed his hold and turned her in his arms toward the craft building. "And over here," he said as he guided her down the side steps and across the snow covered driveway, backtracking over their trail in the snow, "is the space I hope to use as a work shop."

"Do you need all of this for refinishing?" she asked as they walked along the front of the store.

"No," he admitted, "but Ted is a wood worker and has some ideas for new furniture."

"You're already thinking about a partner?"

"Nope," he said and smiled at her. "'If' I do let him work here, I'll provide space for a small fee and a percentage of his sales, and he'll still pay his part of the utilities. He'll also have to buy his own materials."

"Very good thinking," she admitted as Thom suddenly cupped his hand over his ear.

"DEPUTY BAINE," WL-One announced in his ear. "YOU ARE BEING WATCHED FROM A VEHICLE PARKED ON WEBB BETWEEN YOU AND THE BRIDGE."

"What is it?" Eddie asked, looking around and then back at Thom.

"Probably nothing," he said, "but we're being watched." He tapped his earpiece and asked, "How long has he been there?"

"THE VEHICLE FOLLOWED YOU FROM TOWN."

"Thanks. Let me know if it moves." Then he put his arm around Eddie and turned her to face the building as if he was showing her something and he glanced through the trees. He noted the dark silver, four-wheel drive truck parked on the street about seventy yards away. "Apparently, someone followed us from town and has stopped on Webb to watch us."

"Is this normal?" she asked as he turned her back toward the SUV.

"No," he admitted, "but it doesn't surprise me too much."

He gestured to the buildings and asked, "Is there something else I can show you?" and when she shook her head, he led her back to the SUV, opened the door and helped her in.

"Where to?" he asked as he buckled himself in and started the car. "The day is still young unless you're going in to the flower shop today."

"I'm not working until tomorrow," she said as he turned the SUV around and started back up Main.

"Would you like to stop at Hap's or somewhere?"

She thought for a few moments, then said, "I think I'd just like to go home and put my feet up for a while. Could we do that and then do something later, for dinner maybe?"

"Sure," he agreed, suddenly looking forward to a quiet afternoon.

One Hundred-Two

"As you all know," Stran said to the crews gathered in Obscure's Flight Ops Briefing Room, "this mission could have turned out very badly for all of us. Our agents in Angrilat confirmed the freighter arrived with only non-perishable cargo, which obviously means there were no captives onboard."

A few of the crews twisted in their seats feeling uneasy with his implications.

"I guess I don't really need to tell any of you," Stran continued, "what the outcry would be if we attacked the escorts of a normal, legitimate freight shipment, even if it was going to one of Prince Kiese's better known ports. Since the Force has not declared a blockade or an embargo on the prince's shipping or any of his ports, he would have called such an act of piracy.

"My eternal thanks to all of you for your unquestioning response to the abort command. We will try to get better intelligence earlier in our missions and hopefully, avoid any more last minute surprises. Thank you." Stran nodded to Major Kooich and sat down.

"Thank you, Colonel," Major Kooich said as he stood up. "I know all of you are pleased to support these missions without regard for personal benefit or status, so you will not be upset to understand that the Board tallies are unchanged." A soft snicker passed through the group. "For the record, the Tallies remain as follows.

"Major Miiles with one kill.

"Lieutenant Miiles with eight.

"Lieutenant Glean with five and one half.

"Lieutenant Donnr with four.

"Major Mooren with five.

"Lieutenant Kaal with twenty-six."

Someone clapped and Major Kooich glanced at Major Mooren.

"Lieutenant Bradg with ten.

"Lieutenant Tam with nine.

"Captain Haak with thirty.

"Cadet Tigs with twenty-two.

"Cadet Moss with ten.

"My apologies to Cadet Grenn and Cadet Kast. Better hunting next mission.

"Lieutenant Kooich with thirteen and one half and finally Lieutenant Geaardt with one hundred and two. 'Well done' to each and every one of you."

Again, someone began clapping and the room quickly joined in. He held his hand up and looked over the room for a moment as they quieted. Then he said, "If there are no questions, the briefing is concluded. Dismissed."

As the room emptied, Major Kooich turned and glanced at Leeana, Stran and Casi.

"Major," Stran began, "I want you to set up a series of tests that will check the sensory capabilities of each of the crew members. I want to get a feel for the level of perception each has. Can they sense the presence of others or things and if so can they distinguish characteristics? Can they identify who or what they are feeling?"

Casi looked at him, and he felt her self-consciousness.

"That won't be easy," Leeana said. "We'll have to broaden the tests so they don't see a specific pattern in the elements."

"You might talk with Kiile about this," Stran said. "He mentioned once that the Marines periodically check for something similar. Maybe, between what you can think of and some of his comments, we can put together a meaningful test."

"We'll see what we can figure out," Major Kooich said.

⅄

"You know there are others in our small squad, don't you?" Casi asked Stran as they walked across the clearing below Obscure's launch portal. "I know you've told me before that it's a trait that's not seen often, but—"

"And it still is," Stran said. "We know I have it to a lesser degree than you do, but it's still there. But what you have is simply incredible and it seems to be getting better and better with time. That makes me think that if someone has the talent, there might be a way to train it, improve it, nurture it."

"And Cheral is beginning to have it and so is Jill."

He stopped and thought a moment. "Yes, you did say they were exhibiting some of the trait."

"I don't know what I've done to make my capability better," she admitted as they stepped up on STSX's aft ramp. "Whatever I'm doing, I'm not doing it consciously."

"I know," he said as the aft portal closed behind them. "I've been watching you, trying to see if I can see anything obvious. But I haven't seen anything that I would say is directly related."

"Well, I don't want to analyze it too much," she said as she settled into the jump seat.

"We won't," he said and settled into the pilot's chair. "But I followed your thoughts when you searched the freighter and its cargo. I was amazed at how you quickly and systematically searched the ship and the amount of detail you picked out. Bren," he stopped and leaned close to her, catching her hand, "if it wasn't for you and your talent, the entire Peace Force would be in deep hot water today."

She blushed and tried to look away, but he held her eyes and smiled.

"I am so very proud of you, Bren," he said. "And I'm very proud of how you choose to use your talents. But I do worry."

"Worry?"

"STSX, take us back to the ranch, please." Then he squeezed her hand. "I worry about the strain it puts on you, being the only one that can see in such detail and to such a distance. The responsibility you put on yourself with having this talent and ability."

"Yes, I know," she admitted. "I've *heard* you wrestling with your concerns. And I have to agree with you. Somehow, Bernice or someone in the Family expected me to have a special talent. I am as sure as you are that is why they tried to take me, and are still trying to take me."

"In one very odd twist of fate, we were very lucky that Bernice poisoned you out of rage, and missed seeing the potential she had when she had both you and Jill at the same moment. I shudder to think of what might have happened if she had realized, had paused to consider..."

"I know, love," she said and leaned over and kissed him. "I am thankful for you and for you saving me every moment of every day.

And now I realize that she actually did me a favor by poisoning me. She gave us time, time for me to train, for me to strengthen my talents, for new talents to..."

She straightened and looked straight into his eyes. "Love? Do you think the poison and the battle STSX says I had in fending it off might have caused my perceptions to grow, to improve? I didn't have much detail in those sensations until after you rescued me. STSX?" she asked. "Is there any correlation between the treatments you used to help Cheral focus her sensations and those used in my recovery?"

"YES."

"Yes?" Stran was surprised.

"THE PROCEDURE USED FOR THE CAPTAIN WAS FOR A FULL BLOOD RYGONIAN. THE PROCEDURE USED FOR CASI'S RECOVERY CONTAINED A BLEND. CERTAIN CHEMICALS FOR HER KYDDELLAN BLOOD AND THE SAME CHEMICALS AS USED ON THE CAPTAIN FOR HER RYGONIAN BLOOD AND OTHER SPECIFIC CHEMICALS FOR HER TERRAN, HUMAN BLOOD."

"I think STSX and Medical may have just given us a big clue," Casi chuckled, "for what we should do when your testing finds those with fledgling talents."

▲ ▲ ▲ ▲ ▲

Thom pulled into Eddie's driveway and quickly went around and helped her out of the SUV. He paused for a few minutes, watching the street in both directions. Eddie stood close, slipped an arm around him and also watched.

"Is that truck still following us?" she asked.

"I think so," he said, the words just out of his mouth when the truck came from the south and crossed Birch on Fox. "Well we know for sure he's interested in what we're doing." He smiled at her. "You don't have a jealous, ex-boyfriend that I don't know about, do you?"

She punched his arm and turned to the house. He followed her and stopped on the front porch to wait while she unlocked the door. He tapped his earpiece.

"Wally? Thom here," he said. "Give me the registration on the silver truck that's been following us this afternoon."

He waited as Eddie turned in the open doorway and listened.

"An Abe Brownly, huh? Lives on Birch at Mann," he repeated out loud as Wally repeated WL-One's response. "I guess we need to add him into our daily checks."

When Wally agreed, he continued, "Would you mind having Eddie's house scanned for transmitters and recorders, like you do with Carole's place? With all of the people in and about her place today, it might be a good thing to check."

Thom nodded absently as Wally answered him. "Thanks. Same schedule as Carole's. That's great. I'll be in at four for the early beat. You and Carole have a good day off."

When he tapped his earpiece again and turned, he was surprised to see Eddie still holding the door open, waiting for him to finish.

"Sorry to keep you," he said and quickly followed her in. "Thought I better check with Wally before I forgot what I was going to ask him."

"You? Forget?" She eyed him curiously. "I thought you had a very good memory."

"Yeah, I do," he smiled. "I guess I'm impatient. I just wanted to know who was watching us. Tomorrow, I'll figure out why."

"I don't think there's any law against driving around town, seeing what there is to see," she said as she hung her coat in the closet behind the front door. "Here, give me yours," she said as she took his coat and hung it with hers.

"Very true," Thom admitted, "but I intend to find out if there's more to it than that."

"Oh, you do?" She chuckled and gestured to the sofa. "Can I get you anything? Water, coffee, beer, wine?"

"No," he said and settled himself on the near end of the sofa. "I don't think I want anything to drink right now." He patted the space next to him. "Come and relax. That's what you said you wanted to do, not wait on guests."

She slipped her boots off by the front door and was almost to the sofa when his expression changed and he tapped his earpiece.

"Thanks," he said as he got up and turned to the end table at the opposite end of the sofa. "Tell me what you see." He bent and looked at the lamp and its shade. At first he didn't see anything, but when he picked the lamp up, he saw the voice transmitter adhered to one of the sculptured legs. He turned to Eddie and silently mouthed "a glass of water."

She went to the kitchen and quickly returned with a full glass and watched intently as he pried the transmitter off the lamp base and dropped it into the glass. She started to say something, but he held his finger up to his lips and turned to the long legged side table beside the wing-backed chair next to the front window. He checked the lamp with no luck, then he looked the table over and found a second transmitter stuck to the bottom under the single small drawer. He dropped it into the glass with the first.

When she mouthed "how many?" he held up one hand and bent two fingers down, then he turned to the dining room.

"Do you like any particular music?" he asked as he studied the underside of the pedestal table and popped another loose from the back side of the carved edging.

"A little of the popular stuff, light rock and a few of the oldies," she said, playing along as he turned to the hall bath.

"I like a bit of that as well," he said and found the fourth under the back edge of the counter next to the wall.

He stopped at her bedroom door and with a gesture asked if he could go in. She nodded and followed him. "My mom liked the romantic country stuff, but I never developed a real interest in it."

"Too bad," Thom said as he stopped in front of the window centered on the back wall. "I like romantic stuff."

He parted the curtains and felt along the window frame and curtain rod holders, then he checked each sash and the locks. Finally, under the bottom sill shelf, nearest the head of the bed, he found the fifth transmitter. He smiled as he dropped it into the glass of water and cupped his hand over his ear again.

"That's five voice. Any video?" He paused and then said, "Good. Check her car the next time she drives it. Thanks." He tapped his earpiece and turned to her. "Thanks for playing along."

"Sure. What are those?" she asked as he set the glass in the freezer section of her refrigerator.

"Bugs. Voice transmitters," he said as he returned to the living room and sat back down on the sofa, "planted so someone can listen to what you or anyone says while they're here."

She stopped in front of him and stared at him. "You asked about video. Did you mean like video recorders?"

"Yes," he said and patted the space beside him again. "There were none planted. No one's taking pictures of you here in your home. Now, sit down and relax like you were going to a few minutes ago."

Eddie settled on the sofa with a little space between them, hesitating as she considered what had just happened. Then she slowly turned away from him and lay back across his lap and stretched her legs over the arm of the sofa. She closed her eyes and folded her hands in front of her as he slipped a couch pillow under her head.

"How did you know?" she asked. "I mean, even to think about the possibility?"

"Seemed prudent to check," he said and she looked up at him. "When the three of us deputies first got here, someone was planting voice transmitters on our patrol cars and our houses. When Wally and Carole started seeing each other on a regular basis, Wally decided to keep check of her house and for a while, he found a few. When we removed a transmitter, a new one would show up. We ended up with ten or twelve in the office safe along with a number of locating beacons. Wally decided we'd plant a few of the beacons ourselves, just to aggravate whoever was planting them." Eddie chuckled. "It worked. They stopped planting them."

"How did you know where to look?" she asked. "Five's a lot isn't it?"

"On the porch, I asked Wally to have your house scanned," Thom said. "And the scan picked up the five transmitters we found and put on ice. And five is actually about normal for a house this size. With your reception today, it was a perfect opportunity for someone to drop a few inside. Usually, eavesdroppers have to put their devices on the outside of windows, but today allowed someone access to the inside."

"But how did you know where to look?"

"The scan told me where to look," he said and saw the questions still in her eyes. "Think of it as a searching tool, something like a drone, that we can use to detect different things. When a scan is in progress, it can direct us very close to where we should look."

"You mentioned a schedule," she said softly, "like Carole's?"

"Wally will have our tool check on your house and your car twice a day at a minimum," he said, "just like he has it check on Carole's. It will also keep a watch around your house and the block to let us know if anyone that shouldn't be here comes by."

"You're doing this for me?"

"Yes, Eddie," he said softly, "I've tried to not be pushy or do anything that would distance you. I wanted you to make up your own mind about me, but I really do care about you. A lot."

She rolled toward him and put her free arm around his neck, pulling herself close as he curled one arm under her and the other around her waist. She slipped her other arm around behind him and squeezed gently.

"Thank you, Thomas," she said and laid her head against his shoulder.

"You're very welcome, Eddie," he said and gently held her to him. "I probably would have started checking on you and your place, even if you didn't want to be with me."

She tilted her head back, pulled herself up and kissed him, long and tenderly.

⬥ ⬥ ⬥ ⬥ ⬥

"What have you put together, Abe?" Don Nikle's voice asked through the Mountain Phone console.

"I have six names like you asked me to choose," Abe answered as he sat down in the chair beside the console, "nice and pedestrian, just like you stipulated. They're all from modest, unimportant families and should not cause too much notice if they should happen to wander off. Only one is from the valley. The rest are from out of town."

"Good, good," Don said, his voice brighter than usual. "Students, I take it?"

"Yes," Abe admitted. "In their early twenties as you requested. They will be available through the spring semester and possibly into the summer."

"That will work," Don continued. "I have reestablished our link with the Traders and will need to supplement my resources from here. Send me your list."

"Sure. Give me a second," Abe said and went into his den, retrieved the memory chip and returned. "Here it comes." He slipped the chip into the data slot of the console and pressed the Send key.

"If you want any of these delivered, you will have to send some of your associates to do the pickups. I am not a 'Shopper', don't have the skills or the inclination. I'm a data person, not a delivery person. Understand?"

"Looks like your list came through fine, Abe," Don said. "I'll let you know when I need something more."

"Did you hear me, Don? I'm not going to help you with—" The monitor went dark as the link disconnected and Abe cursed loudly.

Wednesday, January 18

It was before seven in the morning when Thom parked his patrol car in the lot in front of the marshal's office and started down the west side of Main. He checked the general store and passed the city hall building with its wide, snow covered front lawn, past Jerry's Café, the cinema and the numerous small shops south to Juniper. When he crossed the street and started back north, he asked WL-One to follow him and scan the back side of each shop as he went. At the bank, he detoured and walked through the drive-thru lanes and then headed past the grocery store. When he passed Sally's Casuals he waved at Sally as she arranged clothes on a rack near the front window and then noted Connie had not made it in yet. WL-One reported everything was normal and he crossed the street to Mary's Flower Boutique. He was about to look through the front window when WL-One called him.

He turned east and slipped between Mary's main building and the storage building on Ash and followed WL-One's concern. He stopped at the iron gate covering the back door to the florist shop.

Looking closer, Thom looked at the damage to the wood and steel jamb, pry marks where someone obviously tried to spring the bolt.

"Any recent records of anyone being here?" he asked the remote.

"NONE," WL-One replied.

He studied the snow and realized there were foot prints around the door, outside the trampled path to the storage building.

"Take a picture," he said and stepped back to give WL-One room. "I wonder why someone would want to break into a florist shop." Then he said, "WL-One, see what the archives or public records have to say about Mary. What her affiliations are, family ties, anything that might be of interest."

"SEARCHING."

"Thanks," he said and retraced his steps to the street.

When he stopped and looked through the shop's front window, he saw Eddie hanging her coat on the pegs by the cool room. He stepped up to the front door and knocked and Eddie came quickly, unlocked the door and let him in. She locked the door behind him and before he could say anything, she wrapped her arms around his neck and kissed him tenderly.

"And good morning to you too," he said as she relaxed her hold and set back on her feet.

"Nice to see you so early in my day," she replied and led him to the back of the shop. "I'll have some coffee in a minute," she said as she prepared the coffee maker and switched it on.

"You know I shouldn't dally," he said and sat down on a stool at the end of her work table, "but for you I'll make an exception."

"Thanks for yesterday and last night, Thom," she said as she set two cups beside the coffee maker and turned to face him, "even if I did fall asleep in your arms. I was a terrible date, host or whatever, but it's the first time I've felt secure enough to relax in a long time."

"It was certainly my pleasure," he said. "I would've held you all night if I needed to."

When the coffee was ready, she filled the cups, handed him one and sat down on the stool next to him.

"You know, Eddie," he said as he sipped his cup, "I like having my first cup of the day with you."

She smiled with a blush. "Me too."

He took a deeper sip and then looked at her seriously. "I need to ask you a question." He continued when she nodded, "On my walk around this morning, I noticed someone has tried to break in through the back door. Can you tell me that damage is old damage and that I don't need to worry about it?"

"I don't remember any damage, Thom," she said as she got up and went to the back door.

When she opened the inside door, Thom pointed out what he saw. "Ask Mary about this when she comes in and then give me a call, please."

"Sure," she said as she closed and locked the inside door. "Is this connected to—"

"I don't know, Eddie," he said and picked up his cup. "When I see something unusual, I just like to check it out and be sure everything is okay."

"I'll ask," she said.

"Will I see you at Connie's for lunch?"

"Sure. Say, twelve-thirty?"

"Twelve-thirty it is," he said as he finished his cup. He stepped to her, pulled her close and kissed her. "Good morning, Eddie. I hope today is the best day ever."

She smiled as he relaxed his embrace and turned toward the door. She let him out and gave him a quick kiss before she closed and relocked it. He waved and she watched him as he walked north past the bakery.

⟁

Thom stepped into the office and sat down at his desk. He switched his monitor on and pulled the remote's monitor from his desk drawer. He got up and poured himself a cup of coffee and returned to his desk. With his first sip, he frowned. *Gotta have Eddie show us how to make coffee,* he said to himself.

"SEARCH RESULTS AVAILABLE," WL-One said in his ear.

"What did you find?" he asked as he set his mug on a coaster beside his monitor.

"FLOWER SHOP OWNER IS WIDOWED, ONE DAUGHTER, OUT OF COLLEGE, MARRIED AND LIVING IN ABILENE TEXAS. MARY'S PARENTS AGED AND LIVING IN RIGGIN. SHE SUPPLEMENTS THEIR RETIREMENT FROM THE PROCEEDS OF THE SHOP. NO FAMILY TIES TO THE REEDS FAMILY OR GOVERNING COUNCIL ARE OBVIOUS. GENERAL SPECULATION IS THAT SHE KEEPS MONIES IN THE SHOP. SHE DOES NOT TRUST BANKS."

"Any information on why she distrusts banks?"

"BANKS FORECLOSED ON HER HOUSE MANY YEARS AGO AFTER HER HUSBAND DIED."

Thom thought about how many times he had heard of that very same situation and reason.

"Thanks," he said and began reviewing WL-One's images from its overnight surveillance.

It was just after eight when Dan Lupis and Kenny came in to start their day. Still obviously half asleep, Kenny hung his coat behind his desk, adjacent to the counter at the front door. Dan greeted Thom and hung his coat on the wall peg behind his desk. They both turned to the coffee urn and filled their mugs.

"Is Wally taking Wednesdays off now?" Dan asked as he walked back to his desk.

"Yeah," Kenny said as he sat down. "He's trying to take off the same days Carole has off, Sundays and Wednesdays."

"I think that's great," Dan said as he unlocked his desk and started to settle into the day's activities. "He probably can't get them all off, but he should take all of them he can."

"Good with me," Thom said as he switched his monitors off and locked his desk. He stood up, collected his coat and walked to the back door. "I've got rounds and should be back in after lunch, one-thirty or so."

"Gotcha," Kenny said and keyed a notation into the activity log.

⋏ ⋏ ⋏ ⋏ ⋏

Wally opened the back door and let Carole enter his office ahead of him. "Hi Dan," he said as he took Carole's coat and hung it on a peg behind his desk, "You said you needed to see me." He hung his coat beside Carole's and turned to look at Dan.

"Sorry to call you on your day off, but you have visitors, Wally," Dan said and gestured to the waiting area near the front door.

Wally turned to greet the couple and remembered them as Dan led the way.

"Wally, this is Mr. and Mrs. Reeds from down near Grants," Dan said. "They said they know you and have something they want to discuss with you."

"Good afternoon, Thad," Wally said and extended his hand in greeting, "and to you as well Betti. Good to see you again. Can we get you a cup of coffee or water?"

"No thanks, Marshal," Thad said. "We just finished lunch at Betti's sister's place."

Wally motioned to Carole. "Thad, Betti, this is my fiancée, Carole Davis. I believe you have already met Deputy Dan Lupis," he continued as he gestured to Dan, "and our Dispatcher Kenny. My other two deputies are out on rounds."

When Thad and Betti responded with their "nice to meet you," Wally asked what he could do for them.

"Do you have a few minutes? I, we, would like to talk to you about some things that are happening down home."

Wally turned to Carole, "We may be a little bit. Make yourself comfortable." Then he turned to Thad and led them into the small conference room in the corner of the office and closed the door behind them.

He gestured to the chairs around the small round table. "Please sit down and we can talk," he said and took a seat in the corner facing the door.

"First," Thad said, "I, we, want to thank you again for your help with our situation down by Grants. I do not know what we would have done if you had not stopped to help."

"You are very welcome, Thad."

Thad hesitated and looked at Betti and she nodded, urging him to continue.

"I do not know how to start, exactly," Thad said. "We have discussed and puzzled this situation for a long time and after the past few days, we decided we had to talk to someone."

Wally listened and did not comment.

"Being here and knowing you a little, Betti says we should talk with you about it," Thad continued, still skirting the issue.

"If I can be of help, I will," Wally said and then waited.

"At home, there is no one we can talk to. Chief Parks is part of the problem," Thad said softly. "We come from a large family of farmers, manual laborers and some with ranching skills. Some of us have the ability to learn complex things while others are less so."

"Get to the point, Thad," Betti urged. "The marshal does not have all day."

"Okay, okay," Thad said and smiled at her. Then he looked at Wally. "For as long as I can remember people in our area have grown up knowing they would be tested and categorized and then sent away in groups to work someplace else, presumably based on the test findings." He took a deep breath, "but this past fall, we realized things were not as we thought they were."

"What happened?" Wally asked and leaned forward to hear.

"It was the last full week of October when a group of workers, sixty or seventy that had been gathered earlier in the month for jobs somewhere, suddenly returned home."

"Isn't that a good thing?" Wally asked.

"Yes and no," Thad admitted. "They could not remember where they had been, but had stories of being held, like captives in confined quarters until their transportation arrived. It made no sense, but they were scared of being collected again and happy at the same time for being brought back home." Thad stopped and looked at Betti again. She nodded.

"About three weeks later, a larger group was collected and taken to a place near Grants where they said a flying transport came to pick them up, but something happened to the transport. It exploded."

Wally noticed Thad was breathing heavily.

"They were detained for another week and then taken to meet a second transport. The people were almost to it, brought to board it, when it exploded too. Everyone was scared out of their minds and ran, breaking free of the Elders and the guards that were containing them—"

"Broke free? Elders? Guards? They were being taken against their will?" Wally asked to be sure he was hearing Thad correctly.

Thad nodded. "Some of them came back home and that is how we came to know the story. Betti's step brother was one of those taken and he told us what was happening. After that, a lot of them scattered, going to relatives or friends elsewhere. Some out of the valley and many have not told anyone where they are."

"Okay," Wally said softly, "What do you want me to do?"

"In a minute Marshal," Thad said and continued, "The collections quieted down and then the judge and a lot of her Elders disappeared. We felt that was a good thing, especially after Harry Woods and the Clotter brothers disappeared, but then the collections started again. We gathered up all of our things and jumped into the truck and left. They tried to stop us and that is when you found us on the highway."

Wally nodded, thinking to himself, finally understanding the bullet hole in the tire.

"Then this last weekend, eleven of our strongest young men were collected and taken somewhere. We were all told their skills were needed for some construction work, but the way they were collected and removed looked like the other collections, just smaller in numbers. Betti got a call from her brother telling us about it and that more and more people are being gathered at the farmstead. He thinks it is starting all over again."

Wally looked at the closed door and remembered Thom's report.

"Marshal?" Betti asked in a soft voice. "You are a real state marshal, right?"

"Yes, ma'am. As real as they come," he answered with a soft smile.

"Then you have authority anywhere in the state, right?"

"Yes, Betti. I certainly do," he said.

"Then you can check out what is going on, right?"

"Yes."

"I know a lot of people are affected by this, marshal," Thad continued, "but we have a son and a daughter down there and we have not been able to contact them. We wanted them to come north with us, but we could not find them when we had to leave. We connected with them after we reached Betti's sister's place and they said they would follow us as soon as they could."

"When was the last time you talked to them, Thad?" Wally asked.

"When we got here and then three days later," Betti said.

"Betti, that was nearly a month ago," Wally said, stating the obvious. He stopped himself and forced himself to listen.

"I know, Marshal," she said, "but we were not sure we should say anything. Chief Parks is one of those in charge of collecting the people and he can be very mean and brutal—"

"Marshal," Thad interrupted, "please do not take offense, but at first we were not sure if we could trust you, even though you helped us. But we have talked to Betti's sister long enough and enough of the town's folk to feel like we can. Many are very pleased that you have come to the valley and they trust you to do the right things when the time comes that they need you."

"I'm flattered," Wally admitted, "and yes, you can trust me. Can you give me details on where they might be containing these people, how many have been collected so far, and especially the names of your son and daughter and what they look like. Anything we can use to find them and the others."

"You will help then?" Thad asked in surprise.

"Certainly," Wally replied.

"Marshal?" Betti asked, smiling softly. "Can I get some water, please? And I'm sure Thad would like that cup of coffee before we continue."

Wally smiled and stood up. "Of course you can. Give me a minute."

One Hundred-Three

After lunch, Shara and Greg went to the horse barn and saddled Danny and Dílis. They took them to the practice arena in the enclosed competition building just north of the barns and paddocks for some exercise. Greg tried to follow Shara's examples on Dílis, but could not begin to match the way she guided Danny through his routines. After an hour of practicing his foot work and coordination exercises, she let him trot and run around the arena in short bursts, alternating the running with walking.

Finally, she traded horses with Greg and ran Dílis through the same routines while Greg walked Danny around the arena for his cool down. He let Danny have short drinks from the trough after each walking lap and after about a half an hour, he let Danny nibble from a feed bucket hung on the fence in front of the bleachers.

When Shara had finished with Dílis' routines and a similar cool down, they led them back to the horse barn.

"Seems like it's been months since I was on Danny," Shara said as she unsaddled him.

"I know," Greg agreed, "but it has only been a couple of weeks."

She led Danny into his stall and removed his bridle. Greg had settled Dílis and was waiting when she stepped out of Danny's stall, hung the bridle on the gatepost and slid the gate closed.

"Feel good?" he asked as they started back to the main house.

"Of course," she said. "It always feels good to be around the horses."

It was dark by the time they had finished with the horses and Greg slowly searched the dimming sky above the ranch. The wind was calm and the sky was nearly cloudless.

Shara stopped beside him and studied the sky. "You know, it seems like it was another lifetime, but just before I met you, I remember telling Uncle Paul how I felt like I belonged to the stars. And now, even knowing that I really do belong with them, among them, as part of my life, I'm still fascinated when I look up and see them."

"I know," he said. "But I see paths through their maze, recognizing them as points along a journey, not just dots on a screen overhead."

"I see them as signposts too," she said and slipped her arm around him, "especially when we get above the planet and get our bearings."

Greg led her into the house and hung their jackets in the coat room. Jill and Nick were sitting on the long couch and Hench and Leeana were snuggled on the loveseat when they entered the dining room. Shara poked her head into the kitchen and asked Matti to bring them a carafe of tea and two cups.

Greg had already settled into their favorite overstuffed chair when Shara joined them and sat down in her customary manner on his lap.

"What have you been up to today?" she asked, looking at Jill.

"Not much," Jill said with a shrug. "Today was a physical training day. Hand to hand and more ropes."

"She's getting pretty quick," Nick admitted. "And she and Rose can still take us guys anytime they want. It's uncanny how they do that."

"Yes it is," Greg said and smiled at Shara. "They do seem to have an advantage, don't they?" Then he turned to Hench, "How're the crews handling the down side of the last mission?"

"Okay. A little disappointed," he said, "but that's to be expected."

"Jill said you called the attack off," Nick said. "She said there weren't any captives, is that right?"

"That's right," Greg said. "The director sent a very appreciative message today, thanking the squadron for its efforts and congratulations for realizing they didn't have captives onboard."

"I'm sure he did," Hench said and squeezed Leeana.

Matti brought Shara and Greg's carafe and cups and turned to the others to see if they wanted anything. She took their requests and then turned to Greg and Shara. "Dinner is about a half an hour away if that is all right."

"Certainly, Matti," Shara said, "I don't know about everyone else, but I'll be ready."

"I'm so glad your appetite came back, Mrs. Shara," Matti said and turned to the kitchen.

When the kitchen door had closed, Greg continued. "The director also mentioned that he wants to arrange another meeting with Casi, but decided to wait until the demand on our time and resources has diminished some."

"Have you had any luck with your testing plans?" Shara asked.

"Some," Hench admitted. "I want to try out one of the tests next week."

Shara turned to Jill, "That makes me wonder. How did your session with STSX go today?"

"He says it went fine," Jill said and shrugged her shoulders. "He doesn't explain things very well so I don't know what he's expecting."

"You need to ask him," Shara said. "Maybe he'll tell you then."

"Yeah, maybe," Jill laughed softly. "But only if he feels like it."

▲ ▲ ▲ ▲ ▲

"Are you having dinner with Eddie?" Wally asked as Thom picked up the stacked folders from his desk and dropped them into the organizer in his desk file drawer.

"That's the plan," Thom said as he locked his desk and stood up.

"You've suddenly started spending a lot of time with her. Is this becoming serious?" Wally pushed himself back in his chair.

Thom stopped and set down on the corner of his desk and looked at Wally. "I suppose I am, and yes, I think it is," he admitted. "I kept my distance and didn't push her one way or the other, but..."

"But she let you know she was willing if you were?" Wally asked with a smile.

"Yeah, something like that," Thom smiled back. "I think I fell for her the first week I was here, but then I found out more about her, how hard she has had it and I knew I couldn't just introduce myself and ask her out. She's been through too much for this to be my decision."

"You know she hasn't been with anyone before," Wally said, "and she may just be responding to your good treatment."

"I know," Thom said. "And that, Wally, is the dilemma. I do want her to respond to my good treatment, but I also know that her response could be like a wilted plant responding to water or it could be heartfelt. I've asked myself 'how can I tell?' and 'how can I be a true friend and not take advantage of her?' If it isn't heartfelt..."

"I wish I had an answer for you, Thom," Wally said.

"Thanks, Wally," he said. "If this is real, then I have to figure out how to tell her the rest without scaring her away."

"Go and have a pleasant dinner," Wally said and waved him toward the door. "And we'll worry about the rest of it when the time comes."

Thom nodded, stood up, put his jacket on and slipped the remote's monitor into its inside pocket. With a wave, he pushed the office door open and left.

⌃ ⌃ ⌃ ⌃ ⌃

Shara pulled the fleece sheets tight around them and snuggled as close to Greg as she could. Her mind absently felt the house, Jill's room, the empty guest room, the house girl's rooms, then checked the apartments, Nick's room and Hench and Leeana's room and then the bunkhouse and the barns. Sensing all was secure and normal, she slipped her arms around Greg's waist and pulled herself tight against him, her head on his arm and her forehead lightly against his chest, feeling the strength in his presence.

She remembered the director's message and how she still felt embarrassed by his accolades over her accomplishment and what it meant to him and the Force. She remembered Greg's worry over her demanding too much of herself, trying to monitor everything around them. Then she remembered the attachments.

"Greg?" she asked softly.

"Yeah," he answered.

"What were those financial displays attached to the director's message?" she asked. "I didn't get a chance to look at them closely."

"The stipend summary?" he asked.

"No, I recognized the deposits and expenses summary. We compare that one to the ranch's bank statements every two weeks." She waited a moment before continuing. "It was the other two that I was wondering about."

"Are you serious, Bren?" he asked as she turned her face up to

72

look at him in the dim light.

"Yes, I'm serious," she said softly. "I haven't seen them before."

"Well," he said, smiling in the dark. "Those are our pay statements. The one with your name on it is a summary of your Shadow's pay, plus pilot's pay, plus mission credits, plus completion credits, plus combat credits and director's bonuses."

"Huh?"

"Your earnings, Bren," he chuckled, "from the Peace Force. You are an active upper-lieutenant, a Shadow and a Q-Ship qualified pilot in the Force."

"But the amounts are big, very big," she stammered.

"Shadows get paid very well, Bren." He held her tight. "Those credits are held in an account in the Rings and can be accessed by yourself, or anyone you chose to be a cosigner, anytime you want them transferred or need to spend them. STSX is your link to them."

"Am I your cosigner?"

"Of course. Who else would be?"

"Are you on my account?"

"Not unless you put me on it."

"How could I? I didn't know I had an account until now. I didn't even know I was getting paid until now." She pushed him back and rolled on top. "You'll have to show me what to do in the morning."

"In the morning?" he asked. "You could do it now. STSX is available."

She kissed him tenderly. "In the morning. I have something important to tell you and I hope it's as exciting for you as it is for me."

"I'm certain it will be, Bren," Greg said and squeezed her. "Tell me."

"I'm a little late, but I went to STSX this morning and let Medical do my eight week check," she said softly, holding her head up to watch him.

"Oh? Only a week and a half late, and what does Medical have to say?" he asked. "Are you all right after your strange eating habits?"

"Yes, I'm fine," she said and slapped his shoulder. "And the baby is fine with one exception."

She felt Greg suddenly stiffen and raise his head to look more closely at her. "An exception? What—?"

"It's a *good* exception, love," she said, reassuring him. "Medical says it can hear the baby's heartbeats. Both of them."

"What?" Greg asked, confused. "Both? There are 'two' heartbeats?"

She nodded energetically, "Yes, love. Two."

"You're... We're having twins?" he asked, his voice happy with the thought.

"Yup," she said and kissed him again.

He squeezed her and held her kiss for a long moment. 'That's wonderful... Incredible...'

Thursday, January 19

It was midmorning when Thom finished his rounds and returned to the office. He had finished his cup of coffee and was pouring his second when his desk phone rang.

"Thom?" the voice on the other end of the connection asked when he picked up the handset.

"Yes, Deputy Baines here," he said.

"George Hattle, Thom," the voice said. "Do you have a minute to talk?"

"Sure." Thom sat down at his desk and took a quick sip from his cup.

"Charley McWilliams was just in," George said, "and we closed on his parcel on the river."

"Really? He got it all arranged and closed?"

"Yes," George said. "We had to set him up with a short-term loan to cover him until you close, but it's his and they're going to start moving this afternoon."

"Well, I'm happy for him," Thom said. "Very happy."

"I talked to our loan manager, Thom," George continued, "and he says there's no reason on our part that would keep us from moving your closing up a bit. If you were interested, that is."

"Interested?" Thom said, nearly dropping his cup. "That would be wonderful."

"I thought you might feel that way," George said. "We don't

74

usually close until the seller has moved out of the residence. It's an insurance thing, but in this case, you have two options."

"Two?" Thom asked.

"Yes. Charley plans to be out of the house by tomorrow night. He's going to get a few of his friends to help with the big stuff, but he'll need the weekend to get out of the craft shop."

"Okay," Thom said.

"That means we can take care of the paperwork any time, but you won't be able to move in until Monday."

"I'm good with that," Thom said. "What's the second option?"

"Keeping your closing date unchanged," George said.

"Why would I do that?"

George laughed. "Then why don't you come by my office tomorrow," he paused, "around nine-thirty."

"I'll be there," Thom said.

"See you then," George said and hung up.

"Everything okay?" Wally asked as he watched Thom lean back in his chair and sip his cup.

"Sure is, Wally," Thom admitted.

"What are you up to?" Wally asked, studying Thom's changed manner.

"I'll tell you tomorrow."

▲ ▲ ▲ ▲ ▲

Shara followed Matti out of the kitchen and took her seat beside Greg as Matti and Cara started serving lunch. Greg noticed Matti's smile when she glanced at him before she returned to the kitchen. He was pleased with the way the house girls took everything in stride, unruffled by the quirky changes and demands they dropped in their laps, often forgetting to warn them ahead of time.

Jill caught the subtle change in Matti and Cara's manner as they set the plates and looked happier than they usually did.

"Okay," Jill said when the girls had retreated to the kitchen. She glanced at Nick, and then at Leeana and the major and they looked back, questioning. "What's up with those two?"

"They're just happy," Shara said and sipped her juice. She glanced at Greg and smiled.

"I see that," Jill said and began eating.

"Can't they be happy without someone being curious?" Shara asked.

"Sure," Jill said softly, "but..."

'You really ought to tell her, love,' Greg said.

'I will,' Shara said and started eating. "Actually, Jill, they are happy for Greg and me," she said and sipped her tea.

"Now what have you done, Shar?" Jill asked and stared at her.

Shara glanced at Greg and then looked back at the rest of them. "I don't know which of us is to blame," she smiled, "but yesterday I had a routine check with Medical and it detected two heartbeats."

"Twins?" Leeana asked before Jill could assimilate what Shara was saying. "It thinks you're going to have twins?"

Shara smiled and nudged Greg's shoulder. "Yeah, that's what it thinks. And I just let the girls know."

"Wow," Nick said softly. "This place is really going to be different. Are you going to be all right with everything that's going on and two kids to worry about and raise on top of it all?"

"We'll do the best we can, Nick," Shara said. "We have some time to decide what we're going to do, but we'll make it work."

⋏

With the lunch dishes cleared and Nick and Jill gone on Remote Four to his dad's place for a visit, the four of them sat around the dining room table discussing the details of their command.

"With Kiile's help and a few suggestions from KKLC and STSX," Hench said, "I think we have a good, first pass for the testing you wanted." He slid his notepad across the table for Greg and Shara to look at. "These are the basic questions that I want to ask, and I'll have a series of things set up around the testing room for them to observe, sense. I'll switch them around so there is no obvious pattern from one person to the next."

"I'm surprised it's as short as it is," Greg said as they read through the list. "Are you sure it's enough?"

"No," Hench admitted and smiled at Leeana, "but I wanted it to be subtle, almost trivial feeling."

"That way," Leeana added, "they won't feel pressured and maybe we can get clearer results." Then she shrugged. "Maybe not. I think the big part of the training will be raising their awareness and alertness so they automatically listen."

"When do you want to try it?" Shara asked as she slid the notepad back to him.

"Tomorrow," he said with a smile, "possibly in the afternoon."

"What do you want from us?" Greg asked. "Or would you prefer we stayed away?"

"No, no," he said and glanced at Leeana. "I don't see any reason why you should stay away."

"Tomorrow afternoon then," Greg said and raised his cup of tea in a toast.

⋏ ⋏ ⋏ ⋏ ⋏

"Your diagnostics look good," Greg said as he studied the data scrolling on the monitor in STSX's nav-com compartment.

"ALL SYSTEMS CHECK. NO ANOMALIES DETECTED."

He scanned the list again. "How's our usage on the core power modules, averages and peaks?"

"MAIN CORE POWER MODULE AVERAGES ABOUT EIGHTEEN PERCENT ON ANY GIVEN MISSION, TWENTY-TWO PERCENT PEAK IN HEAVY COMBAT SITUATIONS. SECOND CORE POWER MODULE AVERAGES FIVE PERCENT USAGE ON ANY GIVEN MISSION, TWELVE PERCENT WHEN SHIELDS ARE ENGAGED AND DEFLECTING INCOMING THREATS."

"Can more power be channeled to the Shields?" he asked.

"YES. MAIN CORE MODULE SHIELDS CAN ALSO BE ACTIVATED."

"What? We still have shields connected to the main Core Modules?"

"YES."

"Can they both be activated at the same time?"

"YES."

He pondered STSX's answers a long moment. "So, if I understand, we can run two sets of Shields, and we can increase the deflective power on both, to provide us with increased defenses."

"YES. THE SYSTEMS ARE INDEPENDENT OF EACH OTHER."

"Are KKLC and you the only ones with two Core Power Modules?"

"No."

Greg stopped and looked up from the monitor. "Who else?"

"TTYF8 AND KVWC33."

"When were they upgraded?"

"MAJOR KOOICH UPGRADED THEM AFTER THEY WERE ASSIGNED AND ARRIVED AT OBSCURE. THIS UPGRADE WAS ACCOMPLISHED WHEN THE ENGINE UPGRADES AND RECODING WAS IMPLEMENTED. THE MAJOR INTENDS TO UPGRADE ALL Q-SHIPS WHEN THE MODULES ARE AVAILABLE. HE HAS ORDERED MORE."

"Very nice," he said softly. "We will use this to our advantage. Does the major know we can do this?"

"INSUFFICIENT DATA. NONE OF THE SHIPS HAVE ACTIVATED BOTH."

"I'll discuss this with the major this evening."

An annunciator illuminated and a soft buzz filled the ship. "INCOMING MESSAGE."

"Display it."

"UNSCRAMBLE

C.DATE 3482.403 1636 HRS LCL 19

TO: COLONEL STRAN GEAARDT HQZL09-ES

FROM: PEACE FORCE HQ DIR AGL36Q

EMBEDDED AGENTS HAVE IDENTIFIED FOUR SEPARATE SHIPMENTS SCHEDULED TO LAUNCH WITHIN THE NEXT SEVEN TURNS. ALL FOUR HAVE DESTINATIONS WITHIN PRINCE KIESE'S DOMAIN. PERISHABLE CARGO IS HIGH PROBABILITY. PREPARE TO DEPART ON TURN

406 AND RENDEZVOUS WITH B GROUP. RENDEZVOUS COORDINATES WILL BE PROVIDED BEFORE YOUR DEPARTURE. PREPARE FOR THREE TO FOUR TURNS ON STATION. EOM."

"Send an acknowledgement," he said. "It looks like the prince has decided to try to spread us out."

▲ ▲ ▲ ▲ ▲

The two large, burly guards paced back and forth across the entrance to the large personnel lifts deep in the Tissl mines as the young food handler's aide pushed the heavy midday meal wagon up the corridor. Small in stature by most standards, the aide stopped at the guards and let them scan the order card mounted on the end of the wagon.

"Where are you going," the guard asked in the local dialect.

The aide stared at the guard like he always did when he asked the redundant question.

"Like the card says," the aide said in his displeased retort. "Shaft Bee Eff Seven, Level Six. Oxygen breathers."

"You always go to Level Nine before," the guard questioned.

"Today it is Six," the aide shrugged. "I go where the card tells me to go," he added and put his shoulder to the levitated wagon, wishing levitation meant 'easier to push.'

The guards separated enough for him to push the wagon into the waiting lift. The aide stopped once inside the lift gates and turned to the console as the gates closed and the overhead lamp illuminated. He stared at the guards' wide backs as the lift began to descend.

The ride seemed longer than usual, even though the food preparation area was subterranean, which meant it should be closer to the shaft levels than if he started from the surface. But today, his mind was alert and he fought to keep his anxiousness under control and unnoticed, this was the first time in the seven turns since he received the names that he had an opportunity to check out Agent Kela's list.

The lift squealed to a slow stop at level Six and the backside gates slowly swung open. He put his shoulder to the wagon and began pushing it down the long corridor, shaft BF7 was somewhere ahead and to his right.

At three different places along his route, more guards stopped him and checked the card on the end of the wagon and finally, the last ones pointed to the heavy metals doors that opened beside them.

"Aspirator on," the guard said and the aide quickly pulled his mask from the pouch on his belt.

"Got it," the aide said as he checked the quantity of breathable gas in the attached canister. "Can't breathe that oxygen stuff very long before it makes me go out of my head."

The guard nodded and patted him on his shoulder. "Go. We will seal it up behind you."

The aide put his shoulder against the wagon and pushed it into the airlock. He stopped before the wagon drifted into the doors on the other side of the chamber. The doors closed behind him and the warning lights changed color. When the correct indication illuminated, the other set of doors slowly swung open.

The guard inside checked the card again, quickly glanced over his aspirator and canister connections and then pointed for him to move along. The aide guided the wagon down the center of the long shaft until it opened up into a wider area filled with tables and benches. Miners were lined up at the mouth of the opposite shaft as it extended farther into the dimness. He noted the guards standing around the perimeter of the chamber as he stopped the wagon near the guard at the head of the waiting line of miners.

Taking a digital pad from the pouch that hung from his belt, he opened the file and prepared to record the distribution of the meals. He depressurized the wagon, then swung its side panel up and slid it into the aperture at the edge of the roof. Ready, he turned to the guard and nodded.

The guard addressed the line of miners and, in the same manner that all meals were distributed, released the first miner to come forward and take a color coded meal container from the open wagon. The aide scanned the microchip in the miner's neck, repeated the number as it displayed on the digital pad and entered the color of the meal he took.

One miner after another, the process continued with the aide dutifully recording the information. But when a number came up that he recognized from Agent Kela's list, he silently composed the details of that individual in his mind and silently broadcast his thoughts to a linked mind, an unseen agent patiently waiting for his connection.

He scanned the next miner and stopped suddenly when the identification displayed on the pad. He tried to stay relaxed, nonchalant and not look up as he realized the miner was the high priority identification noted in Kela's request, but he glanced up at the face as the miner picked up a yellow container and stepped aside.

He formed the information in his mind and was about to send the data when the next miner stepped up and impatiently started searching the stacks of meals, roughly tossing unwanted containers aside in his single minded pursuit. The aide tried to stop him and get the scan, but the miner shoved him aside and shouted, "Where is it? Where is the Green?"

The guard reached the miner and grabbed his shoulder, but the miner resisted and shoved the guard away. He turned back to the wagon when the guard stumbled and fell, but when he saw the aide between him and the open side, he roared defiantly, grabbed the aide and threw him aside.

The aide landed on a table and fell onto the benches between it and the next. He heard something snap and felt fire shoot up his arm. He fell onto the floor between the tables and with some satisfaction, saw half of the guards converge on the possessed miner, riot sticks flashing.

He suddenly felt hot, nauseous, and found it difficult to breathe. He grabbed his arm and painfully pulled it to his side as he rolled onto his back. He wiped the sweat from his forehead and suddenly realized his aspirator was gone, dislodged and flung from his face when he fell into the tables. Panic swept over him, the mask and the hose were both gone. He twisted around and tried to see where it went, tried to unhook the canister from his belt, but only fumbled, making his panic worse.

Then he remembered his link as he turned, still searching for the aspirator. His vision dimming, he tried to push himself up, but he couldn't get his arm under him. He rolled face down and pushed, but he wobbled and rolled aside again. He thought about his link and as he pulled his legs up under him for another try, he formed the Galactic Standard words in his mind, *'Captive 4-4-6-1-6-e, C-o-l-l-i-e-r found. Antidote yellow. Shaft BF7, Tissl.'*

Someone caught his shoulders and pulled him up. He felt

something, a hand, or a mask maybe, cup over his face as he drifted into dark unconsciousness.

Friday, January 20

"Thanks for meeting with us," Wally said as Greg closed the heavy front door behind them. "I hope this isn't too early for you. This is Deputy Ted Marks."

"The time is fine, Wally. Pleased to meet you, Ted," Greg said as he led them through the foyer and into the living room. He gestured to Shara as she got up from the chair near the fireplace, "This is my wife, Shara."

"It's very nice to finally meet you," Ted said and nodded. "Wally speaks very highly of you both."

"Thank you," Shara said and gestured to the couch. "Can I offer you coffee or tea?"

"Coffee would be nice," Wally said and Ted nodded as they sat down.

Greg settled on the loveseat across from them and Shara went to the kitchen.

"You said you had something of importance to discuss, Wally," Greg said. "What's up?"

"I had a visit this week from a Thad and Betti Reeds," Wally began as Shara returned and sat down next to Greg. "They live near that farmstead east of Grants." Wally related the story that Thad and Betti had given him on Wednesday, of people being collected and held against their will at the farmstead and that they had asked for Wally's help. He then explained how Ted and Thom had accompanied Kiile and his Marines in searching out the tunnels down to Grants and near the farmstead the previous week and weekend.

He interrupted his explanation when Matti and Cara brought two serving trays into the living room. Matti gave them each a cup and poured coffee for Wally and Ted. Cara poured tea for Shara and Greg.

"I can confirm there is a collection facility at the farmstead," Greg said casually when the girls had gone.

"You know about it?" Wally asked, surprised.

"Yes," Greg said and nodded. "Last Friday, the same day you,

Ted, and Thom, were helping Kiile check out the tunnels, we detected the arrival and subsequent departure, of a small fighter converted to transport use. I had it followed rather than terminated so we could see if they have any means of removing the people."

"Thad says there is a place at the farmstead, large enough to hold and restrain a significant number of people," Wally explained, his tone becoming more urgent.

"Yes," Greg admitted. "We mapped the facility and think we understand its layout, its composition."

"Originally, they only moved a few male workers," Wally said, "but now Thad says they have collected women and young adults as well. They have not been able to contact their son and daughter."

"Yes, we understand they are no longer discriminating," Greg said. "What are you planning to do, Wally?"

"I feel it is time that I must intervene," Wally said firmly. "I have to stop the collection and apprehend Don Nikle and Chief Parks and possibly Chief Russell. I am asking for your assistance. I need the support of Kiile, some of his men and possibly a couple of your remotes in able to free the captives and put a stop to this atrocity."

"Do you know what you're up against?" Greg asked. "Major Mooren identified approximately ninety-five persons manning the facility, and most likely over half are security forces." Greg pondered the facts a moment. "My latest intelligence indicates they have collected approximately thirty from the local area to be removed."

"I know there are more than the two of us can handle—"

"Only Two?" Shara asked.

"Yes," Wally admitted. "I have to keep a presence in town. After the attack here, I'm beginning to see signs that something may be getting ready to happen in town as well, so Dan and Thom will manage the home front while Ted and I are down south dealing with this." Then Wally paused and looked at Greg and then at Shara, "I can't wait for them to be shipped out. I have to do something while they are still here, and hopefully, I can catch Chief Parks and Don and possibly others in the act."

"I know exactly how you feel," Greg said and Wally saw him glance at Shara.

"Kiile will be here in two or three minutes," Shara said softly, smiling at Greg and then at Wally and Ted. "Major Kooich and Leeana have just finished the crew briefing for the next mission and will be here as soon as they can get away."

Ted stared at Shara in surprise and Wally smiled and sipped his coffee. "Thanks."

▲ ▲ ▲ ▲ ▲

Thom smiled and looked at the large envelope in his hand as he stepped out of the Valley Bank and walked to his patrol car. He glanced around him and inhaled the sweet, cold, sunny morning and slapped the half-rolled envelope against the open palm of his other hand.

As he got into the car, he knew the first thing he had to do, the first place he had to go, before he went anywhere else. He started the car and drove the three blocks up Main and swung into the parking lot in front of the marshal's office. He got out, locked the car, turned to the street and jogged across it.

Trying to retain some semblance of poise and dignity, he opened Mary's front door and saw Eddie turn from her workbench. Smiling hugely, he hurried across the room, caught her around the waist and lifted her up and held her tight.

"Thom? What's—?" she asked in surprise as she looked down at his excited face.

"I got the house, Eddie," he said as he looked up at her. "I just closed the loan and it's... mine!" He wanted to say 'ours.'

"Thom, that's great," she said and bent forward as he slowly lowered her to the floor, her arms tightened around his neck.

He kissed her firmly as he continued to turn, holding her tight against him in the middle of the room.

"I had to let you know as soon as it happened, Eddie," he said as he slowly relaxed his embrace. "I had to tell you first." Then he kissed her slowly, more gently.

"My, my," Mary said through a broad smile, pulling their attention back to the now. "Should I ask what brings all of this on?"

Eddie smiled sheepishly at Thom and then slowly turned in his arms to face Mary, suddenly remembering there were customers in the store, smiling and watching their enrapt exchange.

"Thom just bought Charley's place," Eddie said and straightened the front of her blouse, "the craft shop and all of the buildings and

84

property. One day, he's going to refinish furniture and maybe make new."

"Well, that is certainly news," Mary said and clapped her hands together. "So you're going to stay and be one of us?"

"Yes, ma'am," Thom said and smiled at Eddie. He kept his arms firmly around her as he looked at Mary and then nodded to the three customers politely waiting around the room. "I like it here, very much."

Then he glanced at the clock over the checkout counter and realizing it was still mid-morning and remembering he had work to get back to, he smiled at Eddie, "Lunch? Connie's?"

Eddie nodded and chuckled, "Of course."

⬧

Eddie watched him step out through the door, turn and wave at her and then hurry back across the street. She felt almost giddy as she turned back to her workbench, half ignoring the chatter of the customers and Mary. When she finished the bouquet she was working on and sat down on the tall stool, she turned around and realized the customers were gone and Mary was straightening some potted plants near the front window.

She sighed, still surprised by Thom's entrance and his single minded purpose of coming to tell her first. Ignoring everything else, everyone else, he came to tell her first, to passionately tell her first. She couldn't believe it.

When she looked up, Mary was smiling at her as she came back and straightened the items near the cashiering machine.

Eddie smiled back, "That entrance was a little surprising, huh?"

"Just a little," Mary said happily. "And I'm glad for you. I think there's no question about how he feels about you."

"He certainly gave our customers something to talk about."

"Yes," Mary agreed, "something nice to talk about."

Then Eddie turned serious. "Mary? I know so little about... about any of this. How can I know if... he's the right one? The One I'll be happy with?"

Mary sat down on the stool beside the counter. "No one can tell you how, Eddie. You have to trust your heart and give yourself time to learn about him."

"What if he changes?"

"Maybe he will. Maybe you will," Mary said. "Learning to handle those changes and accepting them are part of any long-term relationship. Discovering each other over and over again can be the best part."

"Sometimes, I'm afraid," Eddie admitted. "Maybe I shouldn't have—"

"Has Thom made you upset or angry?"

"No," Eddie said. "He's done so much for me, he still does, and since we met, he's there when I need someone... but sometimes I get frustrated, waiting for... well, for things like today."

"Give him time," Mary said, "and you time. Show him what's in your heart and learn what's in his and then, if you still like what you see... Well, then you'll know he's the right one."

Eddie smiled. "Thanks, Mary."

⏶ ⏶ ⏶ ⏶ ⏶

Leeana snuggled close to Hench on the loveseat after dinner. Hench held his notepad in his left hand and Leeana with his right arm. "I was very pleased with the first three we tested," he said, referring to his notes. "But after that, the results were not so clear."

"So, you asked questions," Shara said, "and set up distractions or activities around them but out of sight?"

"Basically yes," Hench said. "With the first ones, I staged, calm, but interesting activities, like mission conversations, and inventory assessments, but those didn't work so well."

"That's when I suggested," Leeana added, "that he stage something that would get their attention, like a freight handler appearing to fall off a shipping container."

"Did that work?" Greg asked.

"With mixed results," Leeana chuckled. "Our 'actor' wasn't emotional enough until someone unexpectedly pushed him off the container. Six of our crewmen and four of Kiile's Marines felt that one."

"Yeah," Shara said with a smile, "Maybe there were seven."

Hench nodded, "I didn't count you." Then he smiled at Leeana. "But actually, Shara, I use you as our benchmark. Then Greg second.

If one of you two don't sense something, I don't expect a reaction from anyone else."

"So," Greg said, seeing Shara's uneasiness, "Who are our most sensitive?"

"Not counting you two," Hench said and consulted his notes, "Cheral scored highest at maybe half your sensitivity. Quantification is difficult and very non-linear so my estimates are a little rough."

"I think STSX helped her more than we realize," Shara said. "Who was next?"

"Franni is a little behind Cheral and the surprise is Jill just barely behind Franni."

Shara's mouth dropped open and she glanced at Greg. "Jill?"

"Yes," Hench said with a broad smile. "Being young, that is having just started *hearing,* I was very surprised that she has any perception."

"I had STSX and Medical help 'focus' both of their senses," Shara said and looked at Hench and Leeana. "Cheral and Jill."

"You did what?" Hench asked in surprise.

"STSX said he and Medical could help them enhance the clarity of their sensations," Shara explained, "so I let him try. He has given them multiple sessions with a 'settling' period in between. He says their minds have to adjust after each session, and it seems that it's working to some extent."

"Well, well," Hench muttered. "Do you think STSX can tell TTYF how he did what he did and help Franni?"

"It's worth a try," Leeana said and smiled at Shara.

One Hundred-Four

Saturday, January 21

"What's a beautiful woman like you doing out at this time of night?" Wally asked as Carole came out of Hap's back door and saw him leaning against the fender of his jeep.

She quickly stepped close and kissed him as the other two girls locked up and turned to their cars.

"Waiting for an escort home," she said and playfully rubbed noses. "Know anyone that's up to the challenge?"

"I think I do," he said and led her to her jeep.

He followed her down the alley and up Baxter and parked in her drive. They went in through the garage and he absently checked with WL-One for a status and it reported that no one had planted any bugs and no one was watching her place. Inside, he hung his jacket and utility belt on the pegs beside Carole's jacket and he smiled to himself as he noted that now, she almost always wore the one he had gotten her.

She had kicked her shoes off and had gone to change like she usually did and he went to the kitchen to fix a pot of coffee.

"Can I get you anything?" he asked as he poked his head around the corner and looked down the short hallway toward her slightly ajar bedroom door.

"Yeah, a lager please," she answered and he turned back to the kitchen and the refrigerator.

He had filled an auto-chill stein for her and was pouring himself a mug when she came into the kitchen wearing the sweat pants and top that always stirred his emotions and alluded to the promise of something more to come.

"Have you thought about my idea anymore?" she asked as she took the stein he handed her. "Thanks."

"Yes and I think you make a good point," he smiled. "As you said your place has more space with larger rooms and all," He said as he sipped his coffee and composed his thoughts. "And there's room in the back to add a second garage for my patrol car."

"And with the extra two rooms upstairs," she added as he turned the kitchen light off and she led him into the living room, "you can have your office space and we can still have a guest room."

He smiled at her as he sat down. "You think we're going to have guests? Your folks live just outside of town and your sister and her family will stay there when they visit and I don't have any relatives to come and visit."

"I guess I'm just making excuses," she admitted as she curled up next to him. "I haven't had any use for the upstairs rooms since I bought the place. But three bedrooms will help resale, whenever we decide to move out to the ranch."

"It does," he said as he turned, wrapped his arm around her shoulders and kissed her. "But I've also been thinking about buying my place and keeping it as investment property."

"Investment property?" She looked at him in surprise. "You've never mentioned that you were thinking about that, and now you're going to be like Thom and start buying up local properties?" He smiled, remembering their discussion about Thom over lunch.

"No," he said slowly and glanced sideways at her as he sipped his mug again. "You remember I may have mentioned that Greg's friend Kiile was investigating tunnels that left that facility of theirs?" She nodded. "Well, I may not have mentioned that Kiile discovered one of them comes north and goes under the College and directly under my place on its way out to Brian Woods' place."

Her mouth suddenly dropped open and she stared at him. "Under your place?"

"Yeah. He told me yesterday, when Ted and I were out at Greg's and Shar's talking with him." He squeezed her shoulders and watched her reaction. "I'm going to be the landlord so the state can lease it for use as a police sub-station. Less up-front questions if it's in my name. And once that's done, Kiile's going to build an access from it to the tunnel."

She sat and studied him for a long moment. "You've been busy, haven't you Marshal Lima?"

He slowly sobered his thoughts and expression, set his mug down on the end table and turned to her. Feeling his change in mood, she looked at him and waited.

"Also, I probably haven't mentioned that I'm going to be away for a few days," he said and pulled her close.

"Where?" she asked in a whisper.

"Ted and I, with some of Kiile's Marines are going down near Grants," he answered softly. "Don Nikle and Chief Parks from Hawthorne have started collecting people for the slavers again."

"No, Wally," she said and buried her face against his neck, squeezing him tight, "no."

"Greg and his people have been watching them as well," Wally continued, speaking softly and forcing himself to explain.

"Does this have something to do with the couple that visited you earlier this week?"

"Yes," he admitted, "Thad and Betti confirmed what we were thinking. Thom and Ted have been checking out leads for the past few weeks."

"When?"

"Probably the first of the week," he said. "Kiile and Greg are watching the situation and we'll make plans over the weekend. Thom will run the office and be in charge while I'm gone and Dan will be here to help him."

She held him tight for another long moment. "It's dangerous, isn't it?"

"A little," he said.

"Don't toy with me, Wally," she said softly and slowly pushed herself up to look at him. "I can feel your concern." After a moment, she stood up, set her stein on the end table and pulled his hand. "Come with me," she said as she turned the lamp off and then led him down the dark hallway.

🔺 🔺 🔺 🔺 🔺

Thom glanced at his wall clock when he heard the knock. He closed the oven door, wiped his hands and hung the kitchen towel on the rod by the refrigerator and then went to answer the front door.

"You're off early," he greeted Eddie with a wide smile and let her in. He took her coat and hung it in the small closet by the door. Then he gestured to the living room, dining area and the kitchen. "It isn't much, but it's warm and dry. Can I get you anything?"

She followed his gestures and smiled at his offer. "This looks nice, Thom. Did you spend all afternoon cleaning just for me?"

"No actually," he said as he turned back to the kitchen, "I didn't. Sorry. I dusted when I got off and then sort of... fell asleep on the couch." He made a sheepish face. "I meant to, but I didn't get there."

She chuckled. "It looks like you didn't need to do a lot." Then she spotted his dining room table and bent to look at the clean, polished lines and the claw-foot legs. "Thom? Was this your mother's?"

"Yes, it was," he said and stopped as he opened a cabinet door. "My dad got her the set when they got married." He turned to her, holding up a stein and a stemmed wine glass. "Which would you like?"

"Do you have a good red?" she asked as she joined him in the kitchen. "Diner smells wonderful."

"One 'good red' coming up. I picked up a couple of bottles of the Syrah you like," he said as he proceeded to uncork the bottle. "Well, actually, I asked Hap to order me a case when I found out what you liked. And as for diner, I'm not a cook like Wally, so don't get your hopes up too much. It's just a simple casserole with a side vegetable and a selection of breads and cheeses."

"Sounds nice," she said as she watched him pour.

Stepping close to her with wine glasses in hand, he handed her one. "Thank you for coming, Eddie," he said and then kissed her, gently pulling her to him with his free arm.

"Thanks for asking me, Thomas," she said and squeezed him gently in return.

⚊⚊

Thom had cleared the table after they ate and he served a light desert. He told her about his growing up in the Queens and his early career over coffee and a fragrant, spiced tea he had fixed for her and she talked about her dreams and desires to be a painter and sculptor before her world changed. He was explaining how his mother had gotten him interested in antiques when someone knocked on his front door.

"Expecting someone?" she asked in jest as he got up to answer.

"Actually no," he said and smiled at her. "I was hoping to spend my time exclusively with you." Then he turned and opened the door and she heard his surprise.

"Charley? Come in," he said and stepped back into the living room. "What brings you out on a chilly night like this? Is everything okay?"

"Everything is fine, Thom," Charley said and noticed Eddie sitting at the table. "Good evening, Miss Collier."

"Mr. McWilliams," she replied with a nod, "Nice to see you."

She watched as Charley turned back to Thom. "We finished cleaning out the craft shop this afternoon, Thom, and I thought you might want the keys. George said you closed yesterday and are ready to move whenever I get out of your way."

"You're not in my way, Charley, but thanks for bringing them by. If you discover you've forgotten anything just let me know, and if we find anything that's not mine, I'll get it to you."

"Thanks," he said and nodded to Eddie. "I need to get going. Judy's out in the truck waiting on me. I certainly hope you enjoy it as much as I have. Goodnight, Thom, Eddie."

Thom thanked him again and held the storm door as he left. Then he closed the front door and looked at the keys in his hand. Eddie watched his profile, surprised to see a number of sober emotions cross his face before he smiled, clutched the keys and turned back to her. He took her hand, pulled her up to him and again caught her waist and lifted her up and turned in the room.

"I really have a place, Eddie. I really do," he said and let her down enough so he could kiss her. He held her tight and then lowered her back onto her feet and slowly relaxed his embrace.

He looked at her a long moment and she knew he was thinking of something more he wanted to say. Then his expression changed subtly and he asked, "Will you help me get it organized, putting things away? Wally, Dan and Ted will help when they're available and Carole said she's bringing a couple of her dad's ranch hands to help with the lifting and shoving. And Shar volunteered two of her ranch hands if I end up needing more help, so I think I have the actual moving covered."

"Of course," she said, wondering what he had not said. "What time are you going to start?"

"Meet me for breakfast?" he asked, "and then I'll see when everyone can gather."

She nodded and he led her into the living room. As she settled on the couch, he set a small circular table in front of the couch and then retrieved their cups and carafes from the dining room before he sat down beside her.

He looked at her and his smile sobered slightly. "I wish my mom could've lived to see this day and to meet you. I know she would have liked you a lot."

Eddie leaned to him and wrapped her arms tightly around his shoulders. "Thank you, Thomas. Thank you very much."

Sunday, January 22

The morning sun was peaking over the ridge beside the Guardian Peak as Stran patiently waited and watched Apache Five and Six join up with KVWC33 and LLRT12.

"You know," Cheral said as she watched from the left hand jump seat, "this is really an awesome sight. Eight Q-Ships and five patrol fighters ready to launch and rendezvous with eight more Q-ships in very deep space."

Casi chuckled and Stran smiled as he watched the joining from the pilot's chair. "Yes it is," he agreed.

"Apache Patrol Five is joined," Major Miiles said. "Cadet Grenn is transferring to KVWC33."

A few minutes passed, then Major Bradg announced Apache Patrol Six was secure and Cadet Kast was transferring.

Casi focused her thoughts and said, *'Jill, LTVC21 is your guardian this trip. Contact Major Glean or Lieutenant Debira if you need their assistance for anything. Kiile will monitor the remotes.'*

'Thanks,' Jill answered. *'I'll remember.'*

'I'll let you know when we start back,' Casi said and turned her attention back to the Wing.

"Colonel," Leeana said, "Apache Wing is ready. Outbound fix is loaded and active."

"Apache Leader and Apache Two are ready," Casi said to the Wing and then to Stran, "The Wing is ready."

"Apache Wing," Stran said, "Proceed to the outbound fix. Cloaking on, sensor blocked and shields full," and he pushed the thrust levers forward and pulled STSX's nose up.

During the ascent, Casi opened the mission file and then said to the Wing, "Load rendezvous coordinates Gamma-Fox-Romeo."

"Gamma-Fox-Romeo uploading," Leeana said. "Approaching outbound fix."

"Achieved," Casi said a moment later. "Apache Leader is ready for the jump." *'It's all yours, love'*

"On my Mark," Stran said, "all ships full thrust, match speed with STSX1. Mark."

▲ ▲ ▲ ▲ ▲

Thom unlocked the front door and opened it for Eddie. He followed her through the short foyer and stopped facing the wide, open staircase that rose up before them to the second floor.

"Wow," she whispered and smiled at him. "Sure didn't see this coming when we looked in the windows."

"After I give you the tour," he said with a wide gesture to everything, "let me know how you would arrange things and your ideas on decorating. Like I said, I need your feminine touch."

"Okay," she said, "but you may not like my ideas."

"On the left," he said, smiling at her candid remark, "is the formal living room or sitting room with a small fireplace and the family room behind it, and to the right," he turned with a grand gesture, "is the dining room with the kitchen behind it."

He led her through the dining room, around the eating peninsula and into the large kitchen with a butcher block topped island in the center. At the back, he stopped and turned around in the breakfast nook nestled in the corner.

"Then, connecting through here," he said as he led her through the archway at the back of the kitchen, "is the family room with its grand fireplace." He pointed to the front of the house, "And it's open back to the formal sitting room. Four rooms around the staircase."

Then he pointed out the smaller appointments. The pantry room off the kitchen. The two downstairs half baths, one with a sit-down vanity under the staircase. The coat closet off the foyer. The three back doors, one beside the family room fireplace that led to the flanking porch, another off the breakfast nook into the attached garage and one onto the porch and to the walk to the craft shop building across the drive.

"The only drawback I see with the downstairs," he said as they returned to the living room, "is the formal living room or sitting area gets the car lights as traffic comes down Main and makes the turn to the bridge. The pines help some, but..."

"But heavy curtains would easily handle that," Eddie said as she looked at the valances over the windows. "And the rods and draws are already here."

Thom looked over her shoulder and smiled. "So they are."

"I like the natural wood floors," Eddie said as she turned and took in the look of the adjacent rooms from where she stood. "Area rugs will give you focal centers, but the floors bring all of the rooms together. Heavy curtains with the right colors will keep it feeling warm and connected."

"You'll have to help me pick out the curtains and the rugs," he said and she nodded. "But don't you think my antique pieces will look good? Even in the more modern parts of the house?"

"Yes," she said, "I think they will look very nice, but I don't think they will fill the space."

"No, they won't," he said and smiled. "With two living spaces and three pieces of living room furniture and a couple of end tables, these spaces will just have to look a bit bare until we add more furniture." Then he gestured to the stairs and with a highly suggestive air, he extended his elbow and said, "Madam, allow me to show you the 'private' quarters."

Thom took her arm and together they ascended to the second floor.

"This staircase is beautiful," she said as she stopped at the top and turned around to look back down. "Wide with extra steps so it isn't so steep, it makes you feel so grand, important."

"Yes it does," he agreed. "I have to admit the first time I saw them, I envisioned you coming down them in one of your beautiful long dresses, a shoulder scarf draped over your arms..." He stopped and looked at her, a little embarrassed, "But really, I must say you look just as exceptional in jeans and that blouse as I have ever seen you. You have a wonderful eye for fashion and color and fabrics."

She smiled at him, her turn to blush. "Thank you, Thomas. That's a very nice thing to say."

He turned to the right and followed the balcony that encircled the stair opening, past the first bedroom, the shared, full bath above the kitchen, the second bedroom and then past the full bath over the foyer, to the bedroom over the living room.

"This is the smaller of the bedrooms," he said as he entered and stopped in the middle of the room. Arms spread wide he turned around once and returned to the door. "And it has a decent size closet."

He retraced his steps back past the bathroom and opened the door to the other front bedroom.

"Both rooms on this side of the house, over the kitchen and dining room," he said as he led her in, "are the middle sized bedrooms separated by the bath."

Back on the balcony, he led her back to the top of the stairs and the French doors angled in the corner to the stair's left. He gestured for her to open them and followed as she slowly swung the doors into the room. He heard her surprised inhale as the expanse of the room with the stone fireplace dominantly centered in the right hand wall, the back wall of the house, caught her complete attention.

He followed her in and let her explore the large master bath and dressing room to the right of the fireplace with access to the large walk-in closet.

"You know you're going to just rattle around in all of this space," she said softly as she stepped back into the bedroom. "It almost feels cavernous."

"Maybe," he agreed with a chuckle.

"I'm very surprised," she said and stopped to face him, "that you are able to afford something this large, this grand. I am truly amazed."

He smiled at her. "Mom left me a sizeable inheritance," he admitted as he put his hands gently on her hips and pulled her close in front of him. "My dad helped a number of businesses on his beat, investing in them off and on over the years, but there were a few that wouldn't stop with simply repaying him. They insisted he was a partner and paid him dividends every year. When she passed, the dividends and the investment proceeds started coming to me."

"So you're not just a simple state deputy," she smiled and squeezed him, "living on a meager deputy's wage."

"Well, I really am living on my deputy wages," he insisted, "saving everything else, but a state deputy, especially one with connections, gets paid pretty well."

"Connections?"

"I have a few friends that helped me along the way," he said with a sly smile. "So I decided, with the bank's help, I could buy something nice enough to 'rattle around in.'"

"Well, you managed to do that all right," she chuckled.

"But I'm hoping it's nice enough to entice you to spend enough time here with me so I won't hear it echo. Obviously it was refurbished for a family, or at least a couple, but I think I can get used to it."

He followed her back to the top of the stairs and stopped to look at the view down into the entry area. "Last night over dinner, you mentioned that you had liked to draw and paint when you were young," he said and she turned to look at him, "when your life was happier."

"Yes, I did," she said and waited, watching him.

"Would you like to do that again, your art?"

"I think so. I've doodled some off and on, but with work and mom's condition, I didn't feel like trying. Not seriously."

"If you'd like," he said slowly, "I want you to choose one of the three bedrooms," he gestured to the ones over the kitchen, dining room and living room, "and make it a private studio for yourself. To work on anything you wish to do, whenever you wish to do it."

She stared at him for a long moment. "You want me to have a place here?" she asked softly.

"Yes, but only if you want to, Eddie," he said and glanced at the floor. "It's your choice of course, and I will admit I have an ulterior motive."

"A motive, huh?" She turned her head slightly and looked at him out of the corner of her eye.

"Yeah. Ulterior," he smiled and took her arm and started down the stairs.

They reached the bottom just as a truck pulling a horse trailer pulled into the drive beside the house.

"Looks like Carole and Wally have arrived with the first load," Eddie said as she grabbed her jacket.

He slipped his jacket on and followed her out onto the wrap-around porch.

⋏

"Thanks guys," Carole said to the ranch hands as they finished and left by the kitchen door. "We really appreciate your help."

"You're welcome, Miss Carole," the tallest one said.

They both waved and got into the Lazy D's truck to leave, taking the trailer with them. Carole looked past them and saw Thom leading Wally into the craft shop building and she turned back to Eddie, rinsing and drying glassware as she arranged the kitchen cabinets.

"Wow. What a place," Carole said as she looked again into the living room and back to the kitchen.

"It sure is," Eddie admitted. "He has enough space to do about anything he wants to do."

"He certainly does."

"So what's it like," Eddie asked, changing the subject, "being a week away from tying the knot? Are you nervous?"

"A little," Carole admitted. "Happy, giddy, and yes, a little nervous. In a good way, I think."

"That's good. No second thoughts?"

"No, Eddie, no second thoughts," Carole said and picked a lager out of the cooler that Thom had iced and set beside the kitchen peninsula. "Want something?" She glanced up at Eddie.

"In a minute. Let me get these put away first."

"Actually, I feel like I've been waiting forever for Wally to come along," Carole said as she leaned back against the peninsula. "You look like you're comfortable with Thom."

"Maybe too comfortable," Eddie said with a sigh and turned to look at Carole. "And maybe I'm a little afraid. You know? How do I know if I'm reacting out of gratitude for his support and assistance, or if what I feel for him is real? It's been less than three weeks since we started seeing each other at Connie's and when mom died, he... he was there and knew what to do. He comforted me and cared for me, but," her eyes brightened, "I had to tell him I wanted a relationship, for him to stop being so reserved, so—"

"Polite?"

Eddie nodded. "I'm bouncing back and forth between wanting to take things slow and a burning desire to 'get tangled up' with him.

Does that make sense?"

Carole smiled. "Eddie, the man's very much in love with you and he's trying to make you happy. Believe me, he doesn't want you to be afraid, but he knows you have to have concerns, worries, and even fears. Talk to him. When it's quiet and just the two of you are together, talk to him, tell him your concerns, and most of all, tell him how you feel about him. When you feel like you want to get 'tangled up' together, do it."

Eddie smiled and started placing dishes in another cabinet.

"If you think you love him, tell him and hold onto every moment you have with him."

Eddie stopped and looked at Carole, hearing the subtle change in the tone of her voice, the deep, guarded concern that colored the edges of her words.

"What's wrong?"

Carole took a long sip of her lager. "Eddie, we both have very wonderful men in our lives. They love us above all else and they want to protect us at any and all costs."

"You're scaring me, Carole. What's wrong?"

"They're policemen, Eddie," Carole whispered and stepped closer to Eddie. She put a hand on Eddie's shoulder. "They don't live quiet, pastoral lives." She sighed. "Wally and Ted are going after some of the slavers in the morning. Down by Grants. Thom and Dan will stay and take care of us here."

"Just the two of them are going?"

"No," Carole said and looked at Eddie. "No, they have help. We have allies that you don't know about yet, aren't supposed to know about yet. But that doesn't keep me from worrying about him, them. Every day, I wake up, hoping I've done everything I can to let him know he's the most important thing to me."

Eddie stared at Carole for a moment and then quietly got a beer from the cooler. As she stood up, she looked at the brand. She knew Thom had selected it only because it was the one she liked the most. She looked back at Carole.

"I... think," Eddie said softly, "I'm being afraid of the wrong things and for the wrong reasons."

⋀ ⋀ ⋀ ⋀ ⋀

"I've reprogrammed One to stay in town," Jill said as Rose set a spiced beer in front of her and a Scotch with a splash in front of Nick, "and Two to stay at the ranch. I figure that will eliminate the travel time if we need one of them in either place."

"So you eavesdropped on the marshal?" Doug asked again, still concerned that she shouldn't have done that.

"Doug," Jill said sternly, "Greg told Wally that Five would be listening to everything they did, as a back up to Wally's remote. While he and Shar are away, I'm the one listening to Five."

Nick chuckled.

"Like every time they leave on a mission," he said. "Greg leaves the four of us in charge of protecting the ranch and helping Wally and his deputies."

"And since Jill can keep in touch with the remotes," Rose added, "she gets to call the shots."

"It's not that, Rose," Jill said softly. "Greg just assigned that responsibility to me."

"I know," she smiled and sipped her lager. "But that's probably part of the why."

"Anyway," Nick said, returning the discussion to the topic at hand. "Five will continue to be our link between Wally and us, and that leaves us Three and Four for transportation and immediate support."

"I'm going to leave Four with you two," Jill said, "and we'll keep Three. I gave you the communicator, right?"

"Yeah," Rose said and laid the small box on the table.

"Right," Jill nodded, "That will let you hear Four and let you talk to it when you're not on it." she looked at Nick. "Is that everything?"

"Pretty much," he replied. "Just have your Blues close by. If we need to react to anything, wear your Blues!"

"Yeah," Doug said with more energy than he intended. "After seeing how they protected Shar and then you, Jill, we won't go anywhere without them."

"When were your Kaaspr's last charged?" Jill asked, suddenly remembering that detail.

"New Year's Eve," Rose admitted. "That's when Shar exchanged them."

"Three weeks is too long," Nick said. "We brought you replacements in case we remembered right."

Rose got up and retrieved theirs from their bedroom. She passed them to Nick as Jill pushed a fresh pair across the table.

"Thanks," Rose said as she sat down. "Sorry we didn't help with the attack at the ranch. Are you doing okay, Nick?"

Nick nodded. "It happened too quickly to call for help. Jill had it almost under control before Kiile's Marines got there."

"Aren't they always close by the ranch?" Doug asked, surprised.

"Yeah," Nick said, taking another sip of his drink. "That's how fast it happened."

"Wow," Doug said softly.

Rose changed the direction of the conversation to Wally and Carole's eminent wedding and the talk around town about Thom Baines' display of affection for Eddie Collier in the flower shop yesterday.

"I guess that one really shifted the gossip mill into high gear," Jill admitted. "I don't think anyone knew they were seeing each other."

"It's a very new relationship," Rose said. "I guess it began around New Year's."

"I'm glad for her," Nick added. "And I bet she was happy to have his support when her mother died."

They each nodded and Rose got up and replenished their drinks. "Can you believe Shar and Greg are going to have a baby?" she asked as she returned to the table. "Shar, a momma. Wow."

Jill smiled at Nick and then said, "Would you believe, maybe twins?"

⊼ ⊼ ⊼ ⊼ ⊼

"Thank you for your help today," Thom said as he settled on the couch, strategically centered in front of the stone fireplace and close enough to feel the warmth, "and for the cleaning and sweeping out and for organizing my kitchen and the rest of my house." He raised his wine glass to the fireplace, "To our first evening together in my new house." Then he smiled at her and said, "I like this arrangement with the two chairs, one on either side, but you didn't tell me where you found the round coffee table. It's such a nice match with my couch and chairs."

Eddie snuggled against him with her legs curled up on the couch. "It was my grandmother's," she said softly. "I didn't have a place for it so it was stored over my garage. When I was looking at your furniture this morning while the guys were unloading them, I remembered it."

"Well, it looks very nice," he said and squeezed her shoulders.

"When I ran home to put on some clean clothes," she said, taking a sip of her Syrah, "I got it down and cleaned it up a little. I snuck it in while you were showering and was surprised it had matching carvings."

"Are you sure you want to use it here?" he asked.

"Yes. It fits and I like having something of mine in your home, in your life."

She looked up at him and he turned his head and kissed her gently. "I want as much of you in my life as I can have, for as long as you will let me have you."

She put her head back on his shoulder and watched the dancing flames in the fireplace, remembering her talk with Carole. After a few minutes, she softly asked, "Thomas, if you had your way, how long would that be?"

She felt him inhale and hold his breath before he relaxed and answered. "If I'm overstepping please tell me and please don't be offended," He stared at the fire and didn't turn to look at her, "but—"

"How long, Thomas?" she insisted softly.

"Forever and a year."

She pulled herself closer and buried her face against his neck. Her thoughts raced and she slowly forced her mind to settle before she said anything.

"That sounds like a proposal," she whispered and felt his nod.

"Yes, Eddie. I've been in love with you since the second time I saw you."

"The second time? You didn't even know me then."

"The first time, you made my heart stop," he said and smiled, still watching the fire. "The second time you stole it completely. That's when I found out you were real. Every time I see you, you take my breath away."

"You know I feel the same way about you, maybe not quite from the second time I saw you, and it scares me. I'm afraid of making a wrong decision, of doing something wrong and yet I'm afraid I'm really asleep and this is a dream and not really happening. If it's a dream, I don't want to wake up."

"I know how it can feel, Eddie," he admitted. "I was afraid at first to admit to myself that I had fallen for you, much less admit it to you. I don't want to scare you off and I don't want you to think my feelings are all or nothing. I want to be with you even if you're not ready for anything longer than our now, one day at a time. I've only dated two other women in my life and they were just that, dates, no real chemistry. I couldn't give them any real part of me, but you... you have my heart."

She quietly held him and watched the fire, unable to think of a proper response.

"I'll understand if you decide I'm not right for you, Eddie," he said slowly, "if I'm just a 'date' for you. I don't want to make you feel pressured or uncomfortable, but you asked, and I told you—"

"That you wouldn't lie to me," she interrupted with a soft chuckle. "Thank you for that. I really like knowing how I stand with you and how you stand on issues. You're not like anyone I've ever known, and I like that. I like what you are. I like that when I'm with you, I'm comfortable, secure, and I feel loved and even desired."

She slowly straightened and finished her wine, set the glass on the coaster on the coffee table and then turned and lay across his lap, facing him. She slipped an arm behind him and pulled herself up and kissed him tenderly. He held her tight, feeling her against him, savoring their emotional agreement in the moment.

She lay back in his arms and caught his free hand, opened his fingers and held his palm gently to her chest. "While I'm thinking of the best way to answer your proposal, Thomas, I think it's time for you to seriously take advantage of me."

One Hundred-Five
Monday, January 23

"Morning Wally," Kiile said as Wally and Ted got out of Wally's jeep and he motioned for them to follow him around the barn on Shara's ranch. It was an overcast and gray morning, nearly dawn when Wally greeted Kiile and Ted shook his hand. "Good to see you again, Kiile."

"We'll go down to Obscure and get some breakfast. We have time," Kiile said as they turned the corner and faced the left side of the marine transport, its personnel hatch open and waiting. "I've got two teams of ten heading down the tunnels. It'll be three more hours before they are in place."

"Should we have started earlier?" Wally asked as they climbed through the hatch and entered the ship. A Marine closed it behind them.

"Not necessarily," Kiile said as he gestured to the seats along the bulkhead. "Our surveillance tells us there are no transport ships there, so whoever's there isn't going anywhere yet."

The floor shifted and seemed to float as the transport began to lift. Ted quickly grabbed a handhold at the central passageway.

"We're about twenty minutes away from the farmstead at Obscure," Kiile continued as if he had not noticed Ted's trepidation and unfolded three of the seats attached to the main bulkhead. "So we can get there before my men if we need to."

"I noticed Shara's ranch looked very quiet," Wally remarked as he sat down and buckled in. "Is Greg away?"

"The colonel and most of his fighter squadron are on another intercept mission," Kiile said casually. "They've rescued nearly two thousand captives since they started intercepting the Traders' freighters. But he left one of his ships here to continue guarding the space station and to help if they bring in a transport to the farmstead and it gets away from us. Cadet Thomas and her group are on alert and helping to watch around the ranch and the town."

"Cadet Thomas? You mean Jill Thomas?" Wally asked.

Kiile nodded and buckled his strap.

"I forget they're around," Wally said and glanced at Ted. "Does Thom know?"

"No," Kiile admitted. "The colonel asked her to stay in the background unless they're needed. I presume you're bringing your remote and that Thom knows to call on Five if he needs remote support."

"Yes, I am and Thom knows to call on Five," Wally said.

▲ ▲ ▲ ▲ ▲

Chief Parks sat nervously in Sam's Café, next door to Smokey's Bar and Grill on the south side of Hawthorne. The cute waitress poured him another cup of coffee and he double checked his notepad as the front door opened and Don Nikle stepped in. He made a half-waving gesture and asked the waitress for a second cup.

Don settled into the booth and the waitress set a cup in front of him and filled it. She asked if he wanted anything to eat and he gave her an order. Chief Parks added his choice and she left them.

"You sounded tense," Parks said as Don stirred a sweetener into his coffee.

"Schedule is getting tight and I am short by five," Don said softly as he laid his spoon on the napkin. "The Traders' transport is arriving before daylight tomorrow."

"I thought you told me they could not get any more transports?" Parks asked. "You said that they had to use the small, converted ships."

After a long silence, Don sipped his coffee and continued, "Apparently, they have one left. It was being used for parts and after the others were destroyed, they gathered up the hulks and pieced together one useable ship from all of the parts."

"Does not sound very safe," Parks said and emptied his cup.

"I do not care how safe it is," Don said and curled his fingers into a tight fist. "Once they leave the farmstead, I am not responsible."

"Sure, sure," Parks agreed. "I know. It was just a comment."

He sat up straight as the waitress brought a large tray with their plates and a carafe. She set the plates in front of them and refilled their cups, asked if they wanted anything else and left when they said "no."

Parks tried to keep from fidgeting and watched Don quietly apply himself to his breakfast.

"I can get three without too much trouble," he offered as he spread a fruit jam on his toast. "Probably by early afternoon."

Don looked up slowly with a tight smile. "That would be good," he said tersely. "Any ideas for the last two I need?"

"Possibly one in Clay," he said and took a bite. "But I will have to go to Riggin for the last one. Two if Clay does not work out."

"Back before dawn?"

"Just after midnight," Parks said and washed the toast down with a swig of coffee.

Don nodded and went back to eating his breakfast.

⏶ ⏶ ⏶ ⏶ ⏶

"Apache Leader, KKLC14 and Apache B-Group are in position," Leeana said, her voice breaking the adrenalin filled silence. "The second freighter is escorted by a single Kyddellan battlecruiser and its fighters. Can you confirm the freighter's cargo?"

Casi closed her eyes and *felt* the freighter. The sensation was slightly softer than her own target, but it was clear enough that she could identify the number of crewmen onboard and the contents of two envirocubes in its hold.

"Perishable cargo confirmed," Casi said to the patrol cruiser Brigstoan.

A short moment passed, then the Brigstoan replied, "Apache Leader, both freighters have been hailed. Voluntary submission refused."

"B-Group is cleared for the attack," Casi said in response.

"Commencing on your Mark," Leeana responded.

"TTYF8, Apache Leader is ready," Casi said to the communications link.

"Apache Wing is ready on your Mark," Franni said.

Casi turned her thoughts to Stran, *'Are you ready, love?'*

'Yes, Bren. Go get 'em,' he said.

"Apache Wing, Apache B-Group, Mark!" Casi said sharply and pushed the thrust levers full forward. She held STSX's nose aimed at the approaching, cloaked battlecruiser and freighter.

"RANGE TEN CLICKS. REMOTE SIX DEPLOYED TO RECORD THE ENGAGEMENT," STSX announced.

"Franni?" Casi asked, "Can you feel the Cruiser?"

"Yes. Top side Weapons control centers identified and locked in," Franni said.

"Light them up, Franni," Casi said and a second later, the freighter and the battlecruiser and the deployed fighters appeared on the scanner.

"Very good," Casi said, then turned her attention to Cheral in Apache Patrol Two. "Apache Two. Like we briefed, feel the entire group of targets first. Use your scanner to confirm their positions."

"I am, cousin," Cheral answered. "I have two fighters that are still cloaked. I'll get them first."

'Yes!' Casi said to herself and Stran.

"ONE CLICK."

"Franni. Reverse orientation," Casi commanded and flipped STSX end over end, keeping one pylon 'aimed' at the underside of the rapidly approaching cruiser to allow all three turrets clear coverage.

Positioned so the cruiser would pass between them, Franni flipped TTYF8 and held full thrust, her own pylon aimed at the cruiser's topside.

Repeating their practiced choreography, Casi and Franni methodically pierced the cruiser's hull and tore open the power centers, hangar bays, fuel storage areas and systematically dissected the mass of the ship into disintegrating chunks of debris. In unison, their two Q-Ships cleared the near-space of any and all fighters within the reach of their long-range cannons. When the engines exploded, they were well clear and only emptiness remained.

Casi reached out and quickly sensed the similar progress of B-Group and then the targets were gone.

'Fourteen terran minutes, Bren,' Stran said with a smile just for her. *'Over two hundred targets neutralized with only one loss in B-Group.'*

'*Who?*' Casi asked, surprised. '*I didn't see it.*'

'*MLVC6 lost shield power and collided with a large piece of debris.*'

"KKLC14," Casi called softly, "We understand you lost one."

"Affirmative," was all Leeana said.

"Apache Squadron, Apache B-Group, regroup. Join up on Apache Leader." Then Casi switched communications channels, "Patrol cruiser Brigstoan, Apache Leader here."

"Apache Leader," the Brigstoan commander acknowledged. "Your Squadron certainly makes short work of your intercepts. We have Apache Squadron's freighter and patrol cruiser *Climatus* has boarded Apache B-Group's freighter. Envirocubes confirmed on both freighters. Good intelligence."

"Thank you," Casi said. "Does the Brigstoan require anything more from Apache Squadron?"

"Nothing more, Apache Leader," the commander said. "Thank you again. It's truly a pleasure to have your assistance."

"Our pleasure as well. Apache Leader out."

Casi turned and looked at Stran, sitting quietly in the right hand jump seat. "Let's collect Six and our patrol fighters."

▲ ▲ ▲ ▲ ▲

Fully cloaked, Kiile's transport settled into a small, insignificant break in the thick forest just north of the farmstead's main buildings. With the wide aft portal already open and his troopers lined up to disembark, Kiile retrieved two small belt pouches from a stores cabinet on the main bulkhead.

"Clip these onto your utility belts," he said as he handed one to Ted and one to Wally. "Note the big push-pads on the ends of the pouch," he said showing Wally where they were. "Those activate the transmitters."

"What are they?" Wally asked as Kiile lifted the back of his jacket and secured the pouch on his belt.

"Cloaking transmitters," Ted said with a wide smile. "Thom and I used a couple when we came down with Kiile a few weeks ago."

Kiile nodded. "You won't be able to see anyone that has activated their transmitter," he said and then handed them each a single ear headset with a short boom mic, "Unless you're very close to one another. Speak softly and listen. These will let you hear and speak to the rest of the squad, but they will not tell you where they are."

Wally looked up and as if on cue, the silhouettes of the troopers lined up across the open aft portal wavered and disappeared. Only the clear view of the hazy forest filled the opening and he realized the morning's gray overcast had thickened into a light fog and snow had begun to fall.

"Watch your tracks," Kiile said to the squad as he tapped his earpiece.

Then Kiile turned to Wally and glanced at Ted. "You have your copies of the facility maps?" Wally nodded and Kiile continued, "Stay close and follow me. The veils will merge when we are close and you will be able to see me and each other. They have cleared the roads and the walking trails. We'll use them to reach the main house. Let's go."

They activated their cloaking transmitters and jumped out of the open portal.

⋏

Kiile merged their veils when they stopped to one side of the walk in front of the main house. "Johnny Three has surrounded the house and confirmed there are six people inside."

"WL-One says Don Nikle and two of the deputies that Thom met are there," Wally said as he glanced around.

Then Kiile tapped the earpiece again. "Johnny One, Johnny Two, report."

In their headsets, Wally and Ted heard the two tunnel squads report their status and positions. "Johnny One is just beyond the security check-point in the north tunnel. Only one sentry on duty. He looks sleepy and bored."

Johnny Two reported from just west of the west tunnel's security check-point.

"Neutralize your sentries," Kiile said into his mic, "then wait until Johnny Three and Johnny Four are in position."

"This is really strange," Ted remarked softly. "Standing in the middle of the road and no one can see us."

"Stay alert," Kiile said in a flat tone. "People will run into things they don't see." Then he turned his attention to the ranch house.

"There are three doors into the main house. We have the front door and Johnny Three is positioned at the other two." He nodded to a large building, just to their southwest. "That building is where they hid the converted fighter for the last shipments. Johnny Four is already inside. There is an elevator and a wide staircase connecting to the facility below. "

"WL-One says there are thirty-one people in the various buildings and in the open spaces above ground," Wally commented as he removed the remote monitor from his inside jacket pocket. "Only ten are armed," he said and showed Kiile where WL-One indicated they were.

Suddenly the wail of alarms sounded in every building and people began running.

"Damn! Time to go," Kiile shouted and turned to the front door. He tapped his earpiece and released his Marines, "Engage! All Johnnies, engage!"

In quick succession, four men burst out of the ranch house's front door and ran for the large building Kiile had pointed out moments before. Kiile and Ted sprang after them as a fifth man, in a deputy's uniform, stepped out and turned, firing his pistol at something back inside.

"Halt!" Wally shouted and dashed for the startled deputy as he looked around.

Seeing no one, the deputy started to run after the others, but Wally dove and caught his legs. The deputy tumbled and lost his grip on his pistol, and before he could react, Wally pinned him face down and pressed the muzzle of his 9 mm against the deputy's temple.

Confused, suddenly seeing Wally out of the corner of his eye, Wally had to tell him a second time to put one hand behind his back. When the deputy finally complied, Wally snapped the shackle on first one wrist and then the other. "Good morning Deputy Martin," Wally said without any pleasantness in his voice. "You're a long ways from Clay. Is your boss around here somewhere?"

Wally stood up and retrieved the errant pistol. Then he pulled the deputy up and shoved him back inside the ranch house.

"Johnny Three?" Wally called and dropped his veil. A Marine coalesced near a group of overstuffed chairs in the center of the large room. "Take care of this one. I've got to catch up with the others."

He started to turn when the Marine pointed to the dining room,

"There's a service elevator in the kitchen, Marshal. Our remote indicates it is connected to the food preparation area in the facility below, two levels down."

"Thanks," Wally said and quickly consulted the map image Kiile had given him. Then with his pistol in hand, Wally hurried to the elevator.

⚓

Kiile and Ted stopped at the top of the long, concrete staircase inside the living portion of the large building southwest of the main house. They merged their veils and Kiile tapped his earpiece, "Johnny Four Report."

"Johnny Four," the response whispered in their earpieces, "is spread out on the first floor down the long stairs. Many persons have taken refuge in numerous small rooms around the central chambers. They do not have uniforms but are wearing identification badges."

"Copy," Kiile acknowledged. "Johnny Three, Report."

"Johnny Three has the main house secured," another voice whispered in his ear. "One city deputy from Clay has been detained."

"Very good," Kiile said. "Secure the remaining buildings on the surface. The deputy and I are going to join Johnny Four."

"Will do," the voice said. "The marshal and one from Johnny Three have gone down from the main house."

"Thanks. Johnny Four, we're starting down the stairs now."

⚓

Wally and Marine Thirty-two crouched on opposite sides of the elevator door when the elevator stopped and the doors slowly slid open. As they slipped out and knelt on either side of the opening, Wally realized the alarms were silent and he quickly searched the moderate sized food preparation chamber. It seemed normal except sans people.

"Kiile," Wally whispered into his boom mic. "We are on the second level down, kitchen area. My map shows this to be the detention level."

"We're on the first level with Johnny Four," Kiile answered softly. "Johnny One and Johnny Two are coming up to your level from the tunnels below you. Security is just outside the food prep area. Go to the doors across the room from you and turn right as you leave."

Wally turned to look across the elevator door where Thirty-two was supposed to be kneeling. "Thirty-two," he whispered, "do you have explosives?"

"Yes," the emptiness whispered an answer. "Series Two through Nine."

"I think we should check out Security," Wally said and started across the room to the double metal doors.

"Right behind you," Thirty-two said.

At the door, Wally looked through the clear paned window and saw a number of people in brown uniforms. Some were on either side of a long counter to one side of a corridor that disappeared to the right and others were standing in numerous small groups, obviously discussing the alarms, but not doing anything in response.

"Each is in uniform," Thirty–two said softly beside him. "No civilians."

Wally smiled at the Marine's distinction.

"Johnny One," the Marine said to his boom mic, "Johnny Two, Johnny Four? Are any of you on the second level in Security?"

Wally heard the three negatives and Johnny Two's comment that they were almost there.

"All Johnny's stop and hold position," Thirty-two said, "Do not enter second level for four minutes." Thirty-two turned to Wally, "Take the respirator from the transmitter pouch and put it on." Wally followed his example as Thirty-two put his on and unclipped a canister with a double blue stripe from his utility belt.

Thirty-two punched the sequence into the keypad on the end of the canister and then turned to the door. He knelt down and slowly pushed his panel open a bit, punched the last button and waited, counting. At the count of three he tossed the canister through the opening and jumped back, the panel closed and at five the canister exploded with a soft 'phoom.'

Wally jumped up and stared into the room through the panel window. Most of the people in the room had collapsed and the few still standing, were staggering and slowly, one by one, stumbled and sagged into silent heaps on the floor.

Thirty-two pushed the door panel open and stepped into the receiving area. He glanced at his wrist unit and said, "One minute and thirty seconds in your time and the room will be safe without the respirators." Then to his boom mic, "Second level, main receiving area is secure. Connecting wings are still hot."

Wally crouched in front of the long counter and checked his map. "This near corridor looks like it goes to the detention areas and the far corridor," he pointed to the other end of the counter, "goes to another large area. WL-One indicates it may be billeting, possibly the Security personnel quarters." Then Wally tapped his own earpiece, "WL-One? What is the status of the billeting area?"

"THIRTY-FIVE DEAD WHERE YOU ARE, SEVENTEEN STILL REMAINING IN THE AREA BEYOND THE MOUTH OF THE CORRIDORS. FORTY-EIGHT NON-HOSTILES RESTRAINED IN THE CHAMBERS AT THE END OF THE FIRST CORRIDOR."

Wally repeated the remote's assessment and Thirty-two addressed his boom mic, "Johnny One and Johnny Two, to second level Security, on the double."

They dropped their veils and slowly stood up as the sound of many running boots came from the stairs across the room.

Wally sighed in relief as the sounds entered and filled the room and the troopers of Johnny One and Two shimmered and solidified.

Immediately, the Marines formed two groups and arranged themselves in front of each corridor. Thirty-two had positioned himself at the mouth of the far corridor and Wally at the mouth of the first, and on Thirty-two's pumping arm signal, they moved in.

At the first opening on his left, Wally slowly peeked into the large room and saw rows of double decked beds and clothes lockers along the walls and others in a double row down the middle of the room. A pistol barked and the door jamb burst just above his head.

With the deputy's pistol in one hand and his own 9 mm in his other, Wally dove through the opening, firing in return as he hit the floor and rolled under a bed and stopped against its locker. The chamber filled with the rapid, continuous din of gunfire and returned fire as the Marines charged in from both sides and engaged.

Suddenly, the crescendo fell silent and Wally slowly sat up. He quickly ejected the spent clip from his 9 mm and replaced it with a full one, then he pushed himself up and stepped out into the aisle between the rows of bunks. He saw Thirty-two at the other end of the row and was about to wave—

"BEHIND YOU!"

Wally spun and crouched at the same time, two 9 mms barked in a staccato duet. The first round went above his head, but the second caught his shoulder, slamming him backwards. Wally's three shots hit the man squarely in the chest as he rose up from behind the desk by the opening into the room.

Dazed and angry, Wally tried to push himself up. He was surprised to see Thirty-two leaning over him and helping him up, asking if he was all right.

"More stupid than hurt," Wally admitted out loud. Thirty-two chuckled as Wally steadied himself and absently rubbed his shoulder. The pain startled him, making his knees go weak and then he looked at the tear in his jacket.

After a quick inspection, Wally realized something was broken. Thirty-two pushed here and there and Wally stumbled when he pushed on the spot. "Collar bone, sir."

Wally shook his head and muttered, "Damn!"

A Marine stood beside the man behind the desk. "Sir, this one's dead. He's a police chief. His name tag says 'Russell.'"

Wally half smiled and shook his head. "I knew he had to be here somewhere. He's the chief up in Clay. I collared one of his deputies up at the main house."

"So the police are in this?" the Marine asked before he remembered himself, "Sir."

"They were," Wally said, "Now there are only four left, one deputy in Clay, and two deputies and the chief in Hawthorne. All of the others have been collected, or otherwise eliminated. The last of the Council of Elders, Don Nikle, should be here somewhere too."

Thirty-two turned Wally to another Marine, "Take the marshal to the transport."

"No!" Wally said sharply, then softer, "No. We'll release the captives first. Is the area outside secure? Can we bring them out safely? How're your troopers?"

"We lost one, they lost ten, eleven now and six surrendered," Thirty-Two said. "You got four of them yourself, sir. Johnny Three says the surface buildings are secure and the remotes have the grounds under surveillance. It should be safe to bring them up, sir."

"Thanks," Wally said and then stopped to look at Thirty-two. "What is your name, Corporal?"

Thirty-two smiled. "Corporal Mosl, sir."

"Corporal Mosl," Wally said and extended his left hand, "it's very good to know you, sir. Please call me Wally."

"Thank you, Wally, sir," Thirty-two said, "Good to know you too. Shall we tell the guests their stay is over?"

"By all means, Corporal Mosl, by all means. Please lead the way."

⋏ ⋏ ⋏ ⋏ ⋏

Carole had arrived at Hap's a little early and was in her apron and wiping tables when the other two waitresses came in and put their coats and purses in the back room. Mel was cleaning and arranging the working side of the bar and Carole absently listened to the sounds of the cook getting the kitchen ready for the day.

She tried to not think about Wally's trip, but she still worried and wondered what was going on, what he was facing.

"So, how was your day off?" the pert brunette asked as she checked the shakers and napkins on a nearby table.

"Oh, morning, Tina," Carole said. "It was busy, and nice. We helped Wally's deputy, Thom, move yesterday. Eddie and I mostly cleaned and arranged things while the guys handled the heavy stuff."

"Where'd he move to?" Tina asked as she stopped to chat.

Carole pointed down Main. "Thom bought the craft shop, the house, buildings and the property they sit on."

"Really? I heard all kinds of rumors and old lady talk about Charley," Tina said with a curious smile. "What's Charley going to do?"

"He's already done it," Carole said and moved to the next table and checked the chairs. "Charley bought forty acres down by the Double J, went back to South Dakota and brought his sweetheart back to live with him on it."

"Charley has a sweetheart?" Tina nearly dropped the salt container she was holding.

"Apparently," Carole smiled. "I haven't met her yet, but Thom says she's very nice, and is very happy to be here."

"Wow," Tina said. "Someone's happy to be here, at this time of year? Are you sure she's not mental?"

Carole chuckled and turned to wipe the table in the booth when

116

she felt the room begin to spin. She reached out and grabbed the table to steady herself, then slowly, as the spinning began to slow, she eased herself into the booth.

"You okay?" Tina asked, noticing the change in Carole's manner.

Carole absently nodded and then suddenly grabbed her right shoulder. The sensation of a sharp pain made her jerk and she looked at Tina. She felt scared.

"What is it?" Tina asked as she slid into the bench on the opposite side of the booth.

"Wally's hurt," she said, the words out of her mouth before she realized how absurd she sounded.

𝗔 𝗔 𝗔 𝗔 𝗔

"Are you sure you want to do this?" Thom asked Eddie as he helped her in and closed the passenger door to his patrol car.

"Yes," Eddie said and she buckled her seat strap as he got in. "You're off your normal schedule and I think you're going to need someone to keep you awake after midnight. Four in the afternoon to four in the morning is quite a bit different from four in the morning to four in the afternoon. Besides, I don't have anything big happening at work until Thursday when we start getting flowers ready for Wally and Carole's wedding."

"Okay, but only if I can drop you back here if you get sleepy," he said and started the car.

"I told you, if I get sleepy, I want to sleep here." She smiled and held his eyes. "After last night, I don't want to be anywhere else."

"Well," Thom said and smiled back, "after last night, I guess I really don't want you to be anywhere else either."

He backed his patrol car into the craft shop parking lot and pulled out onto Main, then took Baxter north. "We'll make one full patrol around town and then get a bite to eat. Think about where you want to go."

"Maybe we should stop in at Hap's and check on Carole," she said. "She told me Wally was going after some of the slavers down by Grants. That's why you changed your shift."

Thom stared at her and shook his head. "I didn't know she told you."

"She probably shouldn't have," Eddie admitted, "but it helped me put things in perspective. I'm new to this and we had a nice talk. I'm new to us and I'm new to your world of law enforcement. She's willing to worry a little to have time with Wally and I think I understand how she feels."

"I hope she doesn't worry too much," Thom said. "Wally tries really hard to keep things simple and as worry free as he can."

"That's what she said, but you and I know he can't always do that." Eddie watched the street as they crossed Juniper. "After we talked, I realized that I'm a little like her. I want more 'last nights' and all of the times we can have together, and..."

He waited in the warm silence of her company and when she didn't continue he smiled and glanced at her as he turned onto Ash and then pulled into the marshal's office parking lot.

"I'll be right back," he said as he got out and locked the car doors behind him. He opened the back door to the office and slipped in quickly. It was only a couple of minutes before he stepped back out, locked the back door and hurried back to the car.

"Take a look at this," he said, handing her a thick book. He pulled out of the lot and picked up his patrol route. "If you're going to ride with me a little, or a lot, I'm going to get you an *official* jacket. If you look on page forty-nine or there about, you'll find jackets. I thought they had some stylish ones, cut specifically for a female officer." He glanced at her, "Of course, you'd know better about that than me."

"That's nice, but why do I need a policewoman's jacket?" She looked at him with her fingers between the pages.

"They're ballistic jackets," he said, his expression turning serious. "I know you're not going to be with me if I have to do anything dangerous, but I want you to be as safe as possible in case the unexpected happens."

"Unexpected?"

"Eddie, I couldn't live with myself if you got hurt because I didn't prepare for the unlikely possibility. Besides, I think some of them would look good on you."

She smiled, realizing he was down-playing the truth of the dangers associated with his work.

"I can even get ones tailored to your tastes," he said, his bright smile returning, "even ones for different occasions and seasons."

"Seasons, huh?" She smiled at him and the implied future in his words. "Okay, Thomas, I'll look at what they have and what I want."

"Thanks," he said and reached over and took her hand.

It was full dark before they finished patrolling all of the streets in town, following a crisscrossing pattern that let him see a significant part of the town twice. Everything seemed normal and quiet and Thom pulled into Hap's back parking lot. He noticed Carole's jeep as he helped Eddie out and walked her to the back door.

"Hey guys," Carole greeted, seeing them immediately as they stepped in. "Booth?"

Eddie nodded and followed Carole to a booth near the back. Thom took her coat and Eddie slid in and patted the space beside her. Thom placed their coats on the seat between Eddie and the wall and sat down as suggested.

"And what have you two been up to?" Carole asked, noticing Eddie's pert glow.

"I'm riding shotgun tonight," Eddie said and covered Thom's hand with hers.

Carole started to ask more, but caught Eddie's 'I'll tell you later look.' "What can I get you?" Carole asked instead.

Eddie looked at Thom. "Can we share the Queso?" Thom nodded with a smile. "Okay, the four cheese Queso and chips, peppers on the side, and a bowl of your chicken and dumpling soup."

"Half size ham and Swiss on rye, mustard, and a small order of the homemade potato chips," Thom added and looked at Eddie. "Coffee for both of us. And a fill up for my insulated carafe when we're finished?"

"Coming right up," Carole said and entered their order in her hand unit as she went to collect their coffee. Returning quickly, Carole set a mug in front of Eddie and placed Thom's mug with the deputy's star in front of him and proceeded to fill them. "Have you heard anything?" she asked in a whisper and sat down at Thom's gesture. "I had the strangest feeling this morning that Wally got hurt, but that's silly. I know I'm just worrying too much."

He tapped his earpiece and said softly, "WL-One, report marshal's status, please."

A moment passed, then he heard an answer in his ear, "FIVE IS RELAYING WL-ONE'S MESSAGE: 'ENGAGEMENT SUCCESSFUL.

FORTY-EIGHT CAPTIVES FOUND AND FREED. FIFTY-FIVE
SLAVE TRADER SECURITY PERSONNEL KILLED, FORTY-ONE
SURRENDERED. ONE MARINE KILLED, MARSHAL SUFFERED
A BROKEN RIGHT COLLAR BONE IN ENGAGEMENT WITH
POLICE CHIEF RUSSELL FROM CLAY. ALL PEACE FORCE
PERSONNEL, MARSHAL AND DEPUTY MARKS ON STAKE
OUT, WAITING FOR POSSIBLE ARRIVAL OF A TRADER'S
TRANSPORT BEFORE DAWN.'"

Thom slowly repeated what Five had said.

"Wally did get hurt?" Carole asked absently and rubbed her
shoulder. "How...? Do you know what time he got hurt?"

Thom tapped his earpiece and asked.

"Ten forty-six this morning," he said and saw Carole's face go
white.

"That's about when I felt the room spin and a pain in my
right shoulder." She looked at Thom and then at Eddie's startled
expression. "How on earth, Thom? I'm not—"

"Don't ask me," Thom said and squeezed Eddie's hand. "I know
you two are very close, closer than most, but this... I don't have a
clue."

Carole glanced at the pass-through window and quickly got up
and retrieved their Queso.

"Who's Five and WL-One?" Eddie asked softly when Carole
stepped away.

"They're two of our tools," he said. "I can't explain right now, but
I can tell you when we're back in the car."

"Okay." Eddie nodded as Carole returned and set their appetizer
on the table.

Carole glanced around the room and sat down again. "Thanks,
Thom," she said. "Wally said I should talk to one of you three if I ever
need to catch him when he's away."

"That's fine, Carole. It's obvious it isn't anything serious or Kiile
would have let me know." Then he smiled, "I think Wally needs to
get you an earpiece, and maybe..." he looked at Eddie "he'll let me get
one for Eddie."

Carole smiled at the thought and then got up and started around
the room checking on her other customers and Eddie watched her as
she went.

"I know there's a lot going on that I don't know about," Eddie said and started into the Queso. "So please don't be offended if I ask too many questions."

He squeezed her hand again. "I won't be. I'll always tell you all I can, and I'll let you know if I can't."

"Fair enough," she said and he picked up a corn chip.

He hesitated and looked at the peppers. "Do you like hot and spicy foods?"

"Yes," she said as she scooped the cheese sauce with a chip and piled a pepper on top. With a bright smile and her eyes dancing at him, she stuffed it in her mouth and ate it.

One Hundred-Six

Thom and Eddie finished dinner and Carole filled his insulated carafe and gave him two insulated cups before they stepped out through the back door.

"Thanks, Carole," Thom said, "We may be back for more coffee before you close up."

"Sure thing, Thom. Take care of this one, Eddie," she said with a wink. "See ya when you come by."

Thom helped her into the car and then got in. He dug deep into his pants pocket and then reached out to Eddie.

"Here," he said, "I want you to have your own key to my place."

"What?" She asked, more than surprised by his gesture. "Are you sure?"

"This is the house," he said and curled her fingers around the key. "All of the other keys are in the cabinet in the kitchen. You know where I hung them."

She nodded absently as he started the car and drove across Main, beginning their second patrol, taking a completely different route across town.

"You're really sure?" she asked again.

"Eddie," he said. "I don't have anything you can't have or use."

"I don't know what to say, Thomas."

"Then just say 'thank you.' "

"Thank you."

"You asked about Five and WL-One," Thom changed the subject after they had passed the elementary school and turned north around the block and started back west.

"Yeah," Eddie nodded, "you almost sounded like your 'tools' were more like people you knew rather than things you use."

"Well," Thom smiled. "We rely on them so much that they can seem that way sometimes. WL-One is the name of the tool that scanned your house after the reception you held." He touched the earpiece. "With these, we can communicate with it, with each other and answer calls when we are not in the office. It can also give us some warning and back up when we need an extra hand."

"Do all police forces have them?" She turned in her seat to see him better as they passed under streetlights. She leaned back against the door and knew he was watching her and liked what he saw.

"No," he said softly. "I don't know of any others that do."

"So how did you get it?"

"It was a gift from a friend Wally knew when he was a kid in foster care. I know that doesn't explain much, but..." Thom tried to add clarity, but just got more and more tied up around the details he couldn't tell her about. "As for Five, it belongs to Wally's friend and now, today, Wally has WL-One with him and Ted and we have Five to relay any information and to fill in where WL-One can't. Our earpieces don't have enough range to reach all the way down to Grants, but WL-One and Five can."

Eddie sat quietly, trying to understand Thom's cryptic explanation and figure out what she should ask next. "Why is it called Five?"

"It's the fifth one assigned to Wally's friend."

"Carole said Wally and you guys have allies here," Eddie said, remembering. "She said I wasn't supposed to know about them yet."

"Only a very few here in town know about them, Eddie," he said and looked at her, "And as soon as I can, I will tell you too. But, I can't just yet."

"I wish you could," she admitted, "but if you tell me you can't, I know you can't. Will you be able to soon, or is it one of those 'wait and see' sort of things?"

"I don't really know when, Eddie," he said and absently shook his head, "but it isn't a 'wait and see' thing."

It was after nine when Thom stopped at the Stop 'N Shop to buy some snack items. Eddie watched him through the store front window as he visited with the young girl and the middle aged man behind the counter. She noticed how he slowly looked around the store, smiling at the few customers that had stopped in while he kept up his conversation. After a few minutes, he stepped out, looked around the parking lot and then got back in.

"Everything okay?" Eddie asked as he got back in and started across River to the east.

"Yeah," he said, "But maybe not. I don't know what it is, but something's nibbling at my senses."

Eddie waited and Thom tapped his earpiece. "One, Two, Five. Have you seen anything unusual?"

"NOTHING," Five reported and Thom shook his head.

"Now, it's One and Two and Five?"

"Sorry, but yes."

"How many are there"

"We have just the one, but we have access to seven at different times." He glanced at Eddie. "And there are others we don't have access to. Right now, we can only access five of them. The other two are away."

"DEPUTY BAINE, THERE IS A DISTURBANCE ON SPRUCE AND ESTER, IN FRONT OF THE ELEMENTARY SCHOOL. RUN SILENT. HURRY. A WOMAN IS BEING ABDUCTED."

"Damn!" he muttered and turned at the intersection with Hurst. "Looks like someone is trying to make a woman go somewhere she doesn't want to go. Can you shoot a pistol?"

"What? A pistol?" She looked at him with startled, wide eyes. "Not since I was a kid."

"Okay," he said calmly. "This could get dicey, so I'm going to tell you this just in case. I don't expect your support, okay? Just to protect yourself if you have to."

She nodded slowly as she straightened herself in the seat.

"In the glove box, there is a semiautomatic 9 mm pistol, like the one I'm wearing. Please take it out and get a feel for its weight."

She opened the glove box and removed the pistol from its holster.

"Now, if you should need to use it," he smiled at her, "and only if you feel your life is in danger, you just pull the hammer back," he showed her where it was and what to do, "then point and pull the trigger. It will fire each time you pull the trigger after that." He looked at her as he reached over and released the Safety. "I know this is not what you expected tonight, and it's certainly not what I expected." He took her left hand and squeezed it.

He cut over to Amos on Cedar and then turned south until he got to Poplar.

"THE VEHICLE IS JUST NORTH OF SPRUCE, BLOCKING THE ENTRANCE TO THE SCHOOL'S PARKING LOT. THE WOMEN WERE TRYING TO LEAVE WHEN THEY WERE STOPPED."

"Okay, Eddie," he said as he turned the corner onto Ester and switched the roof mounted flashing lights on, "Duck down and stay out of sight."

When he stopped with a quick warble of the siren, he stepped out and stood behind the open door, the headlights showing directly on the patrol car's Hawthorne Police Department door emblem. He knew Five was on the other side of them, waiting for his orders.

"Stand up with your hands up!" Thom shouted seeing the struggle behind the car.

He stepped around the door and heard Eddie open her door. He turned his head to look and saw her step around her door, following his example.

"Get back," he said in a loud whisper as he moved closer to the front of the Hawthorne car.

"No, you need back up," she said in a soft voice and quickly crossed in front of his car. "There are two of them."

"Damn!" he muttered to himself. "Stay behind me then," he said to her and moved around the front of the Hawthorne police car. "Stop! Put your hands up!" He shouted and held the 9 mm aimed squarely at the large man's back.

The man turned and Thom saw the second man slowly stand up.

"There's another woman in the car," Eddie whispered to Thom.

"Release them!" Thom shouted as the large man slowly rose and turned, revealing the disheveled woman lying on her side on the snow packed drive, trying to sit up, a shackle dangled from one wrist.

"Well, if it isn't Deputy Baines," the large man said as the headlights flashed on his badge.

"Explain yourself Parks! You are out of your jurisdiction," Thom said, watching the deputy standing behind the chief and just beyond the woman. Then quietly he said to Eddie, "Stay behind me. Keep me between them and you at all times."

"I am," she said.

"We just have a runaway here, Deputy," Parks said, gesturing with his hands at the woman.

"NEITHER ARE RUNAWAYS. THEY GO TO THE COLLEGE HERE. THEY STARTED IN THE FALL. THEY HAVE BEATEN THE WOMEN. THE WOMAN IN THE CAR IS BARELY CONSCIOUS."

"Well, Chief?" he said and watched the deputy. The chief's gestures became more animated with each passing moment and Thom was sure the deputy would take advantage of the distraction. "Put them in my patrol car and we'll check out their story down at the marshal's office." Then to Eddie he added softly," I don't like this, it's going to go downhill any second."

"That's really not necessary, Deputy," Parks continued.

"Parks! Put them in my car! You can either come down to the office with them or you can leave. You do NOT have authority here!"

"What?" Parks demanded and swung his arms wide.

The deputy made his move and Thom spread his left arm wide, opening his loose jacket to shield Eddie as he and the deputy fired. Two shots hit Park's deputy in the chest, one centered and one low, and Thom slammed back against Eddie. He felt her 9 mm fire under his right arm and he saw the chief spin aside, his pistol disappearing into the darkness.

Thom lost his footing and fell back against Eddie and suddenly the void between him and the chief erupted in a blinding flash of light. He continued to fall and felt Eddie cushion him as he stopped. The bright light faded and he rolled over to look at her.

"Are you all right?" he asked and saw her nodding her head as she grabbed his shoulders. She was shouting something, but he couldn't make it out. She suddenly sounded a long way away.

Then someone pulled him away from her and he tried to fight back, he did not want to leave her. Then he was looking up at the black night and someone with a red headband was slapping his face and shouting at him.

⋏

When Thom slammed against her, Eddie fired the pistol once and then automatically wrapped her arms around him as he pushed her backwards. His weight knocked the wind out of her when they hit the ground and she wasn't certain if she saw a bright flash of light or if she had hit her head.

Then Thom rolled over and lay on top of her, asking if she was all right and she tried to assure him she was. His speech slurred and he asked her again if she was all right.

Suddenly out of nowhere, someone was bending over Thom and rolled him aside, shouting at him, and then she started slapping his face and yelling for him to "stay with her, to stay with Eddie."

Abruptly Eddie realized there were four people in dark, almost black suits. Two were women wearing brilliant red headbands and the other two were men. Confused, she wondered what they were doing, where they came from and slowly she looked down at her blood covered arms and blouse.

"Thom?" She looked at him on his back, at his blood soaked uniform shirt. "Thoomm!" she shrieked and tried to reach him.

"Give Jill a minute, Eddie," one of the women with the headbands said and grabbed her shoulders, stopping her.

"Thom!" she yelled again as her eyes filled with tears. Then slowly she started to hear more people speaking and suddenly the space around the chief's car filled with men in white camouflaged uniforms. Someone was helping the woman on the ground and others the woman in the car.

"Jill, the Medic and a corpsman are here," one of the uniformed men said as another knelt down beside Thom. "Give him some room. The transport is here and waiting."

"Nick," the voice said and Nick's familiar face atop another nearly black uniform emerged from the darkness. "Take Three and get Carole. Eddie's going to need her for support. Hurry."

"Jill?" Eddie asked, confused as Jill turned to look at her. "Rose, bring her over here and then you and Doug take Four and try to find the chief's trail. He can't be far." Then to Eddie, Jill said, "Hold his hand Eddie. Let him know you're here. Talk to him. Keep him awake."

Eddie took his hand like they told her to and she leaned over and kissed him. "Don't you dare leave me, not now, not after we've found each other."

She stiffened her resolve and talked to him about the times they were going to have and the things they were going to do. She was completely lost in Thom's face and the one sided conversation and didn't realize Carole was there until Carole put her arms around her and began talking to her, telling her he would be all right. If anyone could help him, she knew their friends could.

"Twelve," Medic Wrth finally said and turned to the Marine that seemed to be in charge.

"Sir?" Twelve said.

"Take him up to Medical," then, when the Marine acknowledged the order, Medic Wrth turned to Eddie, her expression warm and caring. "Are you with him?"

She nodded, suddenly unable to speak.

"This is Eddie, Meara," Carole said softly. "They belong to each other."

"We'll do everything we can, Eddie," the Medic said and Eddie absently nodded.

"Twelve, take Eddie and Carole with him to Medical," Medic Wrth said. "The hand scanner is encouraging, but I will look him over better when we're settled there." Then she turned to Eddie, "I've given him an injection that will keep him calm. His pulse is strong and he's young. Let's go and see how bad it is. Oh, Twelve, bring the women they were trying to steal. I'll treat them and let them sleep until you can arrange to have someone speak with them."

Eddie got up with Carole and suddenly stopped. "Jill? Is that really you?"

"Yes, it's me, Eddie," Jill said. "Can you tell me what happened? I'll get the video from Five, but please tell me."

Eddie slowly explained what she knew, from her point of view. "I know Chief Parks and his deputy were trying to take the two women against their will and Thom was trying to stop them. Thom warned me the situation was deteriorating and he stayed in front of me. He could've ducked, but he stayed in front of me."

"We sort of met the chief and his deputy when we went down to Hawthorne with Thom on New Year's Eve. He really didn't like Thom being there and asking questions. Thom suspected he was deeply involved with the slavers and now he has the proof Wally needs to put them away."

Eddie looked at her in surprise. "His assignment? You were there?"

"Yeah, Clay and then Hawthorne," Jill said. "Rose and I were his escorts, his backup."

"Cadet Thomas," Twelve said as he stopped and extended his hand. "These are the deputy's and Miss Eddie's pistols. We'll return his patrol car to the marshal's office and then one of my men will bring the key fob to Miss Eddie on the transport." He looked around the parking lot and the small group of people the lights and activity had started to draw, "And we'll clear the area and visit the 'witnesses' before we leave."

"Thank you, Twelve," Jill said, taking the pistols, "I'll be on the transport for a while." Then she turned to Nick. "Take Carole up to the transport on Two, and I'll bring Eddie on Three. Carole, I guess when we get there we might as well tell Eddie everything. I think Thom will be relieved he doesn't have to hide it any more. Come on, Eddie. I know you were asking about the remotes, so I'll introduce you to Three."

She led Eddie away from the glare of the lights as the Marines settled Thom in a litter and strapped him in. Remote Three drifted down and stopped at head height and extended its stirrups.

"Eddie, this is remote number three," Jill said, "We just call it Three."

"How many?" Eddie asked, remembering Thom's explanation.

"Kiile's Marines have six for each transport, so that's eighteen, and we, my brother that is, have ten and each fighter has six, so that's..." Jill stopped, seeing Eddies completely befuddle expression. "Sorry Eddie. Greg says I babble too much and he's right. Come on, let's get you up with Thom."

Jill showed her how to mount and they were ready when Two drifted down and stopped beside Three.

"I guess I'm ready, Nick," Carole said as she followed Jill's example, remembering her previous ride and slipped her foot into Two's extended stirrup and grabbed the hand hold.

Tuesday, January 24

The night passed slowly as Carole and Jill sat with Eddie beside Thom in the transport's Medical chamber and the two women slept in two of the other Medical chambers. Having explained all they could think of to Eddie, they had settled down for the long wait. The Medic was pleased and told Eddie the two bullets had gone completely through Thom and if he had not been wearing his jacket, they would have wounded her as well. She told her they missed his vital organs and did only minor damage, nicking one lung and a rib.

The Medic assured Eddie that Thom would be up and around in a day or two.

As she reached the hatch to leave the room, Medic Wrth looked back at Eddie, "You're very lucky to have a partner that cares enough to take the shots to protect you." The Medic shook her head. "I think Kiile needs to talk to Wally. I didn't know he had women deputies, but he really should have issued you protective gear." The Medic left before Eddie could contradict her thought that she was a deputy.

Jill slowly looked around the small room with its four Medical couches. "You know, the first time I saw a room like this one was on Kiile's transport when Shar found and rescued Nick." She smiled at Eddie. "I sat in a chair just like you are, for what seemed like days. It took Nick nearly a week to get back on his feet after being exposed to the freezing cold for nearly four days."

"Where was he? What happened?" Eddie asked as she absently rubbed Thom's hand and fingers.

"Up on the reservation, in the valley west of Chief Joshua Mesa," Jill explained. "Old Judge Bernice Reeds stole him and had him staked out in a very desolate and wild area and left him to die. After we found him, Kiile showed up with his transport and a band of Marines. I sat with Nick in a room like this while Shar tracked down the guys that had taken Nick." Jill sighed. "We got all three and eventually got old Judge Bernice."

After a few more moments had passed, Jill continued. "Nick's recovered in a Medical unit three times now, Uncle Jim once, my dad once, Dusty at the ranch once, and me once." She smiled and glanced at the floor. "And Shar once. I have no idea how many times Greg's had to use one, but Cheral scolded him for using it too often."

"Who's Cheral?" Eddie asked.

"Oh, you knew her as Meg," Jill said. "She worked at Hap's. Undercover."

"I remember Meg," Eddie said. "She's one of you, your—?"

"Yeah," Jill smiled and then continued. "She was my brother's navigation and communications officer for three years. She got shot, really bad, in Pitcarthy, Pennsylvania a year and a half ago and was out of commission for nearly six months. Greg said she was a whisper away from dying. That's why she has that limp and one slightly drooped shoulder."

"Oh my," Eddie said and covered her mouth in surprise. "I had no idea. What's she doing now?"

"She's a fighter pilot."

Eddie's eyes went wide. "A what?"

"Fighter pilot."

"I expected you to say she had gone back to school, or taken a better job in a better restaurant, or..." Eddie paused.

"Well, she did go back to school," Jill giggled to herself, "Just not like you were thinking." Jill saw the strange expression cross Eddie's face and quickly tried to calm her thoughts. "Eddie, I know you're getting a huge dose of our alternate realities and I really know how hard this is to accept. I, we all went through the realization and then the adjustment, but it's the love of our friends and our special ones that make it understandable, keeps us steady and keeps things in perspective. I didn't know I had a brother until he and Shar rescued me from the slavers, and then when I found out I had one, I also found out he's an undercover investigator, a cop. He's also a fighter pilot and now commands a squadron of heavy fighters and three squads of Marines. And Shar is a fully qualified fighter pilot."

"It's a steep learning curve, Eddie," Carole added. "And a lot to comprehend, but to be with Wally, I was happy to accept it and embrace the comfort it gives me to know I have friends looking out for me and for Wally, even when I don't know it. They're here for you and Thom too. And we're here for you too."

"I know Thom's here for me. I know it more now than ever," Eddie admitted, "and I'm going to be here for him." She smiled at Carole and then at Jill.

"Uh, oh," Jill said suddenly and turned to the door. She stepped out into the corridor and looked both ways. "Where's Twelve or Twenty-two?" she asked the Marine standing in the opening to the cargo bay.

The Marine pointed across the corridor and she rapped on the closed hatch.

When the panel opened and Twelve stood in the opening, Jill explained, "Can you alert Kiile and the marshal? There's a Traders' transport descending toward their location. You should also call LTVC21 down for support. When they find out the captives are not there, they'll surely try to run for it."

"Yes, ma'am," Twelve said and then smiled. "Thank you for the warning, Shadow Thomas." Then he turned to the cockpit and the nav-com officer.

▲ ▲ ▲ ▲ ▲

It was a couple of hours before dawn when Jill and Nick drifted up Kelly Street on Three and stopped near Rose and Doug in the trees beside a gingerbread house.

"Four followed him here," Rose said, pointing to the single story house across the street. "He stopped at a house on Poplar and when no one answered, he worked his way up across campus. He stopped at a Hall on the north side, east of the Library but couldn't get in. Then he stopped at a house at the corner of Birch and Mann. When no one answered, he came here."

Jill looked at the house across the street and then up and down the street. *'Three, see what's behind the house.'*

When Three circled the house and reported what it saw, Jill put the pieces together.

"Rose, if I remember what Greg said, this is the old sheriff's house," Jill explained. "It was around here somewhere that Greg got shot the day he took Shar's sports car. The day—"

"Of the car wreck!" Rose said, finishing Jill's statement.

"Let's get closer," Jill said and they remounted the remotes.

As they crossed the street, Three began to report on the activities it could hear inside the house.

"He's in a back room," Jill repeated as Three confirmed the chief's location. "He's looking for something."

"Probably weapons," Doug said.

"Probably right," Nick agreed. "Should we just break in from the front and the back and catch him?"

Jill nodded. "Rose and Doug can take the front and we can..." Jill suddenly sensed something was wrong with that decision. "Wait! There was something else Greg said about this place, about... the back yard... the fences..." She looked toward the back yard and the trees barely discernable in the coming half-light. "That's it! Greg said the back yard is guarded! Fortified! There are laser weapons protecting the back yard."

"Wow," Doug said.

"Then let's all go through the front," Rose suggested. "He'll know he can't go out through the back and we'll have him, maybe before he can find a gun or whatever."

"Sounds good to me," Nick agreed. "Jill?"

"Yeah, I guess," Jill said. "Kaasprs ready? Let's do it."

⋏

Chief Parks had emptied all of the boxes he found in the single bedroom closet and found nothing for all of his fumbling around. With his right hand stuffed deep in his pants pocket, knowing the burnt arm was broken, he tried to tighten the cloth he had wrapped around his singed hand and another around his upper arm to stop the bleeding. It was of little help and he returned his attention to the puzzle. He tried to think of anywhere else the sheriff might have hidden his small arsenal. He knew the sheriff had collected rifles and pistols of many calibers, collected from cleaning out the homes of his many 'collections' for the Family. But where the sheriff had stashed them eluded him.

The dizziness was stronger as he turned from the living room and into the dining room, but there were no cabinets or buffets or safes or anything that would hold long guns and none of the drawers revealed any hand guns.

He was beginning to think someone had searched the house after the sheriff went missing when the front door burst open!

He turned in a start and saw the four figures in dark blue-black body suits suddenly pour in, his eyes focused on the two wearing red headbands and Don Nikle's conveyed fears of those that wore the headbands suddenly exploded in his mind.

Without thinking, he panicked, bolted. He jerked the back door open and dove into the dark, stumbling over something unseen and then a second something as he tried to run for the back fence, driven by the anticipation of safety beyond.

The high-pitched whine of a motor drive somewhere in the tree tops was the last thing he heard and the sudden burst of light all around him was the last thing he saw.

⋏

Jill and the group drifted to a stop behind the marshal's office and dismounted. Rose and Doug took stances to watch the areas around them as Jill unveiled and knocked on the back door. The lights were on and she knew Deputy Lupis had already started his shift when they arrived, but she figured he might not have the office open for business. After a moment, Dan opened the door.

"Deputy Lupis?" Jill asked, still wearing her Blues and her headband, "may we speak with you?"

"Miss Thomas?" Dan said in surprise. "Yes, come in. I almost didn't recognize you wearing that—"

"I know," Jill said quickly, "but this is urgent. You need to know that Thom was shot last night."

Jill and Nick quickly retold the events of the night and explained that the Medic expected Thom to be back home later this coming night. She explained they had followed Chief Parks and what happened at the old sheriff's house.

Dan's shoulders drooped as he listened, suddenly looking very vulnerable and depressed.

"Are you sure Thom's going to be all right?" he finally asked. "And Eddie's all right?"

"Yes, Dan," Jill said as convincingly as she could. "The Medic says they will bring him and Eddie back to his place a little after dark tonight."

"We know this leaves you terribly shorthanded," Nick said, "so we figured we can help out tonight."

"Help out?" Dan asked, puzzled. "You've already been helping with everything."

"Well, with Wally and Ted away," Jill continued, "and Thom out of commission, you certainly can't cover the day patrols and the night patrols by yourself. So we, Nick and I, will drive the overnight patrol until Wally gets back."

"You two?"

"Yes," Nick said firmly. "With the remotes and Kiile's Marines, I think we can manage if an issue arises. And we can call you if something happens that we either can't or shouldn't handle."

Dan rubbed his chin. "Yes, I... guess that would work. You said Thom's going to be all right?"

"Yes, he is," Jill said and smiled. "We'll meet you back here, a little before four this afternoon?"

"Yes, that will work," Dan said and nodded. "Before four. If you see him, tell Thom that Mandy and I will be praying for him and wishing him a speedy recovery."

"Sure will," Nick said as they stood up. "Maybe you can see him tomorrow."

"Rose says all's clear," Jill said to Nick, then turned to Dan. "See you this afternoon."

Dan locked the door after them, but when he looked out of the window, he only saw the half-lit, empty parking lot.

One Hundred-Seven

"Just like Jill said it was," Kiile said, standing beside Wally in the dark doorway of the large farmstead building. "My remote reports the freighter is passing over Grants and heading this way. LTVC21 is following."

"Jill told you?" Wally asked in surprise and wincing from the twinge in his shoulder as he jerked his head to look at Kiile. Even with his right arm in an improvised sling, tied tightly across his chest, the movement was uncomfortable and he tried to hide the stab of pain.

"You really should've gone to Medical," Kiile said, glancing at him in the darkness. "You're not going to be any help in a fight."

"I can still use my left hand," Wally insisted.

"You're worse than a crusty ol' Gunny," Kiile muttered, then said, "Yes, Jill sensed the freighter coming and told Twelve it was coming."

"After seeing her at the ranch, after the attack, I suspected she was 'communicating,'" Wally admitted. "And when the two Marines helping her called her a Shadow, I knew it had to be true. But now, she's sensing things?"

"A new found capability," Kiile said with a guarded tone in his voice.

"Her secret is safe with us."

"Carole knows?"

"After we were 'asked to stay' at Obscure the week after Thanksgiving," Wally said with a smile to himself, "I felt it was necessary to keep her informed about everything. She helps me sort out puzzles and solutions, so the more she knows the better we work together."

"Good. She can be trusted," Kiile said confidently, then nudged Wally's left shoulder. "They're landing."

Kiile flipped his night vision head gear into place and scanned the clearing immediately to the south of the large building, then tapped his earpiece, "All Johnnies, stay veiled and then close to twenty terran yards when it settles. Thirty-two, be ready to greet them when they open the loading hatch."

"Sure hope Thirty-two can pull this off," Wally said softly.

Kiile tapped his earpiece again as he flipped the night vision head gear up, "Twenty-eight, get into the nose strut well and be ready with a Series Seven,"

Wally remembered Kiile explaining that was how they disabled the other freighters, by blowing up the electronics and control bay just forward of the nose landing strut. He remembered Kiile saying Shara had passed that trick to him through Seventeen.

"It's on the ground," Kiile said, interrupting Wally's thoughts. "They'll have to unveil to greet ground support."

A scant moment later, the dark shadow of the freighter's hulk solidified in the slowly brightening darkness. The large loading hatch latches banged and the lift mechanisms squealed softly as the hatch began to swing open and up. A ramp slowly unfolded, extending until its tip settled onto the ground beside the twenty foot, dimly illuminated opening.

Wally followed Kiile as they moved forward, closer to the ship, invisible inside their veils, and watched Thirty-two as he walked up the ramp to meet the loadmaster standing in the opening. Unseen, he knew two Marines had gone up each side of the wide ramp and into the hold.

Suddenly, the loadmaster drew his hand weapon and turned to something inside.

⚔

Thirty-two stepped up onto the ramp, holding a large notepad before him, hiding the Kaaspr he held ready in his other hand. He walked slowly maintaining an air of discipline, hoping it was the way Security would normally receive a freighter. He had donned a Security Officer's uniform and planned to enter the ship unveiled. If all went well, four Marines would sneak in behind him and secure the cockpit before they suspected they had been infiltrated. If all went well, that is.

As he neared the top, he saw the five other cargo handlers rearranging containers to make room for the expected envirocubes.

The loadmaster asked for the bill of lading in Galactic Standard and Thirty-two was about to hand him the notepad when he heard a hatch to his left open inside the cargo bay. Someone beyond it shouted and he saw the unmistakable reflection of a laser flash.

The loadmaster shouted an order to the handlers, grabbed the hand weapon from his pouch and turned toward the opened hatch.

"Drop it or die!" Thirty-two shouted, tossing the notepad aside and dropping down on one knee with the Kaaspr aimed directly at the loadmaster's guts.

Out of the emptiness of the cargo hold, three laser tracks exploded on the cargo deck and stopped the handlers as they ran for the cockpit. Two Marines dropped their veils and materialized in front of the handlers.

The loadmaster froze, undecided as he saw the two Marines and realized he was the inescapable target of a third. Slowly, hearing the sound of heavy boots running up the ramp and seeing the Marines coalesce in the cargo bay around him, he lowered his weapon and let it drop to the deck.

"Cockpit is secure," Thirty-two heard in his ear.

Then he stood up and looked at the loadmaster. In Galactic Standard, asked, "Where are the other four?" When the loadmaster did not answer, he gave a hand signal and sent men searching.

Quickly, the cargo bay filled with Marines as they unveiled and began shackling the six crewmen. Two Marines entered from the cockpit with one of the piloting crew.

"One resisted," one of the two Marines said with a shrug as he reported to Thirty-two.

The unmistakable whisper and hiss of laser fire drifted from somewhere aft of the cargo bay and Thirty-two cupped a hand over his ear.

"The other four have been found," the voice said. "One objected."

▲

"I have one other thing I have to do before I let you send me to Medical," Wally said to Kiile as they walked back into the large building. "Can you take me to see the captives we have released?"

"I can do that," Kiile said and smiled.

The Marines had collected all of the captors, staff, aides, security and now the freighter crew and secured them for suitable processing, so he felt the weight of the mission was reduced enough to allow him to assist Wally in his pursuit.

"I believe all forty-eight have been moved to the main ranch house," Kiile said as he opened the door from the large building. Dawn was fully upon them as Kiile gestured to the ranch house across the wide drive. "I understand they have been given access to the necessary facilities and have had the chance to clean up as best they can and have been given rations and drinks."

When they entered the front door, the room fell into a hush, and in surprise, Wally noted the changes made in the large living room since he had last passed through. The furniture was pushed back against the walls and every space large enough to sit on was occupied.

A Marine greeted them as they closed the door.

"Is everyone okay?" Wally asked in a voice loud enough that the room would hear him.

"I believe so," the Marine said and glanced at Kiile.

Kiile nodded and gently pushed Wally into the narrow path through the amassed people. Wally took the hint and slowly walked through the crowd, asking if they had everything they needed? Many of the men stood up as he and Kiile moved among them, shaking their hands and muttering their thanks.

Wally stopped at the far side of the room and turned to face them.

"I know you don't know me or any of the men that have come with me," Wally said. "I am State Marshal Wally Lima, assigned to a permanent post in Riggin. It is mine and my deputy's job to protect you the best we can. And I will tell you, we will do everything we can to ensure there will be no more forced collections and shipments to jobs elsewhere. If any of you need anything from us, see anything you think I should know about, please call my office and let me know. Very shortly, I will have deputies stationed in Clay, Hawthorne, Grants and possibly one that can come regularly to help you here."

A soft murmur went through the room and Wally continued.

"You are all free to return to your homes or go where ever you wish. I would though, like to ask that you stay here until midmorning to allow us to clean up the area and properly take care of 'our' captives"—someone chuckled—"before you go out and go your ways. You have my sincerest apologies for not being here before this happened, but because it did happen, I can now bring those responsible to justice. If you need anything in the meantime, food, drink, phone, anything, please just ask one of the Marines.

"Now, I have one additional thing to ask," Wally added and looked around the room, "Is there a Sam and Glory Reeds, son and daughter of Thad and Betti, present?"

At first, no one moved or said anything and Wally felt he needed to explain further. "I ask because Thad and Betti came to me when they could not reach their kids, and I told them I would find them and bring them back to be with their folks."

After another moment, someone near the dining room stirred and nudged a young fellow. A slender lad of twelve or thirteen years, Wally judged, slowly uncurled his long legs and stood up.

"I'm... Sam, sir," he said softly and Wally smiled warmly.

Slowly the young girl beside him stood up. Wally estimated her to be around nine.

"I'm Glory, sir," she said and took Sam's hand.

Wally motioned them forward and people moved to let them by.

"I have a phone number here," Wally said and held out a business card with a number written on the back, "for you to call your folks. It's you mother's sister's number and they would really like for you to call them. Then you can let me know if you want to go and be with them or if you want to stay here."

Wally gestured with his left hand to the phone console on the nearby desk and then turned back to Kiile.

"You have more deputies coming?" Kiile asked.

"Yup," Wally smiled. "I will have two in Grants on Monday, two in Hawthorne and two in Clay by Wednesday. They will report via remote and will be assigned to my office, permanently. And I'll have another assigned in Riggin by Friday. Now all we have to do is pick up the current deputies and Chief Parks and ask them to join their partners in crime."

"CHIEF PARKS AND ONE OF HIS DEPUTIES ARE NEUTRALIZED," WL-One said in Wally's ear.

"What?" Wally looked at Kiile and repeated WL-One's report. He was going to ask for more details, but Sam stopped beside him and tugged on his sleeve.

"My father asks that you bring us to Riggin, sir," Sam said with a wide smile and Glory smiled brightly as she hung on his arm.

"It will be my pleasure, Sam," Wally said.

Softly, the room began to clap and Sam and Glory smiled even more.

Wednesday, January 25

Thom saw the muzzle flash as the deputy fired from behind Chief Parks and fear for Eddie gripped his mind as he spread his jacket with his left hand in reflex, his pistol flashing in his other hand. He saw the deputy's third shot go high as he felt something hit his chest and slam him backwards. When he hit the ground, he knew he was hurting Eddie, falling on top of her, and he rolled over to see her, but the pain in his chest blurred his vision and kept his arms from working properly.

When he saw her contorted face, the expression of pain, he shouted, "Are you all right?"

She said something, but he could not hear her so he asked again. He tried to push himself up but his arms did not work and suddenly someone grabbed him and rolled him over. His mind shouted to Eddie, fearing Parks had grabbed him. *Eddie!* his mind shouted. *Eddie! Watch out!* Then with a sudden twitch, his whole body jerked and the hoarse, shouted words slipped out, "Eddie! Watch out! Watch..."

Startled by the sound of his voice and feeling someone gently catch his shoulders and press against him, holding him down with their head tightly beside his, he slowly smelled her scent, felt her hair across his face and heard her soft sobs as she whispered his name.

"Eddie," he whispered, recognizing more of her with each passing moment as his arm found its way around her waist.

"Yes, Thomas. I'm here," she whispered in return, embracing him from where she lay beside him on his bed. "I'm here."

Stiffly, Thom found her with his other arm and slipped it tightly around her.

"Are you all right?" he asked with a cough. "Are you..."

Eddie reached across him and grabbed a glass from the night stand and put the bent straw against his lips. "Take a sip. Your mouth is too dry to be talking." When he drew on the straw, tasting the light, sweet juices, she continued softly, "I'm all right, Thomas. I'm fine. You protected me."

He studied her face for a moment after she took the glass away

142

and seeing the concern, and fatigue in her tightly smiling face, he reached up and pulled her head to him, pressing her cheek against his. "Are you sure you're all right? I was so scared—"

"I told you, I'm fine," she said and firmly squeezed his shoulders. "But you're not! Not yet, anyway."

He looked at the ceiling and then around the room. "I remember the deputy shooting..."

"Yes," Eddie admitted with a sigh. "You killed him, but his first two shots hit you. They knocked us down."

"And Chief Parks?"

"Seconds after we were knocked down, four people in blue-black body suits arrived," Eddie said. "I was completely dumb-founded when I recognized them, Jill Thomas, Rose Mitchell, Nick Jordan and Doug McIntire."

Thom smiled and slowly nodded. "Makes sense."

"Now it does," Eddie admitted and explained the details of that night as best she could remember. "Jill and her group followed Chief Parks to the old sheriff's place out on Kelly just past your old place and when they pressed him, he bolted through the back door. Jill said the back yard was some kind of a trap and the chief was killed before he could escape. She said you'll need to take a look at that place when you're back on your feet."

"How long...?"

"Two days and nights. It is late morning on Wednesday. Kiile's Marines got you onto their transport and into that strange couch they call Medical. Late last night, it and their doctor said you were healed enough to come home and that you'd be able to walk and do most normal things today," she said and smiled at him. "But no heavy lifting, hand-to-hand combat or gun fights for at least a week."

"Medical? Jill? And the...?" he asked out loud and then realized she had been talking about Jill and the others in their suits. "Then you know?"

"Yes," she said and kissed him on the cheek. "Carole and Jill stayed with me on the transport with you and I've been introduced to your 'allies' and their alternate identities. I understand why you couldn't just tell me about them."

"Oh, damn! My shift! How's Dan—"

"It's taken care of," Eddie said and held his shoulders when he tried to sit up. "Jill and Nick Jordan have been driving your patrols and Five has followed in case they needed help."

"Jill," he said with a smile as he relaxed. "She's certainly capable." He refocused on Eddie and asked, "And you? How are you handling knowing?"

She pondered the bed beside them for a long moment. "I have to admit I have had a lot to think about in the last three days." She looked at him and continued, "Realizing and accepting how you obviously feel about me and how I was beginning to feel about you—"

"Was?" Thom interrupted, worried.

Eddie put her finger on his lips. "Listening to Carole and hearing what she went through growing up here, depressed with every local boy only interested in her for her inheritance, and then Wally stepped into her life and she was thrown into the middle of this secret society herself. Suddenly, I find myself face to face with the same secret society and I admit I'm scared of it all. But then, I'm still scared of a lot of things. You have helped me understand and embrace so many of my fears.

"I know I'm rambling, Thomas, but Monday night made me face a lot of fears, some perceived and others from misunderstanding. When Jill Thomas, the uppity 'Miss Socialite' I knew in school showed up with Rose, Nick and Doug, lean, mean, full of compassion and armed for battle, leading a full squad of camouflaged Marines intent on saving you, us, my world was turned upside down, again.

"Listening to them while I sat with you in Medical, and hearing about all that Shar and Jill have gone through, with so many trying to kill them both, and what all Shar has done, learned to do, I was completely in awe. I guess I still am. So many people I thought I knew and understood are really so very much more and not at all what I supposed they were."

Thom caught her hand and held it to his chest.

"Thomas, I don't know how I fit into all of this," she said and held his eyes, "but when you were shot and I saw you covered in blood, I saw my world disappearing again. I knew that I don't want to be without you. I knew I don't want another moment without you and I knew I don't want to be left out of your world. And... I knew then... I've fallen in love with you too."

Thom pulled her to him and gently kissed her.

⋏

Eddie pondered Thom's unwavering understanding along with everything else she had to consider as she stood in front of the stove and heated a chicken broth and dumpling soup for their lunch. She absently took two insulated mugs from the cabinet and filled them with coffee.

Realizing how many things she did not understand and how many people she had misjudged and how many were suddenly there when she needed them she wondered if she even knew herself. As she opened the kitchen door to the flanking porch and carried the two mugs out and sat them on the rail, she realized Thom had been repeatedly giving her the opportunity to find out, to get to know herself again. No pressure, no expected direction, just the opportunity.

She stood there for a moment and looked across the snow covered parking lot in front of the previous craft shop; she straightened her shoulders and stood erect, accepting the fact that she was going to learn. The Medic's comment, thinking she was a deputy, nibbled at her senses.

Then she said to the emptiness, "I'm sorry you have to stand out here in the cold. I'd like to think you have much better things to do, but since you're here, I've brought you some coffee to help you endure the time."

She turned and when she opened the storm door to go back inside, she stopped and looked back. Both mugs were gone and she smiled.

"We're not sorry, Miss Eddie," a voice said from the nearby emptiness. "Thank you for the coffee, but please do not feel badly for us. We are part of Twelve's squad, given the greatest privilege, assigned to protect the colonel and the lieutenant and those under his command. They are the most important people on this planet at this time. We are honored to be of this squad and to protect the ones the colonel has identified as important."

"Why us?" she asked before she thought. "I mean, I can understand protecting Thom, the marshal and the deputies, but why am I included? My mind could have been altered just like the women that were attacked. I could have been made to forget what I saw, to forget what is secret."

"Yes, it is obvious that Deputy Baines is important," the veiled Marine said, "because of his profession, his status as a Person-of–

Importance, and because he places the needs of others ahead of his own. Monday night, he proved again that others are more important to him when he protected you, never giving it a thought that he could lose his life in doing so. Your life is more important to him. You were first important because of his feelings for you."

Tears filled Eddie's eyes as she listened, unable to say anything.

"In your work you also show people how important they are by the creations you give them, but you have never been tested like you were Monday night. If Deputy Baines' life meant nothing to you, you would have stayed in the patrol car like you were told to do. If his life meant nothing to you, you would not have taken the pistol with you and you would not have shot Chief Parks, keeping him from killing Deputy Baines when he fell and could not defend himself. You were afraid, Miss Eddie, but you never thought about losing your own life. You thought about Deputy Baines first."

She stared at the emptiness where the voice came from and finally said, "Thank you."

The voice continued, "You were enlightened because you must know we are here to protect you also. You cannot live happily, at peace with Deputy Baines unless you know and understand the secrets. You and your compassion are needed to help others know better and safer times are coming, to show others they are also important in their own ways. Maybe you don't know it yet yourself and maybe you do, but you have already chosen where you want to be and what you want to do."

Eddie chuckled and wiped the moisture from her eyes. "You're quite eloquent."

"The message is from the heart," he said, "our hearts Miss Eddie, and it is meant to raise you out of your doubt and worry. The deputy needs you as much as you need him."

C.3482.409

Cheral spun Apache Two around to face the two fighters searching for her. They had seen her destroy her last target and were closing on the area in space where they assumed she would be in after the strike. But she had jinked down and to one side and *saw* them when they changed course and was away and waiting when they swept the empty space with cannon fire.

146

She knew either Franni or Casi had illuminated the escort fleet with the maintenance codes and had dropped the fleet's veils as the engagement began, but a few had not responded to the codes, hiding with different cloaking transmitters, ones that the Q-Ships did not have the codes for. These two were two of those, feeling confident because they were still veiled and, they assumed, unseen.

But their confidence was shattered as her forward firing cannons speared one as she charged between them and her aft turret pierced the void for the second. Two fiery clouds of smoke and debris stretched out behind her and dissipated. Cheral forgot them quickly and focused on the next unlit *sensation.*

Off to her left, she saw two blossoms as Ani destroyed two more and she absently smiled as she fired, another unseen target disappeared in fire and smoke.

She knew the target opportunities were diminishing, but when she turned and searched for another, she was surprised they were all gone. She checked her blank scanner screen and then *felt* the emptiness, and finally accepted the fact that they were indeed gone.

"Apache Three," Cheral said into her helmet mic, "good shooting."

She was not surprised, but it was unplanned that she and Ani had formed a friendship and had simply found themselves pairing in each engagement. Ani had a natural hunter's instinct and talent that matched her own unexpected tenacity for the fight. They both had the ability to concentrate on their own targets and yet be alert to the field around them. They watched each other's backs and even though they generally fought alone, they both regarded themselves the other's wingman.

"Thanks, Apache Two," Ani replied. "Looked like you did pretty well yourself."

"Thanks," Cheral said as she switched the IFF filter off and the squadron's numerous blips suddenly appeared on her otherwise empty scanner screen, "Looks like we've run out of targets."

"Apache Wing, join up on Apache Leader," Casi's voice said, suddenly filling their helmets.

"Let's see what they've found," Cheral said to Ani and swung Apache Two toward STSX's pulsing position on the scanner.

⋏

As Cheral settled into position to one side of STSX, she was surprised that STSX had remained veiled. STSX and KKLC14 had chosen to be the freighter escort for this engagement, essentially removing themselves from the battles, leaving the command and engagement oversight to TTYF8. Then she realized STSX had kept the entire squadron veiled with one exception, only MKCC5 had unveiled to display the squadron colors to the freighter and to the patrol cruiser *Climatus.*

She listened to the normal mission end conversation between STSX and Climatus, pleased when Casi finally led the squadron to stand off a few clicks and collected the patrol fighters.

▲

When Cheral unsealed her helmet and hung it in the equipment bay, she heard Casi finishing a conversation with someone else. When she glanced at Stran as he stepped out of his EV Suit, she recognized Leeana's voice signing off.

"Good shooting, Cuz," Casi said as Cheral reached the top of the ladder and saw her, aft facing and still watching the echelon on either side.

"Thanks. What's up next?" Cheral asked as she settled on the left side jump seat.

A moment later, Stran entered the central compartment and handed each of them a container of ration tea. He settled on the right side jump seat and strapped himself in.

"Anything new from KKLC?" he asked and opened his container.

"Leeana just passed the squadron status," Casi said and pulled a sip of her tea through the straw. "No losses, no damage. Oddly enough, it was another clean engagement."

"Yeah," Cheral admitted. "It was almost routine. Too easy." She looked at Stran. "It worries me a little. It can't continue this one-sided for long."

"It probably won't," Casi agreed. "The Ring's intelligence informed me that the news of this interception and B-Group's interception has already made it back to the prince. I guess we've really upset him this time." Casi smiled at Stran and then at Cheral.

"Upset him enough?" Stran asked.

"Maybe," Casi nodded. "Intelligence reports something new is happening in the prince's naval yard. New launch preparations have already started." She looked at Cheral. "Keep your fingers crossed."

"How did B-Group do?" Stran asked, intentionally changing the subject.

"The same," Casi replied, "Patrol cruiser *Dorsalt* released one hundred and eleven captives and we released one hundred and six. B-Group will be joining with us at the next rendezvous point in about seven terran hours." Then Casi shifted her focus. "STSX, load the rendezvous coordinates and see if the squadron is ready to move."

"COMPLYING."

"Right now, Intelligence is telling us," Casi continued without skipping a beat, "the next freighter should reach the intercept area in about twenty-two pars, twenty-one hours and seven minutes in terran time."

"APACHE WING IS READY TO MOVE."

"Thanks STSX," Casi said and swiveled to forward facing. "Apache Wing Leader, Apache Leader and Apache Patrol Two are ready."

"Apache Wing is ready," Leeana's voice answered. "All patrol fighters are secure and crews transferred. On your Mark."

"Rendezvous coordinates Gamma-Gamma-Sierra, Apache Squadron, Mark!" Casi said and pushed the thrust levers forward. All ships, max thrust, match velocity with STSX1."

"Roger that," Leeana answered and Casi was sure she heard her chuckle.

⋏ ⋏ ⋏ ⋏ ⋏

Sitting up, with pillows stacked against the headboard behind him, Thom could only stare at Eddie as she came out of his master bath. She was dressed in a form-fitting green blouse with abstract splashes of yellow and ocher that drew attention to her shapeliness, a light scarf loosely draped around her neck and thrown over her shoulder, and tight black pants that accentuated her narrow hips and long legs that reached down into her low topped, fur-lined boots. She had his complete attention.

"Wow," he whispered. "You are unbelievably gorgeous." He shook his head. "But you can't stay here looking like that."

She smiled and put one hand on her hip, "Oh? And just why not?"

He smiled as he slowly swung his legs out from under the covers and over the side of the bed. "I won't be able to keep my hands off of you long enough for you to get out of the door."

She stopped beside the bed, leaned close and kissed him. "I'm glad you're feeling good enough to notice. That's a good sign."

He sat on the edge of the bed and checked the small gauze patches taped to his chest. He vaguely remembered someone removing a very constricting body wrap and remembered how he suddenly felt like he could breathe again. His memories were hazy until this morning, but when Eddie fed him and got him up out of bed for the first time, he realized he felt achy and almost normal otherwise.

"What's the occasion?" he asked as he slowly pushed himself up. Eddie quickly caught his arm and steadied him.

"This," she smiled and said as she stepped back and slowly turned around in front of him, "is for you. I don't want anyone to think you have poor taste." She kissed him again. "And the occasion is that Wally and Ted will be getting back in a little bit."

"They are? I didn't hear." He looked at her and she smiled.

"I borrowed your earpiece" she said and tapped the side of her head. "I let Carole know and she came over to help fix dinner. I hope you don't mind that I, sort of, moved in while you needed someone to watch over you."

"Of course not, Eddie," he said as he caught her hand. "How could I mind?"

"Thanks, Thomas. I put a few of my things in the next bedroom."

He nodded and glanced at the rumpled blanket spread out on the far side of the bed before he turned toward the master bath. "Good. I guess I'd better make myself presentable as well."

"Do you need any help?"

"Want, is a better word," he said and pulled her gently to him. "One part of me wants to just sit and admire how you look, and the other part wants to hold you and ruffle you up something fierce."

"The ruffling will come later," she said happily and pushed him toward the master bath's double door, "now that you're feeling better and are able. I'll be down with Carole. Call me when you're ready to come down."

⚔

"They're here," Eddie said and turned to the kitchen door.

She flipped the parking lot lights on and waited, wondering when she did not see anyone right away. Thom stopped beside her as Carole donned her coat and stepped out onto the porch.

"WL-One and Five say they're just beyond the parking lot," Eddie said softly, "but I don't see them yet."

"Who cleared the lot?" Thom asked when he looked past her and realized the snow was pushed aside and piled along the far side of the lot.

"Oh, Dan got someone to plow it for me this morning," she said and slipped her arm around his waist, "The father of one of Blaire's friends from school. Oh, there they are."

Carole was off the porch and hurrying across the lot as soon as Wally's unmistakable figure appeared at the far side of the lot.

"Looks like his arm is better. Who're the kids with him?" Eddie asked absently as Carole caught Wally in an enthusiastic embrace.

They watched as Wally guided her, the two kids and a Marine across the lot and finally up onto the porch. Thom opened the door and gestured them inside.

"Carole, Eddie," Wally said as he slipped his coat off. "This is Squad Leader Kiile. He leads the Marine squads assisting us."

Kiile greeted them each with a handshake and Eddie asked, "Who might these two be?"

"Sam and Glory Reeds," Wally replied. "Thad and Betti's kids."

"Very nice to meet you," Eddie said and extended her hand. "Sam, Glory, welcome."

"Do your folks know you're here?" Carole asked when she greeted them.

"Yes," Wally said, "I let them know when we landed. They'll be here in a few minutes."

"Wally?" Thom asked. "I thought Ted was with you."

"He was," Wally admitted, "But when we picked up Chief Park's deputy from Hawthorne and Chief Russell's deputy from Clay, he thought he should stay there for the next couple of days to start the transition."

Thom nodded.

"He'll be back late Friday," Wally continued, "and I'll have permanent replacements for Clay, Hawthorne and Grants on site next week."

Eddie led Sam and Glory to the peninsula counter and offered them a soda while they waited. Sam helped Glory out of her coat and hung it on a chair back before they sat down.

"This is a very nice house," Sam said, his eyes wide as he looked around the dining room and into the part of the living room he could see.

"Thank you, Sam," Eddie said and poured their drinks in a glass for each of them. "It belongs to Deputy Baine. He just started moving in last Sunday."

"Is he good, like the marshal?" Glory asked.

Sam quickly shushed her, telling her she should not ask things like that.

"It's okay, Sam," Eddie said and thought about Glory's question. Then she leaned close to Glory and said, "I think the marshal is a very fine man and he has the best, nicest deputies in the whole state. They only want you and the rest of the people in the valley to be safe and happy."

"Good," Glory said and took a big sip from her glass. "I like the marshal."

Eddie smiled and saw headlights flash in the dining room window. She stood up and said, "I'll bet that's your folks."

Sam and Glory were waiting at the kitchen door when Thom answered the knock.

"Good to see you, Thad," Wally said as Thom led them in. "Betti. I'm sorry I couldn't get back yesterday." He was going to say more, but Sam and Glory had completely caught their attention with long hugs.

After a long and happy embrace, Thad praised Sam numerous times for taking care of his sister, and Glory for being strong and listening to Sam while they were separated. He asked the kids if they had been minding their manners and Eddie asked if they had eaten yet. Thad admitted they had not and Eddie insisted they stay for dinner. When he started to refuse, Betti interrupted him and said it would be their pleasure to have dinner with people that rescued their children.

"Deputy Lupis and his wife and daughter are coming shortly," Eddie said and looked at Glory, "Blaire is a little younger than you are, but she's very smart and very grown up for her age. You might like her."

Listening to Eddie, Thom turned to Kiile and asked if he was in a hurry. "I know that babysitting the marshal, tending his wounds and listening to his complaining is enough to drain a man's strength. You'll stay for dinner, won't you?"

When he nodded thanks, Eddie caught Carole's hand and started for the dining room. "Sure am glad you talked me into fixing both roasts tonight. Help me get the leaf in the table and the extra chairs arranged."

Dan, Mandy and Blaire arrived as planned and Thom offered wine or other libations to the adults before dinner. Mandy immediately joined Eddie and Carole in the kitchen to help where they needed it and Betti, a little shy for the company she found herself keeping, offered her assistance if they would want it. Eddie immediately included her in the group of females.

Thad found himself enjoying the company of Wally and the deputies, the normal discussions of sports, hunting and especially with Dan on the subject of dealing with the issues of raising kids. Kiile, dressed in his civvies, blended in, listening to the gentle banter of the evening.

When dinner was over, the dishes rinsed and in the dishwasher, Eddie made sure the women were included with the men in the family room for an after dinner wine or drink and continued conversation. Thom pulled a selection of board games from the closet under the stairs and the kids played on the floor between the living room and the family room, close enough to hear everything the adults talked about and to feel included with those who cared about them.

At some point in the evening, Carole leaned over to Eddie and said, "You know, this feels like family."

⅄

Finally, Thad and Betti decided they needed to get Sam and Glory back to Betti's sister's place and call it a night. Thom and Eddie assured them they were welcome to come back anytime and Sam made a special effort to say good night to Blaire. Kiile thanked Eddie for the dinner and Thom for the invitation and then disappeared across the parking lot.

Carole and Wally helped put the dining room back in order and then Wally turned to Thom as they put their coats on, "Are you able to work tomorrow?"

"No!" Eddie said sharply before Thom could answer. "The Medic said Thom cannot drive until Monday and is not supposed to lift anything before the weekend."

Wally smiled and looked at her. "Can he walk and sit behind a desk?"

"Yes, I suppose he can do that," she said and slowly smiled at Wally's implication of her authority over Thom.

"Good. The Medic won't let me drive either," Wally said, "until Saturday. I told him that there will not be any restrictions on or after Saturday." He smiled and winked at Carole. "You said Dan's doing the four-am to four-pm patrols and you have the four-pm to four-am patrols covered, so I just need to be sure the office is covered, eight to five and was thinking us two invalids could do that."

⚊⚊⚊ ⬥ ⚊⚊⚊

When Wally and Carole left, Eddie locked the kitchen door and the door to the garage and Thom went around the house, closing the drapes where he had them and checked the locks on the front and the family room doors. He found Eddie in the family room standing in front of the fireplace, staring at the embers and the dwindling licks of flame.

"Thank you, Eddie," he said as he stopped behind her and slipped his arms around her waist. "You were wonderful tonight."

"It was nice, wasn't it?" she said as she covered his arms with hers and held them tight. "I really felt like I belonged."

"I am so very glad," he whispered in her ear. "You do belong here. I'll say it again, I love you and I want you to be my partner in all of this, all of whatever happens. I want to be your partner in whatever you do, whatever happens."

She slowly turned in his embrace and looked at him. "But what if I change? Or you change?"

"Eddie, we will change. Together. That's the beauty of it," he said and smiled at her. "Together, we cannot be what we were apart." He pulled her close and held her tight.

Slowly Eddie relaxed and looked up at him.

"Well Thomas, since you have taken my heart, I will say that I can only let you keep it, and the rest of me," she gestured to herself, "for forever and a year. With my sincerest wish that each day is the best we can make for each other."

∧ ∧ ∧ ∧ ∧

"What time is it?" Cheral asked as she took her Blues out of the cleaning unit.

"2242 hrs Galactic Normal Time," Casi said from where she sat in the aft facing double wide chair. "Seven and a half terran hours to Intercept."

Casi looked up and smiled as Cheral drifted past wearing her yellow robe. She settled into the opposite double wide chair. "Feel better?" Casi asked.

"Much better," Cheral said as she fluffed her damp hair. "A shower always helps, even a ship-side one. No offence intended, STSX."

"Did I ever say thanks for you loaning me your robe while I was recovering?" Casi asked, remembering when she woke up from her ordeal of being poisoned, wearing the bright robe and finding her clothes freshly laundered and folded for her. "And your Blues."

"Yeah, I think you did," Cheral said. "You're welcome anyway. I was just glad the Blues came close to fitting."

"Me too."

"What're you reading?" Cheral asked, noticing the technical looking display on Casi's notepad.

"Looking for chinks in their armor," Casi said. "The Kyddellan battlecruiser we engaged was more difficult to penetrate than the converted freighters were. And I'm sensing more than one Kyddellan cruiser in the escorts coming, so I asked STSX to give me anything he has on them."

"Any luck?"

"Not yet," Casi admitted, "but I'm wondering if it might be as simple as their shields being stronger than what we were expecting."

"It didn't look like you had any trouble penetrating," Cheral said, puzzled.

"I did, though. We had to fire multiple, close interval shots to get through and into the ship's structure. And the hits seemed 'soft,' like they had lost a lot of their punch. The multiple shots also make it easier for them to locate us and return fire." Then she asked, *STSX?*

Am I on the right track? Is there a way to increase our penetration?'

'YES. YES. TWO THINGS. PROGRAM ONE DISCHARGE RATE AND ENERGY TO ATTACK SHIELDS ONLY AND ANOTHER DISCHARGE RATE AND ENERGY TO ATTACK THE CRUISER'S STRUCTURE. THE FIRST OPTIMIZED TO OPEN A PATH THROUGH THE SHIELDS AND HOLD IT OPEN. THE SECOND OPTIMIZED TO DISCHARGE THROUGH THE SHIELD OPENING FOR MAXIMUM STRUCTURAL PENETRATION.'

Casi saw Cheral waiting and she repeated what STSX had told her.

'*Can you do that? Do we have the power to do that?'* she asked before Cheral started asking questions.

'YES. YES. PRIMARY CORE POWER MODULE CAN PROVIDE PRIMARY SHIELD ENERGY AND CANNON PROGRAMMING CAN USE SECONDARY CORE MODULE POWER. REPROGRAMMED CANNON DISCHARGES WILL REQUIRE SIXTY PERCENT DURING THE DISCHARGE, REDUCING ENERGY AVAILABLE FOR THE SECOND SHIELDS.'

"And if we use the primary core for primary shields, we haven't decreased our defenses," Casi said out loud.

"THAT IS CORRECT."

"Okay," Casi said, caught up in the whirlwind of thoughts. "If we set up a selectable file to program one cannon in each turret to attack the shields and two cannons to penetrate the structure, firing those three in whatever close sequence you feel is optimum, and keeping the remaining cannon unchanged and independent for lighter targets, like fighters, how will our energy resources stand?"

"ENERGY RESOURCES CAN BE MANAGED. PRIMARY CORE POWER MODULE CAN SUPPLEMENT OR PROVIDE BACKUP ENERGY."

"And if we attack with two or more ships," Casi continued, unaware that Stran, hearing her excited discussion with STSX, had drifted up behind her, "we could attack the shield generation either first or simultaneously with weapons control or ship's control."

"TWO SHIPS, AS YOU HAVE IN THE PAST, WILL BE ADEQUATE."

"I'm impressed," Stran said

Casi jumped at his unexpected and sudden voice in her ear

and was instantly thankful for the seat straps. Stran and Cheral both laughed with her.

"Sounds like you've worked out a solution to the cruiser problem," Stran said. "I forgot to mention that STSX told me both core power modules have shields and we can run both of them simultaneously. He also said we can increase the strength of each shield. We seem to have the reserves."

"How many of the ships have a second core power module?" Cheral asked.

"There are four of us," Stran said, "STSX, KKLC14, KVWC33 and TTYF8. STSX, please tell the majors about the shields. They'll need them today."

Suddenly Casi's expression turned to worry.

"What is it?" Cheral asked and Stran turned to look at her.

"Four won't be enough," she said softly and looked back at Stran. "So far, there are five battlecruisers and another, larger ship that I don't recognize."

Stran looked at Cheral and then held Casi's eyes. "It's the prince's Battleship, *Constellation Destroyer*."

C.3482.410

"Begin transferring the patrol fighter crews," Casi said to the ship-to-ship communications link as she assumed her normal position in the aft facing pilot's chair and watched for the EV activity behind the four other Q-Ships.

She was not happy with the target arrangements they had worked out with Major Kooich and Leeana, but knew it was the best they could do with what they had. She started thinking about the odds and the numbers and—

"STOP."

"You're right, STSX. One thing at a time, do it and then move to the next one. Keep doing it until it's over. I remember."

"Apache Patrol Two. Powering up," Cheral's voice said, interrupting her depressing thoughts.

"Good hunting, Cuz," Casi said.

"Apache Patrol Four, powering up," Wilm said, immediately

followed by Ani in Apache Patrol Three and then by Loni and Gill in Apache Five and Six.

"AFT PORTAL SEALED," STSX said, announcing Stran's return.

A moment passed then Leeana announced, "All majors are secure."

"Apache patrol fighters, 'Release,'" Casi said to the Wing. She felt the slight nudge as the repulsion pads pushed Apache Patrol Two away.

Each patrol fighter reported in and maneuvered into their echelon positions.

"Any change?" Stran asked as he drifted into the cockpit and strapped himself into the right hand jump seat. "I don't feel anything different."

"We have eight Kyddellan battlecruisers and one Kyddellan Battleship," she said as she turned her chair to forward facing. "STSX says there are two hundred fighters in flight, actually one hundred and ninety-eight, escorting the one freighter." She looked at him out of the corner of her eye. "You did say you wanted to draw the prince out of his palace and into the fight, right?"

Stran swallowed and confirmed her sensation. "I did, didn't I?"

Casi chuckled. "I guess sometimes you get what you wish for. He certainly did come."

"And the only way to free the captives," Stran said with a deep inhale and a tight smile, "is to meet him and to annihilate his escorts."

"So, I think," Casi said, "we better go and meet him."

"Casi," a very tense Franni said softly on her private communications link.

"Yes, Franni," Casi answered softly.

"Do you have an origin on the freighter? Something feels odd about it, almost familiar. I don't know what to make of it."

"BETOLLE," STSX said and Casi and Stran looked at each other, "THE LIEUTENANT'S HOME WORLD."

"Yes, Franni," Casi said softly to the communications link. "STSX says it departed your home world. The captives are from Betolle. You knew?"

"No, I mean, I guess so," Franni said, trying to understand. "I knew something was different from the other freighters."

"That's very good, Franni," Casi encouraged. "Now, let's go and stop them. After we whittle their group down to size, you can form up and we'll take out that Battleship."

"Yes, ma'am," Franni said in a much improved voice. "Ready when you are."

Casi smiled and glanced at Stran. *'Ready, love?'*

'Ready, Bren. Go get 'em.'

"Apache Wing Leader," Casi said to the squadron, "Wing status?"

"Apache Wing is ready," Leeana said.

"Apache B-Group," Casi said, "Wing status?"

"QRTT7 and the Apache B-Group are ready," Major Clef said.

"Patrol cruiser Brigstoan, Apache Leader here," Casi called.

"Apache Leader," the Brigstoan commander replied, "Hail refused. Battlecruisers turning to engage."

"Attack commencing," Casi said, then turned her attention to the Wing, "Good hunting. Apache Squadron, confirm cloaking on, sensor blocking on and shields full. Mark!"

Casi shoved the thrust levers full forward and Apache Squadron accelerated, slowly spreading out as they closed the distance to the armada escorting the lone freighter.

⋏

Casi lined up on her assigned battlecruiser and rolled STSX so his right pylon aimed at its top side. She slowed their closure velocity and *felt* for the weapons control center one third of the ship's length forward of the engines.

"Let's try the new program, STSX," she said out loud as the massive hulk of the cruiser grew in front of her.

As they swept over the cruiser's center line, each of the three turrets fired a single, coordinated volley, effortlessly piercing the hull. Somewhere deep inside something exploded, randomly blowing skin panels off and releasing huge jets of fire and oily smoke.

Casi jinked sideways and down, turning STSX for a pass across the cruiser's belly and the flight control center below and behind the cockpit. The three turrets discharged and again pierced the hull cleanly. Another explosion shook the ship, skin panels erupted and a huge cloud of smoke boiled out from the far side of the cruiser. Casi jinked for a better look and saw the upper half of the nose section was torn away, the smoke billowing from the gaping hole where the bridge and surrounding structure had been.

She maneuvered to the side of the ship and fired at the large, rectangular hatch closed over the flight deck and hangar bay. Firing parallel instead of converging shots, the cannon fire raked the hatch, filling the hangar bay with devastating ribbons of white hot energy. Numerous internal explosions erupted, throwing both side hatches out and tore the midship open. Burning and nearly unrecognizable remains of fighters tumbled and spun out into the void around the cruiser.

Casi's last pass found the fuel cells and the resulting explosion separated the engines and sent them spinning aside. The cruiser broke into many large and small chunks and the engine cluster disappeared in one large, final burst of fire and smoke.

STSX swung around and Casi quickly looked for the nearest cruiser when she saw a small explosion well away from any of the ships. Waiting, she *felt* for any escort fighters in that area, but only sensed a Q-Ship.

"Mines, Bren!" Stran shouted as another explosion blossomed and someone in B-Group yelled, "Mines! They've dropped mines to see where we are!"

Instantly Casi thought about the patrol fighters.

"Apache Patrol Two through Six, form up with your carrier ships. Immediately! Form up! Watch for mines!"

Casi *felt* the space where the explosions had occurred. She jerked her eyes open when another mine exploded and she saw the stutter of canon fire converge on the same area. Something small exploded followed by a larger fiery cloud and she *felt* the Q-Ship disappear.

"Shoot the mines!" Casi shouted as she saw another series of small explosions, "Then jink!" She watched with sudden detachment, remote, and separated, as she saw the explosions blossom against the distant cruisers, wide spaced around the spot where she knew the Battleship and the freighter were. Suddenly another, larger fiery burst and the lost sensation dampened her spirits. She gauged the targets and hits by the size of the different explosions and suddenly, a larger flash caught her attention.

"THREE OF B-GROUP," STSX said in a tone that snapped her back to the reality of the situation.

She pushed the thrust levers forward and headed for the next cruiser closer to the prince's battleship.

"Apache Two, Apache Three, target the mines! Feel for them" Casi shouted. "Franni, use your forward cannons to clear the mines. Don't let them know where you are."

Then she focused on the nearest cruiser. "STSX," Casi said absently, "Do all of the Q-Ships have the new cannon program?"

"YES. TWO HAVE NOT USED IT YET."

"Okay. Remind them," she said and lined up on the cruiser's top side. "Whose target is this one? Let them know we're here to help."

"MVSS6, B-GROUP."

Then she shifted her thoughts, "Apache Two? Are you formed up?"

"Right behind you."

"Watch for the mines and take out any fighters as you see them."

"Got it."

Casi fired on the weapons control center and watched the same smoky plumes result as she jinked down and to one side. She *felt* Cheral jink with her and saw other surface explosions near the cruiser's engine cluster and a number of smaller ones around them as Cheral caught the near side mines. Casi shook her head and cut across the belly, aiming for the flight control center.

"I don't believe it," Cheral's voice said, "Two shots and the cruiser is dead and drifting. The engines have shut down and they have no defenses."

Casi felt another series of small explosions near another battlecruiser, followed by a larger burst of fire and the loss of another sensation. *'Damn! I can't let this continue, Greg. I've got to do something!'*

"STSX," Casi said out loud, ignoring Cheral's remarks. "Tell MVSS6 to cut it up. We're going after the battleship. Give me the spec details. I know where the shield generators and the weapons control centers are located, but I need to know what's around them. How deep they are. You know what I need."

STSX did not answer as TTYF8, with Apache Patrol Four in trail, and MKCC5 formed up with her and Cheral. Casi focused on the looming mass of the battleship.

"STSX, pass the specs to Leeana and Colbee," Casi said, and then addressed the Q-Ships, "It has redundant control centers for weapons and flight controls, and two bridges. I'll go after the shield generators and the aft weapons control center. You two decide on which centers you want. Watch for fighters, they will be their best ones." Then she switched to her private communications channel, "Cheral, if this gets too hot, fall back. I have no idea how this thing will break up, or if it will break up at all. Focus on the mines and clear a path, before you go after a target."

"Will do, Cousin."

Just don't get hit, she said to herself. *We might not be able to get to you to help this time.*

STSX's detailed displays of the battleship popped up on the monitor ahead of Casi and to her right. Stran leaned forward and studied the schematics and the 3-D images with her, looking for obvious shot angles.

"They're buried deep, Bren," he said. "The primary shield generator is just forward of the engines and fuel cell storage, almost in the core of the ship."

He saw her close her eyes and felt her mind probe the ship ahead. She found the generator and followed various passages, looking for a path that would link to the surface or at least offer less structure to penetrate. After a long moment, searching every passageway she could detect, she settled on one and swung STSX into position.

Stran tensed a little as Casi pushed STSX closer and closer to the battleship's surface. He felt another Q-Ship disappear.

'I know, love. I'm going in a lot closer.'

Casi glanced to her left and suddenly wondered if the pylon would hit. Then the cannons fired and the flash was brighter than she'd seen it before. She suddenly felt like they were inside the explosion.

She jinked for more space and farther aft, spinning STSX so she could get a look.

"THEIR SHIELDS FALTERED, PRIMARY GENERATOR HAS FAILED. REDUNDANT GENERATORS ARE ONLINE. SHIELDS ARE FULL."

"Okay," Casi said and maneuvered STSX to the opposite side of the battleship, "Let's go for the first redundant generator."

ᴧ

Prince Kiese watched the battle from his raised throne on the primary bridge of the *Constellation Destroyer*. He was surprised when the attack started without any forewarning, without any alerts, just the hailing of the freighter as the barest of foreknowledge. He swung his chair and dais to face the wide monitor and saw the first of his battlecruisers erupt in a huge fiery cloud of smoke and debris.

"Commander Ilser!" the prince shouted as the battle alert sirens began to wail. "How many attackers are there? Where are they coming from?"

The commander turned and bowed to the prince. "We do not have a count, Sire. No targets on any of the scanner frequencies or channels. They are just attacking out of the void."

He watched the small flashes and his anger grew in keeping with the number of flashes he saw. Then suddenly two more of his battle cruisers erupted without firing a shot.

"Why are they not defending themselves?" he shouted.

"There are no targets to fire at," the commander said. "Cruiser *Haevani* has dispatched fighters to spread mines. They will help us determine where the attackers are."

"Finally something," the prince seethed through gritted teeth.

"With the mines, we have destroyed five of their heavy fighters," the commander added after a few centipars.

Suddenly, he saw two small explosions hit the *Haevani* and it disappeared in another huge fireball of smoke and debris.

He shouted and shook his fist. He stood up and screamed at his commander. Then the whole ship shuddered and he was suddenly floating, unable to grab anything with his wildly gesticulating arms. Just as suddenly as it stopped, the artificial gravity reactivated and the prince found himself on the floor in front of his dais.

Servants hurried to help him when the ship shuddered again, twice.

"Launch fighters!" the commander shouted. "Shield generators and weapons control centers are under attack."

The prince pushed his aides away and stared at the monitor. A fifth cruiser disappeared and the space around them filled with smaller, rapidly flickering flashes. "The mines?" he asked.

"Negative. Our fighters," the weapons control officer said as the battleship shuddered again, stronger.

"Launch all fighters," the commander said and then stopped when the communications corpsman said, "sir, we have damage amidship and in the fuel cell storage areas. Primary flight controls have failed and we are on backup. Shields are still strong and weapons are still active."

"Commander!" the prince shouted. "Fire at random! Fire at anything! Fill the void with cannon fire! All ships, fire at something!"

"Yes, Sire."

The prince switched his monitor to view the departure of the fighters. He needed to see something positive for a moment.

⋏

Casi was glad she stayed close in when the battleship's cannons began firing, confirming Apache Squadron was causing more damage than they could tell. She felt the twinges of fear in the battleship's crewmen, and an odd defiance somewhere inside. She suspected it was the prince as she concentrated on firing repeated piercing blows through the exterior plating.

Then she *felt* the fighters as the hangar bay opened and they began to emerge. She swung STSX toward the hangar bay portal and fired volleys through the open hatch as they passed and suddenly, she knew what they had to do. She pulled STSX away from the ship and lined up in the stream of fighters leaving the maw, the one area clear of cannon fire.

'Greg, love. Do you see what I see? They're open on both sides.' she said as she aimed STSX's nose and pushed the thrust levers full forward. "Cheral, break off and go aft. Leeana and Colbee, break off. Get as much clearance as you can possibly get." *'I love you, Cousin. I love you, Greg.'*

'I love you, Bren. Do this,' Stran whispered in reply.

Then Casi shouted, "STSX, Double Shields full front! Drop Visual cloaking, now!" and she began firing at the oncoming fighters and those in the open hangar bay.

⋏

Prince Kiese stared in disbelief as the Peace Force's heavy fighter coalesced on his monitor. He started to say something to his commander but hesitated when he saw the double red stripes angled across the body of the sleek ST-Class fighter. The millipars seemed to turn into centipars, seconds into minutes, as he watched the determined fighter race toward his battleship, firing into the stream of launching fighters. Then it disappeared from view and the whole of the battleship seemed to inhale suddenly and shake fiercely, the floor and walls of the Bridge burst upwards in a horrific, fiery exhale and then everything went dark. The lingering image of the double red stripes was the last thing the prince saw.

▲

Franni watched the battleship in her side monitor as she and MKCC5 followed Apache Patrol Two past the engines and into the emptiness behind the battleship. Slowly Franni turned them to see what Casi had planned and was completely unprepared when she saw STSX materialize on a headlong charge into the river of fighters.

She saw the rapid sequence of flashes as fighter after fighter exploded. She heard herself yelling for Casi to pull up, to break off, to do anything to avoid a collision with the battleship. Then suddenly, STSX disappeared and a dreadful anticipation swept over them, overpowering them, holding them suspended.

Franni blinked and the battleship erupted, bursting into thousands and thousands of burning pieces of debris.

One Hundred-Eight
Friday, January 27

Greg sat on the edge of their bed, quietly watching his beautiful mate as she slept. He hated to think about waking her, knowing how exhausted she felt. She had slept the full ten hours of their return flight plus another six once they got back to the ranch and into bed. He knew how exhausted she felt.

He smiled, remembering her daring attack on the prince's battleship and how uncertain they both felt when the 'opportunity' presented itself. They had seen it together and instantly knew it was their one chance. But it wasn't until afterwards, when the Squadron began hailing them, that they stared at the void and realized how small the odds had really been, how extremely lucky they had really been.

It was when they collected the Apache patrol fighters that the reality of the attack revealed itself, when they cheered their unfathomable victory, when they knew they had destroyed every cruiser and fighter the prince had amassed and deployed, when they praised the patrol cruiser *Brigstoan* for the release of over three hundred Betollean captives. It was then that they realized their spotless luck had finally met its odds and the squadron suffered its first losses, five Q-ships from Apache B-Group.

With a sigh, Greg nodded to himself, pleased that the cadets had learned well, fought well, and had escaped to come home and prepare for the next battles in a suddenly changed war.

Smiling hugely, he threw his robe across the foot of the bed and slipped back between the fleece sheets to wake his beautiful BrenCara. He looked forward to her morning hunger, followed by a quiet breakfast and then their necessary meetings at Obscure.

Å

It was still early, relatively speaking, when Greg and Shara led Major Kooich and Leeana with Jill, Nick, Doug and Rose close behind, into Obscure's launch bay. They had put on clean Blues for the briefing, but at the briefing room door, Greg stopped and waited as the group filed in and Hench began arranging the chairs and podium at the head table. Greg asked Shara to tell Franni that he wanted to speak to Crem before the briefing and then he excused himself and started down the corridor.

Major Mooren met him in the Mess as he got them both a cup of coffee and then sat down at a table. The major took a seat when Greg gestured for him to sit.

"Please be at ease, Major," Greg started softly, "But may I be personal for a minute?" The major was surprised but nodded and he continued, "Thank you. Casi and I have noticed that you and Franni have become an exceptional team. Franni has settled into her work and is happier now than we've seen her since the two of you arrived. And I must say that her talents have certainly blossomed."

"Thank you, sir," Major Mooren said, questions still colored his expression. "She will be very pleased to know we've earned your compliment."

"It also appears to us," Greg said, "that yours and Franni's relationship has also improved. Would that be a fair thing to say?" Greg smiled and watched him.

"I believe I would say it has," he replied, still curious.

Greg sipped his coffee and looked at the major as he picked up his cup. "Okay. The point is, Casi is of the opinion that Franni has become attached to you and has definite feelings for you."

"Sir?"

"Come, come, Major. I think you have also grown in your attachment to Franni. I see it in how you two work together, eat together, spend time together, laugh together, how you support her training, praise her accomplishments and how she supports you, and even fusses over how you look."

"Sir?" the major asked in surprise, "Are we that obvious?"

Greg nodded. "And with Casi, it's very obvious. Crem, may I suggest you just ask her?"

"But, sir? What if—"

"I doubt she will," Greg interrupted. "I might also note that if Franni does not want a long engagement, I am available and I can arrange a time with the director."

▲ ▲ ▲ ▲ ▲

'*Hench says he is ready to start,*' Shara said as Greg left the Mess.

'*We're on our way,*' he replied and hurried up the spoke.

Turning at the door, Greg followed Major Mooren into the Briefing Room. As Major Mooren found his seat beside Franni, Greg noticed Leeana and Shara were already sitting behind the long desk and Major Kooich was standing at the podium. Greg crossed the room and Major Kooich smiled and thanked him for taking the time to join them. Someone in the room chuckled.

"I will thank you for your patience in advance," Major Kooich said. "We have a lot of information to cover this morning and I will try to not keep you too long." He glanced around the room. "Therefore, I will begin.

"In this last mission, we had four sorties, and all of the mission goals were successfully met, though we did sustain losses this time." Major Kooich shook his head and stiffened his posture, as if trying to shake off the bad thoughts everyone knew he was feeling. "It is my understanding that we caused the release of over thirteen hundred captives with those four sorties and well over twenty-five hundred in all since the campaign began. A mission very, very well done!"

The pilots and crews clapped until the major called for their continued attention.

"Unfortunately, we all know that success was not without cost," the major continued. "Apache Squadron's B-Group lost six ships in the last two sorties, one due to a shields failure and five during the last sortie due to the mines dispersed by Prince Kiese's fighters."

Major Kooich paused a moment before he continued.

"But we honor those fallen by succeeding where we can. We believe, and Intelligence is confirming our belief, that we were successful in terminating the Knobaal Warlord, Prince Kiese, on our last sortie." The room burst in cheers and clapping and the major quickly held his hand up. "We are confident in the fact," the major glanced at Shara and grinned, "but it still has to be confirmed."

Shara glanced at Greg with the barest of a smile.

'*You were absolutely fabulous, love. We know without confirmation,*' Greg said and turned back to the meeting.

"As a point of interest, as of this date, Apache Squadron has tallied seven hundred and eighty-seven kills and B-Group has tallied an additional three hundred and sixty-five kills, for a command total of eleven hundred and fifty-two. Congratulations Commander." Major Kooich turned, extended his hand in Greg's direction and nodded. "And under the colonel's new training program, Apache Squadron's nav-coms and cadets have tallied six hundred and ninety-eight and one half of those kills. My congratulations! You are indeed fighter pilots!

"I want to thank each of you majors," Major Kooich continued when the clapping subsided, "for literally taking a back seat, and allowing your budding fighter pilots the opportunity to train and show us their capabilities. And my eternal gratitude goes to LTVC21 for accepting the comparatively inglorious assignment of watching the home front and providing air support for Marshal Lima and his deputies and in the capture of the Trader's last freighter east of Grants." Major Kooich caught Major Glean's eye and nodded.

"Now, for the tallies you've been waiting for, again separated by pilot's name and beginning with the cadets.

"Cadet Gill Kast in Apache Patrol Six, made it onto the board. In sequence, the sorties are tallied as two, two, three and ten, for an initial board total of seventeen.

"Cadet Loni Grenn in Apache Patrol Five also made it onto the board with three, four, six and eleven for an initial board total of twenty-four.

"Cadet Wilm Moss in Apache Patrol Four with three, four, three and ten, adding twenty to his tally for a total tally of thirty.

"Cadet Ani Tigs in Apache Patrol Three with nine, nine, eleven and sixteen, adding forty-five for a total tally of sixty-seven."

Someone started clapping and Major Kooich let it continue a moment before he called again for their attention.

"Cadet Captain Cheral Haak in Apache Patrol Two with ten, nine, eleven and eighteen, adding forty-eight for a total tally of seventy-nine." Again, Major Kooich had to call the group to order. "Captain Haak has surpassed the number of cadet solo kills set by Lieutenant Geaardt when she was a cadet, though Lieutenant Geaardt's cadet record of sixty-two for a single sortie still stands."

Again, he had to wait for the crews' applause and whistles to settle down.

"For the Q-Ships, Lieutenant Emly Bids in JCCV4 made it onto the board with three, three, three and eight plus one half of a battlecruiser, for a total tally of seventeen and one half.

"Lieutenant Lori Tam in KCMM9 with four, two, three and eight plus one half of a battlecruiser, adding seventeen and one half for a total tally of twenty-six and one half.

"Lieutenant Mri Bradg in LLRT12 with four, two, three and five plus one half of a battlecruiser, adding fourteen and one half for a total tally of twenty-four and one half.

"Lieutenant Franni Kaal in TTYF8 with ten plus one half of a battlecruiser, ten plus one half of a battlecruiser, fourteen plus one half of a battlecruiser and twenty-eight, adding sixty-three and one half for a total tally of eighty-nine and one half."

Major Kooich smiled at the cheering and clapping group and spotted an abashed Franni and a cheering Major Mooren near the middle of the group. Finally, he held his hand up and continued.

"Lieutenant Colbee Donnr in MKCC5 with three, four, three and twenty-eight, adding thirty-eight for a total tally of forty-two.

"Lieutenant Meecia Miiles in KVWC33 with six, five, eight plus one half of a battlecruiser and eighteen, adding thirty-seven and one half for a total tally of forty-five and one half.

"Lieutenant Leeana Kooich in KKLC14 with four plus one half of a battlecruiser, five plus one half of a battlecruiser, six and thirty-six plus one half of a battlecruiser, adding fifty-two and one half for a total tally of sixty-six.

"And last but not least," Major Kooich said and noticed the sudden, intense silence in the room, only the sound of the ventilators whispered.

"Lieutenant Casi Geaardt in STSX1 with eleven plus one half of a battlecruiser, twelve plus one half of a battlecruiser, None while acting as freighter escort and on the last sortie, one battlecruiser and thirty-eight of its fighters, one half of a battlecruiser shared with B-Group's MVSS6 and twenty-four of its fighters, and one battleship with forty of its fighters, for a sortie total of one hundred and two plus one and one half battlecruisers and one battleship. The battleship which she single handedly destroyed was Prince Kiese's personal Kyddellan battleship, *Constellation Destroyer*. With this mission, Lieutenant Casi Geaardt has added one hundred twenty-eight and one half, and has raised her total campaign tally to two hundred thirty and one half."

When the room exploded in clapping and cheering, Major Kooich just sat down and smiled at Shara. There was nothing more he could say or add. Then Greg, Leeana and the major joined in, adding their applause to that of the crews.

▲ ▲ ▲ ▲ ▲

At the time STSX and the director arranged, Greg and Shara waited in the forward, double-wide cushion chair across from STSX's stacked sleeping couches. Shara snuggled on Greg's lap, holding his free hand gently on her tummy.

"Greetings Colonel," the director's voice said as STSX completed the connection. His image appeared on the monitor suspended between the chairs and above the fold-out table in the seating area. "Lieutenant."

"Good morning, sir," Greg said in return. "Squad Leader Kiile is running a few minutes late. He is organizing the post-mission inspections and repairs."

"Very well then, while we are waiting for Squad Leader Kiile, I'd like to discuss your last mission status report," the director said. "You said that Apache Squadron's B Group suffered six losses. I understand they are your first losses."

"Yes, sir," Greg answered, explaining the situations surrounding each loss. "I believe their five losses can be attributed directly to their inability to sense the locations of the mines. We had five looking for them."

"Five?" the director asked in surprise.

"Yes," Greg continued. "Casi, Lieutenant Franni Kaal, Captain Haak, Cadet Ani Tigs and myself are all able to sense targets, even small targets like the mines."

"I must think about this in detail. Is this a new talent?"

"In a manner of speaking," Shara said. "We have, or rather STSX and Medical have, developed a way to enhance and grow that capability once it is confirmed. Cadet Thomas has also developed the talent."

"That is extraordinary. And you think B-Groups suffered because they did not have this talent in their ranks?"

"Yes, sir," Shara said firmly.

"We must discuss this in greater detail," the director said with a broad smile. "You also said that Prince Kiese was terminated on 3482.410 and you have asked for an investigation to confirm his loss."

"That is correct," Greg said. "His aura ceased when his battleship exploded."

The director's expression went neutral and he looked straight at Shara, "And that brings me to you, Lieutenant. Please tell me how in the galaxy you managed to penetrate Prince Kiese's battleship's defenses, its shields and then single handedly destroy it? All in mere centipars."

Greg chuckled to himself, feeling Shara's discomfort.

Shara inhaled and started by explaining the trouble she had with the Kyddellan battlecruisers on the previous mission and how she and STSX devised a cannon firing sequence to penetrate the shields and deliver full strength shots. She linked with STSX to be sure she had the terminology right and then explained how she and STSX worked out a cannon fire control procedure to simultaneously attack the shields and penetrate the structure. She explained that STSX made the program a selectable file so they could use it when they engaged Kyddellan ships and not use it when they did not need it, and that they had equipped all of the ships with the file.

"So you simply created a way to pierce the shields and then shoot through the 'hole' while you held it open?" he asked, repeating her words to convince himself he was hearing her correctly. "Is that how you immobilized two battlecruisers with two shots each, and destroyed one of them with a third shot?"

She grimaced, "Yeess. Once I got past the shields, it was pretty easy to lock onto the proper targets. I focused on the ship's flight and intra-communication control center and the weapons control center. STSX follows my thoughts so all I have to do is see what I need for him to shoot at." She glanced at Greg and saw him trying to hold his mirth in check.

"He just shoots where you feel? You don't use the physical gun controls?"

"Yes. No," she confirmed. "We both guide and command STSX that way. The physical controls are redundant as a backup, but are not necessary on an ST-Class fighter."

"Then, how do you explain the high kill numbers for the non-ST-Class fighters?" he asked, "since they cannot fire where the pilot feels."

"Any one of us five," Shara explained slowly, "can sense where the unseen targets are, but when the colonel or I see them, STSX displays a false target on everyone's scanner displays and they fire at the false targets. If I can get a sense from one of the other three and can pass it on to STSX, then they can be displayed."

"I see," he said after a short moment, "but then what did you do? Your entire engagement with the battleship lasted six or seven centipars."

Shara slowly recounted the events and pointed out that when she went after the fighters, she noticed they were dispatching them from both sides of the battleship. She explained that when she realized she could see all the way through the battleship, she decided to go through herself, firing as she went, using the forward turret to clear her path of fighters and setting up the aft two turrets to fire outward and aft relative to STSX's axes. That way, she figured, they would stay ahead of the destruction, unless of course, something blew up around them. For that, she said she had hoped STSX's double shields would be enough.

She chuckled to herself. "The battleship wasn't shielded inside and it just, sort of, came from together, around us."

"From the mission reports I have received," the director said, letting his shoulders drop, studying Shara closely, "this wasn't the first time you've created new tactical maneuvers to achieve your goals." He raised an eyebrow and waited.

She squirmed but did not look away. "Well, no, sir. It wasn't. Sometimes ideas just come and seem like the right thing to do at the time."

"And you've been showing the flight trainees how to use them and how to do the same thing." He did not take his eyes off of her.

She inhaled and then said, "It's only right to show the crews how to do something that works, no matter where it comes from. I mean, I don't show them the ones that don't work. Uncle Paul's teachings are great, but sometimes they're too... cumbersome."

"So you just improvised," he said with a broad smile as she nodded. He hesitated a long moment and then continued. "That is exactly what I like. Lieutenant, I think some of your new ideas will be added to our syllabus, though I am not sure I will include fighting a battleship from the 'inside' as a proper engagement tactic."

STSX announced Kiile's arrival and opened the aft portal. Kiile entered quickly and took the opposite double-wide chair at Greg's gesture.

"Sorry I'm late, sir," Kiile said as the director's image filled the second monitor facing his chair.

"Your timing is fine," the director said. "We had things to discuss while we waited. And now, since you are here, I would like you to explain the details of your hostage rescue and the capture of the Traders' last freighter."

"Yes, sir. Certainly, sir," Kiile said and began recounting the operation from its inception, the request from Marshal Lima for their assistance.

▲

"Colonel," the director said after he had finished examining every detail of the mission reports and adding comments where he felt the reports understated the facts. "I have sent STSX a number of Letters of Commendation and a couple of promotions that I would like you to present to the appropriate members under your command. In some cases, you may have suitable insignias on hand in the standard Field Commissions Kit that you keep for such occasions. You can distribute the ribbons and medals after you get back, but I would like you to award the Letters as quickly as you can. In a time of war or conflict, no one should wait to know how grateful I am, how grateful the Force is."

"Yes, sir. It will be an honor," Greg admitted. "Back, sir?"

"Yes," the director smiled. "You are to attend a ceremony in the Rings to help me introduce the Apache Squadron and your new training command in one week. Let us say day 420, 1900 hrs my time."

"Oh my," Shara said and looked down, holding her abdomen. "Will I fit in my Dress Blues?"

Greg laughed and smiled at the director. "We will be there, sir."

▲ ▲ ▲ ▲ ▲

"Thom?" Eddie called as she walked past the breakfast nook and into the family room where he laid, still stretched out in a t-shirt and sweatpants on the couch in front of the fireplace.

"What?" he asked and raised his head up to see her.

"We have a letter," she said as she lay back down beside him, propped up on one elbow.

"A letter? From who?" he asked, slipping his arm around her to keep her from rolling off the couch.

"The Marine on the porch said it was from the colonel. Which one's the colonel?"

"Shar's husband, Greg," he said as he took the envelope in his free hand and stared at the notation, AGL36Q. "It's from the Peace Force director," he said softly as he handed it to her to open.

"Why are you getting a letter from him?" Eddie asked as she opened the envelope and studied the contents. "You get paid by the Peace Force too?"

"With everything that's happened since you found out about them, I guess I forgot to tell you," Thom whispered. "Why?"

"This says they're giving you, each deputy and the marshal, a twenty percent raise and one year's salary as a bonus," she said and looked at him. "That sounds like a lot."

"It is," Thom said and smiled at her awed expression as he explained the amounts and how they converted to local dollars. He squeezed her hand and pulled her tight against him. "Remind me, what were we talking about before you got up?"

She slapped his chest playfully and laid her head on his shoulder. Thom ran his fingers through her hair as he looked at the letter again, "You know, there's another message in the envelope."

"Really? What does it say?"

"It seems," he said, reading from the letter, "the director has received a report that says one Daniel Collier has been located, alive."

Eddie jerked her head up and stared at him. "That's not funny."

"That's what Greg says, Eddie," Thom said, "And I know neither Greg nor the director would ever lie or kid about something like this. He goes on to say first reports are that he was discovered in a place called Tissl and is amnesic, possibly the result of reconditioning."

"Reconditioning?"

"They may have tried to remove his memories," Thom said, touching her cheek gently with his hand. "But this confirms he is alive, Eddie, and maybe he can remember with time."

"Can it really be true?" she asked softly. "What happens next? When—?"

"Hand me my earpiece," Thom said and she rolled up on top of him and stretched to reach it on the coffee table. When she hooked it on his ear, he smiled up at her, feeling his body respond to her presence. "You sure you don't remember what we were talking about?"

He tapped the earpiece and connected with Five through WL-One. "Greg? Thom Baine here. Have you got a minute? Eddie has to talk to you." Then he repositioned the earpiece on her ear.

⏶

"Greg?" Eddie asked, "Thank you for answering."

"Good afternoon, Eddie. You're very welcome," he said, "Are you still at work?"

"No," she answered, surprised at his casual inquiry. "I got home about a half an hour ago. We finished all of the arrangements for Carole and Wally and now we just have to set them all up in the morning. Hope the weather cooperates."

"Very good. What can I do for you?"

"The message," she started, "we received about my dad. Is it true? Do you know what's going to happen?"

"To the best of our knowledge, it's true, Eddie," he said. "You will be asked to help with a DNA sample for comparison sometime in the coming week, just to be sure the ID we have is correct. So far, everything agrees. Our mission this week has created some confusion among the slave traders. Capitalizing on that, the director sent a small squad of Marines, like Kiile's, to Dangcee and Tissl to extract your dad, plus about a hundred others identified as stolen people and humanoids. Once they are safely under our protection, they, he will start medical treatment and evaluation and, if possible, rehabilitation."

"Sounds like that might take a long time," she said, her voice reflecting her quickly changing, uncertain feelings as she remembered her mom's struggles before she died.

"It may," Greg admitted, "but he has been found and we will keep you informed while we do everything in our power to correct a very big wrong. Thanks to Thom's initial investigation, he has a chance, slim as it may be, to recover and come home. If not, at least he's no longer a slave."

"Thank you," Eddie said and smiled. "Thank you."

Eddie tapped the earpiece and smiled at Thom, her surprise slowly turning to happiness as she gently tossed the earpiece back onto the coffee table. "It also means you were right. Dad didn't leave us because he didn't like us anymore. He was taken from us." She kissed him gently. "Thank you, Thomas. Thank you for everything."

He returned her kiss. "You are very, very welcome, Eddie. But I believe we were discussing something before we were so rudely interrupted," he said and kissed her again. "Do you remember what it was?"

She chuckled and shifted her weight slightly, smiling, "I think, Thomas, that I was about to be taken advantage of."

▲ ▲ ▲ ▲ ▲

When Greg and Shara returned to Obscure, formally attired in their dress Blues, they descended into the launch bay with Jill, Nick, Rose and Doug closely behind. They were pleased to see Kiile's men had set a small table with a podium to one side in front of the north wall. They had arrayed a small cluster of folding chairs in front of the table.

'Crem asked Franni,' Shara said as they stopped in front of the table and saw Major Kooich and Leeana come out of a hatchway and down the half flight of stairs.

'And?' Greg asked, turning to look at her.

'She's ecstatic! They have asked us to officiate.'

'Very good. Since we alerted the director to the possibility, we should be able to get his audience without any serious delay.'

'Franni asks if this evening, after your meeting is too soon?'

'Tell them it will be our pleasure.'

"Colonel," Major Kooich greeted as they joined them at the table. "Kiile should be here in a few minutes."

"Has everyone had time to eat and get some down time?" Shara asked as she noticed a few Marines entering from a door to the northeast of the presentation area.

"Yes," Leeana replied as Nick and Doug set two large envelope boxes on the table. "The crews have not stirred much. Some spent a little time outside while the rest retired to their apartments and spent some quiet time doing whatever they needed to do to relax."

"They seemed pleased that you had called a meeting this

evening," Major Kooich said as he glanced through the first envelope box.

"Can you and Leeana join us after the ceremonies?" Greg asked Leeana.

The major stopped and looked up at his request.

"We have been asked to officiate a joining," Shara explained, "and the director is available when we are ready."

Leeana smiled. "Franni and Major Mooren?"

"Yes," Shara said with a huge smile.

"I knew you were right," Leeana said, "after you mentioned it and I started watching them."

"We'll certainly assist," Major Kooich agreed and smiled at Leeana.

As Shara took a seat behind the table with Leeana, she absently wondered what memory sparked the smiles she saw them exchange.

▲

"This assembly was called to honor each and every one of you," Greg said addressing the assembled fighter crews and Marines, "for your part in making this Campaign a success. Today, I only have Letters of Commendation to hand out and the presentations are with the sincerest gratitude and thanks a commanding officer can offer. Actual medals, stars and camouflaged uniform patches will arrive by Special Courier next week and I will have a 'Pining-On' ceremony as our mission duties allow. I did not want to wait until then to let you know how the Force feels, how we feel about you and your accomplishments. Now then, USL15. Please come forward. USL15 has a few Letters to present to the newly recognized Apache Marine Battalion."

When Kiile stopped in front of the table and beside Greg, he turned, saluted and then turned to face the assemblage. A lance corporal took his place beside Kiile and opened the first envelope box. Kiile began reading names from his notepad and with each name read, a Marine stood and went to the front. Kiile then announced the commendations contained in the letter presented by the lance corporal.

Each Marine received a ribbon for Meritorious Conduct in the Face of Enemy Fire. Some also received Distinguished Service Stars for Actions Beyond the Call of Duty. Kiile's five corporals acting as squad leaders, Twelve, Seventeen, Twenty-Two, Thirty-One and Thirty-Two, received promotions to sergeants.

When Kiile had finished awarding the Marines, he turned and saluted Greg, stepped back one step and turned back to face the assemblage.

"USL15," Greg said as he faced Kiile and smiled. He glanced toward the assembled Marines with a knowing smile. "On behalf of the director, for service beyond the call of duty and for unwavering support for your teammates and Shadows, the director has decided that henceforth you will be addressed as lieutenant."

Greg saw Cheral in the front row of folding chairs and caught a glimpse of her surprise, her eyes dancing over her hands cupped over her mouth.

The launch bay suddenly filled with clapping, cheering and a chorus of deep 'hoo-rahs.'

"Lieutenant Kiile," Greg continued, forcing the cheers to subside, "is further awarded an Apache Battalion Commander's Insignia, a ribbon for Meritorious Conduct in the Face of Enemy Fire with a Braid of Distinction with a black slash for each combat encounter under the Campaign." Greg looked at the audience of Marines with a puzzled expression and said softly, "I didn't know they made Braids that long."

As he had hoped, a few chuckles drifted across the crowd.

"Lieutenant Kiile is also awarded," Greg continued, "two Distinguished Service Stars for Actions Beyond the Call of Duty and a Gold Ribbon for Exceptional Bravery and Courage under Enemy Fire. Congratulations Lieutenant."

Greg extended his arm and Kiile clasped it. Then Greg stepped back and saluted.

Kiile returned the salute, turned and slowly returned to his ranks.

Major Kooich stood up and stepped to the podium.

"Colonel Geaardt," he said. "Will you please bring your four personal Defense Squad cadets forward?"

Greg turned and faced Jill and Nick, defensively standing to their left just beyond the podium. "Cadet Thomas and Cadet Jordan, front and center." Then he turned to face Rose and Doug, standing in mirrored defensive positions to their right, "Cadet Mitchell and

Cadet McIntire, front and center."

Major Kooich handed Greg four envelopes as his cadets stopped beside him, saluted and turned to face their peers.

"For outstanding service in threat determination and quick response in the protection of Headquarters, your commander and his lieutenant, and the defense of and support of the local law enforcement officers, Cadet Thomas, Cadet Jordan, Cadet Mitchell and Cadet McIntire are awarded full Shadow Ribbons and a Distinguished Service Star for Actions Beyond the Call of Duty and are hereby promoted to the rank of under-lieutenants.

"Furthermore," Greg continued when the applause died down, "Lieutenants Thomas, Jordan, Mitchell and McIntire have been listed as trainees in Apache Squadron's Second Flight Training Class and will each receive an Apache Squadron identity pin."

Startled, Jill asked no one in particular, *'What? How did he know we wanted to train?'*

'Seems your sister might have mentioned it,' Shara said softly.

'You've earned it, sis,' Greg added. *'Each of you have.'*

"In addition, for their assistance in the capture of this facility and in the capture of the Traders' Data Collection Complex, you are each awarded two Ribbons for Meritorious Conduct in the Face of Enemy Fire and a Gold Ribbon for Exceptional Bravery and Courage under Enemy Fire. And for their parts in the rescue of six captives during the capture of this facility and for the rescue of two of the Force's Persons-of-Importance in the Data Collection Complex attack, you are each awarded two Distinguished Service Stars for Actions Beyond the Call of Duty."

The applause was significantly louder as Greg shook each of their hands, handed them their Letters and offered his congratulations.

Greg turned back to the podium as the new lieutenants resumed their previous defensive positions.

"Now, Major," Greg said and raised his hand for silence. "I believe this brings us to your flight cadets."

"Will the five flight cadets please come forward?" Major Kooich asked.

As they came forward and arranged themselves in front of the table, Major Kooich continued. "A very short while ago a cadet under Colonel Geaardt's tutelage caught the attention of many people in the

Rings, the director's included, by accumulating Sixty-Eight combat kills while flying as a cadet in only a two week time span. Sixty-Seven of those were while flying solo. Because of that accomplishment, the director challenged Colonel Geaardt to train a test group of cadets. He wanted to see how much of the outstanding performance was the individual and how much was the teaching. Today the director says it is obviously both.

"At the completion of the 26 January engagement, three of the cadets have experienced six weeks of exposure to the colonel's training, and two have only experienced two weeks of exposure. The director gave me the following assessment to share from this morning's mission briefing.

"Cadet Captain Cheral Haak in Apache Patrol Two has set a new cadet record by accruing seventy-eight solo combat kills in her six weeks of exposure.

"Cadet Ani Tigs in Apache Patrol Three has accrued sixty-seven solo combat kills with six weeks of exposure.

"Cadet Wilm Moss in Apache Patrol Four has accrued thirty solo combat kills with six weeks of exposure.

"Cadet Loni Grenn in Apache Patrol Five has accrued twenty-four solo combat kills with two weeks exposure.

"And Cadet Gill Kast in Apache Patrol Six has accrued seventeen solo combat kills with two weeks exposure."

The bay again burst in applause and Major Kooich raised his hand.

"These five cadets have completed the Flight Training Syllabus and have shown their capability in actual combat and are each awarded a Space Pilot Ribbon and a Campaign Fighter Pilot Ace's Cross. In addition..." he waited for the clapping to subside, "Cadet Ani Tigs, Wilm Moss, Loni Grenn and Gill Kast are promoted to the rank of under-lieutenant."

Amid the clapping and cheering, Greg and Major Kooich walked the line of five, saluted and shook their hands, handed them their Letters and offered their congratulations to each of the new fighter pilots and officers.

When the new officers had returned to their seats, Major Kooich paused and studied the chamber again. Then he continued. "When the director suggested the new cadet training program, Colonel Geaardt proposed an addition, based on very sound combat situational reasoning. He proposed that all Q-Ships should have two pilots instead of one, reasoning that if there is only one pilot and a pilot is incapacitated, we will likely lose both crewmen and a Q-Ship. So, he proposed adding all of the nav-coms under his command to the cadet training program. Will the eight Apache Squadron nav-com lieutenants please come forward?"

Major Kooich read their names as they stopped in front of the table. "Lieutenant Leeana Kooich, Meecia Miiles, Debira Glean, Colbee Donnr, Franni Kaal, Mri Bradg, Lori Tam, and Emly Bids.

"The director is pleased to admit that Colonel Geaardt has successfully accomplished in mere weeks what the Academy spends four years accomplishing." He paused, "Each of these nav-coms have completed the Academy's entire Flight Training Syllabus, have been exposed to the demanding situations confronted in combat, have learned how to improvise and adjust when the situation does not fit the textbook examples and they have survived with confidence, determination and a very respectable showing on the tally boards."

A soft chuckle drifted across the audience and Major Kooich turned to face the nav-coms.

"It is my pleasure to award each of you a Space Pilot Ribbon, a Ribbon for Meritorious Conduct in the Face of Enemy Fire and a Campaign Fighter Pilot Ace's Cross."

Major Kooich and Greg walked the line, saluted and shook their hands, handed them their Letters and offered their congratulations as the audience clapped and cheered.

Major Kooich turned and faced the chamber. "Will the five previous Space Pilot cadets please stand?" When they did, the major continued. "I present to you the first Graduating Class of Apache Squadron's Combat Training School, henceforth to be known as Class ASCT-One."

Everyone stood and the applause and cheering continued for many minutes as the new pilots returned to their seats. Finally, Greg held up his hand and continued.

"Major Hench Kooich and Lieutenant Leeana Kooich," he said and looked at them. "Please come forward."

When they were standing before the assemblage, Greg turned to the audience. "For their performance as Apache Wing Leaders and as the Terran Campaign and Apache Squadron second in command, Major Kooich is hereby promoted to the rank of colonel and

Lieutenant Kooich is promoted to the rank of captain." Greg turned and clasped their forearms and handed each a pair of lapel insignias. "Congratulations."

Then he turned back to the crews and the marines. "I would like to present Colonel Hench Kooich and Captain Leeana Kooich of KKLC14."

Everyone stood again and clapped loudly. Greg noticed they held the cheering to a more respectful and dignified level as the applause slowly subsided.

"I have but a couple more announcements to make," Greg said and watched the chamber as everyone slowly settled and the clapping reluctantly ceased. "Lieutenant Geaardt. Will you please come forward?"

Confused, Shara looked at Greg as she stood up. He smiled and waited as she took a place in front of the table.

"Colonel, if you would do the honors," Greg said and stepped to one side.

Colonel Kooich stood and stepped forward. "Certainly." Then he turned to the assembled pilots and Marines. He looked across the launch bay, cleared his mind and then began.

"I have only known Lieutenant Geaardt since 3482.315, the 23rd of October in local time, but for those of you that do not know this remarkable young lady," Colonel Kooich began, "you should make the effort to do so. In my opinion, it is your unfortunate loss if you do not.

"This evening, we simply do not have the time for me to enumerate the achievements she has accomplished, her passion for what is right, or her indomitable spirit in the face of adversity and in some cases, overwhelming odds. But I do want to highlight her outstanding support as co commander in the Terran Campaign and the management of Apache Squadron. I know she is extremely compassionate and caring of the crews under hers and the colonel's command, though I also know she can be a bit of a thorn in their sides if they mess up or do not live up to their potential."

Somewhere in the audience, Franni smiled at Crem.

"Lieutenant Geaardt has taught others how to improvise and be flexible in applying the teachings presented, how to think quickly and minimize dangers when possible, and moreover, how to turn a bad situation into a win, both on the field of combat and off. She is an accomplished Flight Leader and Q-Ship qualified Fighter Pilot, a dedicated wingman and at times, a concerned mother hen, always watching out for her wingmen and her squadron mates."

Colonel Kooich cleared his throat.

"Okay, enough of the character hype," he said abruptly and a few in the audience chuckled. "As you all know, Lieutenant Geaardt has not settled quietly into a background role of a managing co-commander. She has fought alongside many of you, led numerous interception attacks across this sector, not to mention the many defensive situations she has faced around her own beautiful planet, on the ground and above it. She puts what she teaches into practice, she leads. In the last sortie alone, she single handedly destroyed a Kyddellan battlecruiser and she is the first fighter pilot ever, to single handedly destroy a battleship, and it's of no small import that it was Prince Kiese's battleship, *The Constellation Destroyer*. She has shared the destruction of numerous other battlecruisers with her wingmen, while increasing her individual fighter kills. She left her cadet status with a record sixty-eight kills on the tally board and today has a tally of two hundred thirty and one half."

He paused and held up his hand when the clapping started. "I'm not done yet."

Another chuckle rippled across the audience.

"Her highest tally in a single sortie was sixty-two as a cadet and her single sortie tally is now one hundred twenty-eight and one half."

He looked at the silent audience, the flight crews were smiling and the marines were stunned.

"You may clap now," he said and the room exploded in applause and cheers.

As the applause slowly subsided of its own fruition, Colonel Kooich turned to Shara.

"For the reasons mentioned and many that have not been repeated or enumerated, Lieutenant Casi Geaardt is awarded a Campaign Fighter Pilot Ace's Cross with twenty-three stars, a gold Ribbon for Exceptional Bravery and Courage under Enemy Fire with six Braids of Distinction, two Ropes of Distinction with a total of one hundred and twenty-eight embedded stars, six Ribbons for Meritorious Conduct in the Face of Enemy Fire and a Grade Promotion to the rank of captain." He extended his forearm. "Congratulations Captain."

Again, the cacophony of cheering and applause filled the bay and required numerous appeals to bring the noise back under control.

"Colonel, if you will," he said and Greg stepped up beside him.

Colonel Kooich handed Shara the captain insignias and Greg handed her the Letters as he took her forearm.

'Well done, Bren. Well done,' he said softly. *'I couldn't be more proud.'*

'Is this for real?' Shara asked, smiling at Greg in return.

'Yes, Bren. You have again out done yourself. Now please hold still so I can position your Ace's Cross.'

'How can I? You're getting awfully familiar there,' she said, her eyes dancing as his fingers brushed her breast.

'Sorry, love. Force of habit.' He winked at her.

'We'll discuss that habit when this is over and I can participate.'

After a long moment, Greg and Colonel Kooich stepped back and turned to face the chamber. "I present to you, Captain Casi Geaardt."

Saturday, January 28

The morning had dawned uncharacteristically bright and sparkling for a late January day in the mountains. The winds died gracefully Friday night and left an almost magical glittery gleam on the snow covered pastures of the upper valley as the sun rose above the Rim Mountains north of the Guardian.

In the excited, expectant calm under a bright and perfectly clear blue sky, people began to arrive. They parked in the wide pasture east of the Lazy D, just above the county road and the band of trees that flanked the entrance of Carole's newly named CW Ranch.

The guests, all friends, neighbors and family from across the valley and some from out of state, filled a large white reception tent on a wooden platform erected and set in a level spot to one side of the prominent rock shelf in the center of the pasture. The shelf was the altar that Carole and Wally chose to have their ceremony on and on which to eventually build their home and life.

For the wedding ceremony, the guests stood or sat just below the rock ledge where huge bouquets and sprays of flowers from Mary's

Flower Boutique announced the joyous event with their brilliant colors.

Wally, attended by Thom as his best man and with Dan and Ted, patiently waited with Shelly as Carole's bride's maid and Eddie and two other close friends as the bride's attendants. They stood on the rock ledge as the music played and Marty escorted Carole up the path through the guests and up the short, temporary staircase onto the ledge and gave her away. Carole's brilliant white, long-sleeve, sparkling sequined and layered gown and train stole the show as it should, worthy of the most prestigious magazine covers.

Finally, after the new Lima's were announced to the guests, after they had greeted each as they passed through the reception line in the tent and after the endless pictures had been taken, Carole and Wally began to mingle, their excitement affecting everyone. Even Carole's new white western boots, occasionally poking out from under her gown solicited a comment or two. Marty and Rusty, every bit the proud parents, mingled and boasted about Carole and Wally, or about both of their two 'exceptional' girls. Thom recaptured Eddie and would not let her stray more than a few feet from him as they visited and chatted with the guests.

⋏

Somewhere in the gaiety of it all, Carole had slipped away and changed into a more modest dress, one better suited for visiting, eating and dancing and Wally exchanged his rented tux for slacks and a sports coat. Thom and Eddie were visiting with Carole and Shelly when Wally returned with a glass of champagne for Carole. He listened as they talked about the different folks that came and explained the relationships of many that Thom and Eddie did not know. Then Wally smiled and leaned close to Thom.

"Is it my imagination," he asked, "or is there something different about Shar? Has she gained a little weight around the middle?"

"What do you mean?" Thom asked, turning with the group to search her out in the crowd.

Carole looked at Wally and laughed. "It's not what you think," she said and winked at Eddie. "And yes, she is gaining a little weight."

"It's not what I think?" Wally said, staring at her laugher.

"No, it isn't," Carole said. "When we were with Thom on the Marine's transport, Jill told us Shar's expecting, twins. As small as she is, it's normal that she's just beginning to show a little early."

187

Wally smiled and admitted how little he knew about such things.

⚔

To one side of the guests, near the southern open flap of the tent, Greg stood with his arm around Shara and took in the breath taking view of the valley stretched out below them.

"Do you ever wish you had a grand ceremony like this?" he asked.

"Not really," Shara said and glanced into the tent. "I have all of the important parts, and more excitement and happiness than I deserve." She squeezed his waist. "And you?"

"Bren, I've got all I've ever wanted," he said and smiled down at her, "and you're giving me more than I could've hoped for."

"There you two are," Cheral said as she walked up behind them with Kiile in his civvies and stopped beside Shara. "I know I've said it more than once," she said and looked at Shara, "but I have to say it again. You are one incredible woman, Cousin."

"I just do my job, Cuz," Shara said.

"I know, but it's the 'way' you do it that makes you so incredible." Cheral raised her wine glass in a silent toast and took a sip. "To the best cousin ever," and she looked up at Greg, "and to her exceptional spouse, the best friend I've ever had."

Greg smiled and nodded, then glancing at Kiile asked, "How many of those has she had already?"

"I'm serious, Greg," she said, all humor set aside for the brief moment. Then her smile returned, "But to celebrate this grand occasion and your amazing feat, I'm going to have a couple more of these before this gathering is concluded."

"I'm glad it all worked out," Greg said.

"You know," Cheral continued, "if your kids are anything like you two, you are really going to have your hands full. You are 'not' going to have a normal family."

"I'll take that as a compliment," Greg said as Shara turned and spotted Carole visiting with a small group near the bar at the far end of the lunch buffet table. Greg pointed to an empty table, "Let's take that one and sample the spread Marty and Rusty have put out for everyone."

As they sat their glasses down to hold their places, Jill and Nick stopped and asked if they could join them.

"Certainly," Greg said and gestured to the empty chairs. "We're just going to get a plate and see how good Jerry's catering is."

When Greg and Shara had gone, Cheral leaned forward as Jill and Nick settled into their chairs. "It sounds like you had your hands full, again. Kiile filled me in on what happened while we were gone."

"It was hectic," Nick admitted, "but I think Jill feels left out when all of you are gone."

Jill swatted his arm, "I do not."

"Well, Jill," Cheral said softly, "now that you're enrolled in your brother's new and rather prestigious flight training program, you probably won't be left behind."

Jill smiled and started to say something else, but stopped when she saw Greg and Shara coming back to the table.

Cheral just smiled. "I think we'll get a plate now," she said and caught Kiile's hand as she got up.

"Cheral, Jill," Shara said in a hurried, hushed tone as she set her plate down and Greg smiled and settled into a chair. "Come with me. Eddie's wearing a ring!"

Shara and Greg's adventure continues in
Paladin Shadows Series Book 10,
Garda Nua: Part 9 The Proliferation of Talent.

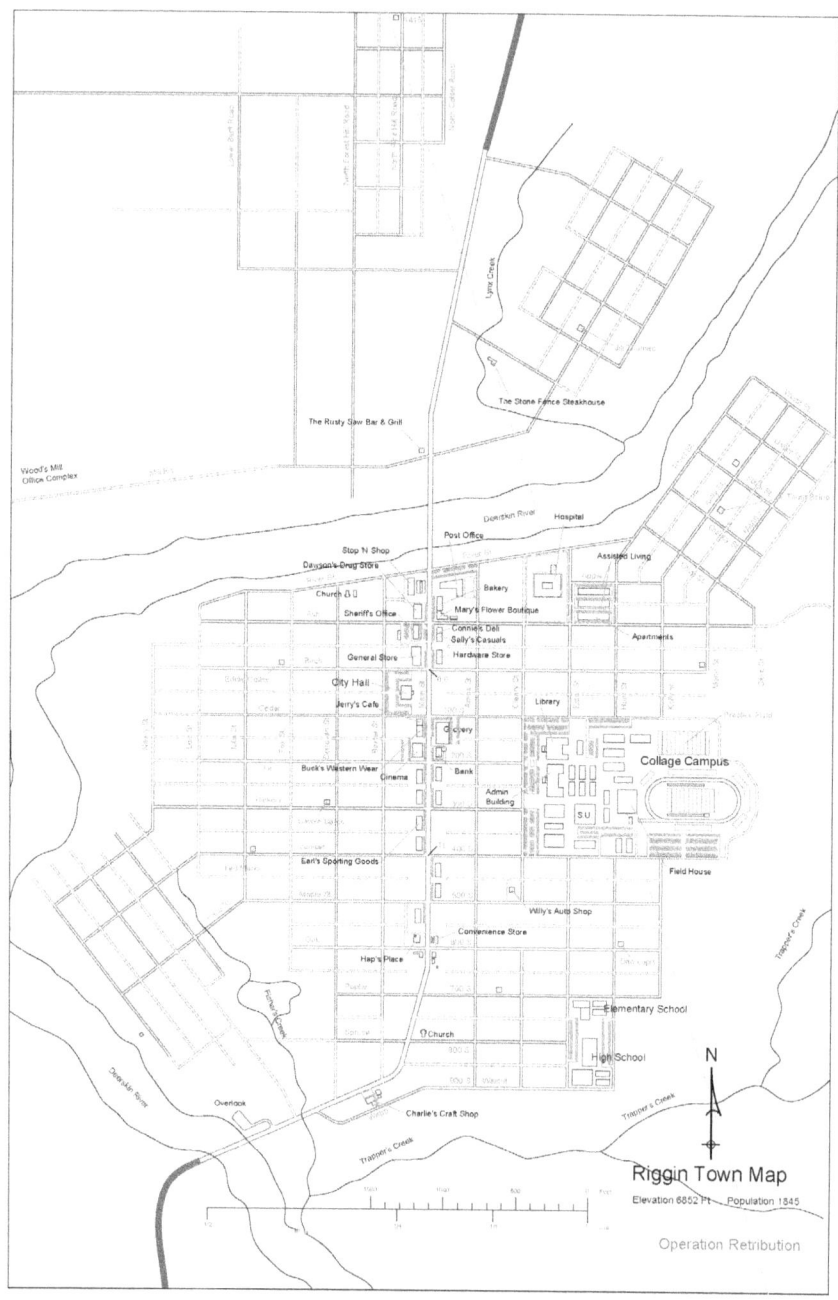

Riggs Valley Map

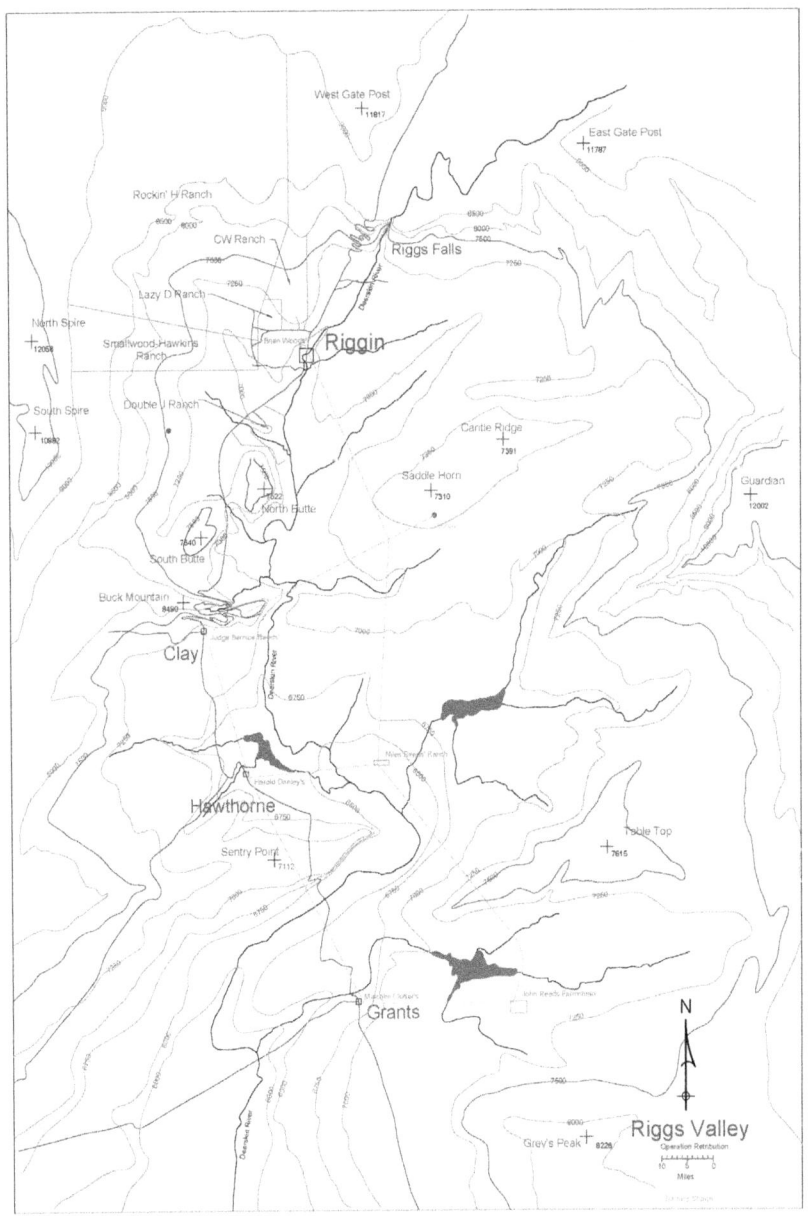

Glossary

Characters:

-A-

Ahaar	Key agent for the Trader's Union.
Arkir, Captain	Captain of the freighter, Dai Horizon.

-B-

Bernice Reeds; Judge	See Reeds, Bernice; Judge
Bren	Short version of Greg's nickname, 'BrenCara,' for Shara. Old Country meaning: "Special Raven Haired Friend."

-C-

Cadet Pilots	Cadet students training in the art of space combat.
	Apache Patrol Two: Captain Cheral Haak
	Apache Patrol Three: Cadet Ani Tigs
	Apache Patrol Four: Cadet Wilm Moss
	Apache Patrol Five: Cadet Loni Grenn (Reported Jan 11)
	Apache Patrol Six: Cadet Gill Kast (Reported Jan 11)
Camerso	Gentleman's Gentleman to Prince Kiese.
Cara	Second house girl at the Smallwood-Hawkins Ranch.
Cassel, Brendon	Coleen Malone's second husband, mate. (IAL01-SS3)
Cassel, Coleen	Husband/mate to Brendon Cassel, second marriage. Previous marriage: Coleen Reese. Maiden name: Coleen Malone.

Chairman Sorgat	Principal Officer in the Trader's Union
Clark, Della	Daughter of Widow Clark and sister of Steve. College student in Riggin.
Coleen Malone	See Malone, Coleen
Coleen Reese	See Reese, Coleen
Colette Marsin	See Marsin, Colette
Collier, Eddie	Floral Arranger at Mary's Flower Boutique. 23 yrs old. Daughter of Daniel Collier. No siblings.
Collier, Daniel	Eddie's missing father.

-D-

Danley, Harold	Banker in Clay, one of Bernice's Elders.
Danny	Shara's black stallion.
Davis, Carole	Waitress at Hap's Place. Shelly's younger sister by one year. 23 yrs of age.
Davis, Marty	Married to Rusty Davis. Father of Shelly, Carole and Todd Davis.
Davis, Rusty	Married to Marty Davis. Mother of Shelly, Carole and Todd Davis.
Davis, Shelly	Raised in Riggin, wife of Lt. Jim Woods. Mother of Carrie Anne Woods. 24 yrs of age.
Davis, Todd	Older brother of Shelly and Carole Davis. Moved away from the valley before Shelly graduated from high school.
Deputies, Special	Thom Baine. See Baine, Thom.
	Dan Lupis. See Lupis, Dan.
	Ted Marks. See Marks, Ted.

Dílis	Shara's black-faced roan. Greg's favorite and named by him. (Pronounced Jee + lus)
Director Korveel	Merchandise Director for the Trader's Union.
Director, Peace Force	Identification AGL36Q

-E-

Elders, The Family	Brian Woods (deceased)
	Harry Woods (deceased)
	Harold Danley (captured)
	Malcolm Clotter (captured)
	Charley Clotter (captured)
	Dave Barns
	Don Nikle

-G-

Geaardt, Stran	A Shadow. An undercover agent. A Major in the Galactic Peace Force. GPF ID: HQZL09-ES. Pronounced "Gee (as in Geese), + art."
Geaardt, Casi (Casey)	A Shadow. An undercover agent. Stran Geaardt's partner, wife. HQZL09-ES2 GPF ID. Pronounced 'Casey.'
Geaardt, Moira	Registered name of Coleen Malone
Greg Malone	See Malone, Greg
Grenn, Loni	Cadet Pilot of Apache Patrol Five, Class 1 Patrol Fighter.

-H-

Haak, Cheral	Captain in the Galactic Peace Force. Cadet in the Peace Force Flight Academy. Cadet Pilot of Apache Two, Class 2 Patrol Fighter. Granddaughter

	of Paal Haak. Previous Upper-Lieutenant Nav-Com on Q-STSX1.
Haak, Paal	Commander, Galactic Peace Force Academy, Retired. Grandfather to Cheral Haak
Hank	Forman at the Smallwood Ranch.
Hawkins, Andrew	Deceased brother of Paul and Nancy Hawkins. Married Katherine Reeds. Father of Clea Hawkins. Shara's Grandfather.
Hawkins, Nancy	Sister of Paul and Andrew Hawkins. Second wife of Dave Ashley, no children.
Hawkins, Paul	Brother of Andrew and Nancy Hawkins.
Hawkins, Clea	Unplanned daughter of Andrew Hawkins and Katherine Reeds. Married to Henry Smallwood. Mother of Shara, and surrogate to two daughters.

-J-

Jordan, Robert (Bob)	Owner of the Jordan Double-J Ranch. Nick's father.
Jordan, Darcy	Nick's Mother. Darcy Reeds married to Ben Jordan. Deceased.
Jordan, Nicholas	Aka, Nick. Friend and class mate of Jill Thomas.

-K-

Kast, Gill	Cadet Pilot of Apache Patrol Six, Class 1 Patrol Fighter.
Kiese, Prince	Warlord Prince of Knobaal.
Kiile	A Marine Squad Leader in the services of the GPF. (Pronounced as Kī īle.) GPF Marine ID: USL15-EFM

	(Upper Squad Leader, Earth Force Marine)
Kooich, Hench; Major	A Shadow. Major in the GPF, commander of Q-KKLC14. GPF ID: RWKR17-SC.
Kooich, Leeana	Major Kooich's partner (wife). Lieutenant in the GPF, Nav-Com officer on Q-KKLC14. GPF ID: RWKR17-SC2.
Korveel, Director	Trader's Union Merchandise Director, under Senior Chairman Sorgat.
Kraast, Director	Trader's Union Intelligence Director, under Senior Chairman Sorgat.

-L-

Lima, Wally	State assigned Deputy to Riggin. Assigned to Riggin after Sheriff Black and his six deputies disappear. 26 yrs of age.
Lupis, Dan; Deputy	Special State Deputy assigned to Riggin under Wally Lima. Wife Mandy. Daughter Blaire (age 7).

-M-

Malone, Coleen	Married to Tom Reese (1), and to Brendon Cassel (2). GPF Planet-side ID: IAL01-SS. Registered Moira Geaardt.
Malone, Greg	Great Nephew to Gary Woods. Son of Coleen Reese (Malone). Stran Geaardt's registered birth name. Born March 17, same year as Shara Smallwood. GPF Terran ID: IAL02-SS
Malone, Shara (Shar)	Greg Malone's wife. Maiden name: Shara Smallwood. GPF Planet-side ID: IAL02 SS2.

Marks, Ted; Deputy	pecial Stat Deputy assigned to Riggin under Wally Lima.
Mary	Owner of Mary's Flower Boutique.
Matti	House girl at the Smallwood-Hawkins ranch.
McIntire, Doug	Significant friend of Rosalee (Rose) Mitchell's. (IAL38-SS)
Mitchell, Rosalee (Rose)	Friend of Shara Smallwood and Jill Thomas. Doug McIntire's significant friend. (IAL37-SS)
Moss, Wilm; Cadet	Cadet Pilot of Apache Patrol Four, Class 1 Patrol Fighter.

-P-

Parks, Chief	Police Chief in Hawthorne

-Q-

Q-STSX1	Colonel Stran Geaardt & Nav-Com Lieutenant Casi Geaardt. Campaign Commander for Trader's Union Offensive; Terran and non-terran forces.
Q-KKLC14	Major Hench Kooich & Nav-Com Lieutenant Leeana Kooich. Campaign Commander's lieutenant and Wing Commander under Colonel Geaardt.
Q-KVWC33	Major Daaws Miiles & Nav-Com Lieutenant Meecia Miiles
Q-LTVC21	Major Neel Glean & Lieutenant Debira Glean
Q-MKCC5	Major Aiilx Romaan & Lieutenant Colbee Donnr
Q-TTYF8	Major Mooren & Nav-Com, Lieutenant Franni Kaal

Q-LLRT12	Major Deni Bradg & Nav-Com Lieutenant Mri Bradg
Q-KCMM9	Major Pti Fila & Nav-Com Lieutenant Lori Tam
Q-JCCV4	Major Ronl Bids and Nav-Com Lieutenant Emly Bids. Joined Apache Squadron after supporting the attack of 4 January and getting repairs done at Obscure.
Q-QRTT7	Major Amel Clef and Nav-Com Lieutenant Pela Clef. Apache Squadron B-Group Wing Leaders.

-R-

Ranch Hands	At the Smallwood Ranch: Jimmy, Tom (Tommy), Billy and Dusty.
Reeds	Terran family name of the controlling Family in southern Riggs Valley.
Reeds, Bernice; Judge	Great Aunt of Shara Smallwood. Head operative in the Family affiliation with the Traders and Slavers. Riggs Valley Circuit Judge.
Reeds, Thad & Betti	A stranded couple that Wally helped on his way through Grants on his way back to Riggin (Dec 20). Son Sam, age thirteen, and daughter Glory, age nine.
Reese, Coleen	Married to Tom Reese (1), mother of Hew and (by an Affair) of Greg Malone. Maiden name: Coleen Malone.
Reese, Tom	Husband of Coleen (Malone). Distant relation of Gary Woods. GPF Planet-side ID: IAL01-SS2.
Riviera, Ensign	QuickSilver Tracnav Surveillance Specialist.

Russell, Chief	Chief of Police in Clay.

-S-

Shara Malone	See Malone, Shara
Smallwood, Shara (Shar)	Unplanned daughter of Henry and Clea (Hawkins) Smallwood. Youngest of three. 28 yrs old. Born June 20 (solstice), same year as Greg Malone.
Smallwood, Henry	Full blooded Apache, American Indian. Married Clea Hawkins, father of Shara Smallwood.
STSX	Q-STSX1 is a late generation, Shadow Class Corvette, nicknamed as a type as Q-Ships, operated under the command of Stran Geaardt. The latest in the long evolution of the GPF's Shadow ships. The name is synonymous with the ship's central computer system ID.

-T-

Thomas, Jack	Married Amy Woods, daughter of Gary Woods. Father of Jill. Financial Officer at the Woods Lumber Mill. (Father of Greg Malone by pre-marital affair with Coleen Reese.)
Thomas, Jill	Daughter of Jack Thomas and Amy Thomas (Woods). Six years younger than Shara Smallwood and Greg Malone.
Tigs, Ani; Cadet	Cadet Pilot of Apache Patrol Three, Class 2 Patrol Fighter.
Tina	Pert, brunette waitress at Hap's Place.
Townsley, Thomas, Colonel	Watch Commander, space station S.S. QuickSilver.

-W-

Wardly, Anne, Lt.	Staff Assistant and Aide to Admiral Baker, space station S.S. QuickSilver.
Woods, Harry	Son of Horace Woods. Longtime head of the Woods Lumber and Mill (Retired). Father of Gary, James and Brian.
Woods, Gary	Son of Harry Woods. Father of Bill Woods.
Woods, James	Son of Harry Woods. Father of Amy Woods.
Woods, Brian	Son of Harry Woods. Unmarried. Current head of the Woods Lumber and Mill.
Woods, Bill	Son of Gary Woods; no siblings. Father of Jim Woods, Lieutenant (USAF).
Woods, Jim, Lt.	Son of Bill Woods; no siblings. Married to Shelly Davis, father of Carrie Anne Woods.
Woods, Amy	Daughter of James Woods. Married to Jack Thomas, mother of Jill Thomas.

Places and Things:

-A-

Angrilat	A Principal commercial complex in the Kyddellan System
Antheria	Major Commercial Planet in the Tunst System. Known as a Heavy World with a gravity index of 2.02 times Galactic Standard.
Aridont	City on Listera, cite of water rioting.

-B-

Baile	Planetary system of the planet Rygon.
Betolle	Planet in the Daneets System. Home

	planet of Lieutenant Franni Kaal and her hometown of Casimir.
Brekshiir	A wrist mounted laser weapon, consisting of one or multiple optics and fired by a unique sequence of mental commands. Specifically designed for the GPF Shadows.
	Brekshiir 170 Single Optic wrist Unit, 50 pulses with a range of 300 yds in air.
	Brekshiir 490 Wrist Clusters is the most common in the GPF, consisting of 4 laser units, 50 pulses each with a range of 300 yds in air. Individually fired or in combination.
	Brekshiir 710 Wrist Clusters, upgrade of the 490. 70 pulses with a range of 300 yds in air.
Brigstoan, Patrol Cruiser	GPF Patrol Cruiser designed for interception and boarding of suspect transports. Operated with a standard pilot crew, fifty aerial marines, a separate pilot crew and a Medical staff.

-C-

C.Date	A date referenced to the galactic calendar. A galactic year is comprised of one thousand galactic turns.
	Example: C.3482.329 is the 329th day of the galactic year 3284. It is also the 310th day of the current story year, November 6th.
Caldite Throwing Dart	A coveted and highly guarded GPF tool, used to inject a sedative or toxin upon impact.

Casimir	City on the planet Betolle, home town of Franni Kaal.
Cellystoan	Planetary system in which the Warlord Prince's home planet, Knobaal, orbits.
Centipar	One hundredth of a par. Similar to a terran minute.
Clay	Town in central Riggs Valley, 93 highway miles south of Riggin.
Colbr	Planetary System with three agricultural planets: Copus One, Two and Three.
Corsecain	Planet in the Gashii system. Prominent for numerous bloody battles in the Moulit Wars.

-D-

Dangcee	Mining colony on the fourth planet of the Greel system.
Double J Ranch	A 43,138 Acre (67.4 sq. miles) horse ranch owned by Nick's father, Bob Jordan, situated between the North Butte and Riggin.

-G-

Galactic Peace Force	Galactic policing organization headquartered in the Gridelin Rings.
Galactic year	Equivalent to 1000 terran days, or 2.7397 standard terran years. See C.Date.
Grants	Town at the south end of Riggs Valley, 186 highway miles south of Riggin.
Greel System	Planetary system in which the Pico Mining Company has established numerous mining colonies.

Greymn	Major Industrial complex on Omerai Two, renowned for its weapons manufacture. Model 40 is hand weapon most widely used by the Trader's Guild.
	Greymn Model 40: 40 destructive pulses with a range of 400 yds in air.

-H-

Hawthorne	Town in central Riggs Valley, 128 highway miles south of Riggin.

-I-

IFF	Identification, Friend or Foe. An identification system to determine if an entity, craft or forces are friendly, and to determine their bearing and range from the interrogator. The system is capable of transmitting a hail to another system on command.

-K-

Kaaspr	The standard issue brand of hand laser weapon for the Galactic Peace Force. Model 106 is the current standard laser hand weapon used in the GPF. Replaced the previous standard, Model 88.
	Kaaspr Model 106: 50 destructive pulses with a maximum range of 350 yds in air.
Knobaal	Home planet and seat of the Royal Throne of the Warlord Prince Kiese. Located in the Cellystoan planetary system.
Kyddel	System in which Angrilat's home planet resides.

-L-

Lazy D Ranch

Martin Davis' 15,455 acre ranch (24.15 sq miles).

-M-

Millipar

One one-thousandth of a par. Similar to in concept but equivalent to 3.456 terran seconds.

-O-

Omerai Two

Industrialized planet in the Kyddel system, noted for its arms manufacturing.

-P-

Par

A fundamental galactic unit of time. Twenty-five pars in a Galactic Standard Turn (Day). Similar to a terran hour.

-Q-

QuickSilver

Planet Earth's multinational, manned orbital space station. (S.S. QuickSilver.)

Q-Ships

Nickname for the Galactic Peace Force's two man Recondite Corvettes. Specifically used by Shadows in their various roles of information gathering, defense and protection.

-R-

Riggin

A small college town in the northern point of Riggs Valley, western United States, planet Earth.

Rockin' H Ranch

A 1,263,950 Acre (1975 sq. mile) horse and cattle ranch belonging to Paul Hawkins and Nancy Hawkins (deceased), situated NW of Riggin.

Rygon

Home planet of the very old Geaardt

family name, located in the Baile
System.

-S-

Shadow
Undercover agent of the Galactic
Peace Force with specialized
training and abilities in clandestine
operations and information
collecting, generally thought to be
able to hide in plain sight.

Smallwood-Hawkins Ranch Horse ranch belonging to Shara
Malone (Smallwood). 209,275 Acres
(approx. 327 sq. miles) split off of
Paul Hawkins' larger ranch to its
north. Situated West of Riggin.

Books by Aidan Red

Paladin Shadow Series
Terran Assignment Triptych
Book 1: Things are not as they seem.
Book 2: When luck is not enough.
Book 3: Fate has a different idea.
Terran Recruits Triptych
Book 4: In the wake of chaos.
Book 5: Terran Talents join forces.
Book 6: New rules of engagement.
Operation Retribution Triptych
Book 7: The training phase.
Book 8: Taking the fight off-world.
Book 9: Luring the Prince into the open.
Garda Nua Triptych
Book 10: The proliferation of Talent.
Book 11: When a planet is stolen.
Book 12: Right does not ask permission.
Assignment: Casha-Six
Book 13: No Warning
Book 14: The Best Laid Plans
Book 14: A Change of Heart

Eight's Warning
Book 1: The Past Hunts.
Book 2: The Past Attacks.
Book 3: The Price of Escape.

More Books by Aidan Red

Keeper and His Tiger
Book 1: An Unexpected Complication.
Book 2: Deadly Undercurrents.
Book 3: The Trap.

Fearin' the Banshee

About the Author

Aidan Red's passion for aviation and aircraft design, engineering, and a deep interest in space and space travel go back many years. An avid reader from an early age, Aidan, with great trepidation, ventured into the world of writing during college. With real world experience in business aviation, Aidan's creative side led him to create an alternate world where the beautiful Riggs Valley was born and Shara's life became chronicled in his epic science fiction series, Paladin Shadows.

Paladin Shadows consists of the five triptychs (three-part works), *Terran Assignment, Terran Recruits, Operation Retribution, Garda Nua* and *Assignment: Casha-Six*. In between the Paladin triptychs, Aidan has penned two, three book series, *Keeper and his Tiger,* and *West's Ghost Ranch* and a novel, *Fearin' the Banshee.*

Unpublished books in his various series are scheduled for release on a regular basis in the coming months.

Visit *www.RedsInkandQuill.com* or *www.AidanRedBooks. com* for more information on Aidan Red's books and where to purchase them.

www.ingramcontent.com/pod-product-compliance
Lightning Source LLC
Chambersburg PA
CBHW070824180626
46818CB00001B/381